The Jabbok Condition

By Larry Wood

A story of blackmail and betrayal

One man's fight for survival

The Jabbok Condition

All Rights Reserved

Copyright © 2013 by Larry Wood

ISBN-13: 978-1490962184

For Helen

For her faithful love and encouragement

"The same night he arose and ... crossed the ford of the Jabbok. And behold, Esau was coming ..."
-- Genesis 32:22; 33:1

Chapter One

He came out of a fitful sleep abruptly, ill-tempered, the moment the telephone began its shrill, unwelcome ringing. He grabbed at his pillow and drew a corner of it over his exposed ear to block out the hated intrusion. The telephone continued its incessant ringing. He rolled onto his back and kicked at the sheets wrapped about his legs. Awake, but his thinking still muddled, he focused his growing anger on the protracted ringing. Less than two hours of sleep only increased his mean disposition.

A bolt of lightning illumined the large upstairs bedroom and he was suddenly aware of the storm outside. The heavy oak furnishings in the room appeared briefly as ominous, silent figures, and then faded quickly into cheerless shadows as a steady rain lashed an unnerving cadence against the unyielding window panes. A crash of thunder followed another bolt, jerking him upright in the bed.

The telephone continued its attack. Begrudgingly, he managed to place his feet on the floor and peer at the bedside clock through tired eyes. The digital glowed 2:40 a.m. He had returned from a bedside vigil at the hospital, undressed hurriedly, and fallen into the bed, naked, at one o'clock, too exhausted to note the approaching storm.   The ringing persisted.

"Okay, dammit!"

He spit the angry curse into the next blare of the telephone, ran his fingers through his hair and grabbed at the receiver midway of the next ring. It slipped from his grasp, banged against the small end table and fell to the hardwood floor. He fumbled in the darkness for the elusive instrument, retrieved it and mumbled another cheap curse. He cupped his hand over the mouthpiece and slowly drew a deep breath. His senses were clearing, albeit reluctantly.

"Hel " His voiced cracked. He cleared his throat and tried again. The greeting carried little enthusiasm. "Hello."

His garbled salutation went unanswered. He repeated it, his voice now full, distinct. Still no answer. In a second he was altogether awake, and angrier. It had not been a good night and so little sleep made him all the more irritable. He was tempted to slam the receiver down, but he could hear traffic in the background on the other end of the line. Or was it line disturbance? He couldn't decide. No. The caller was still there, he was sure of it. Someone in trouble, maybe. "Who is this?"

Lightning bathed the room again, a brilliant reminder of his aversion to lightning. As a small boy he had learned to fear it, and had never forgotten a frightening electrical storm which knocked a telephone receiver from his young hands as he talked, splintering the thing. That frightening experience was seared in his memory. Too, he could remember vividly his mother hiding her head under a pillow at the slightest hint of electrical turbulence. He wanted off the line as soon as possible.

A hoarse, grating voice asked, "Captain Campbell?"

"Who is this?"

No response. He waited. Then, "Who is this?" he demanded again. "One question at a time, captain," the husky voice said. "This is Captain Campbell, right? CID, Vietnam?"

He stood and took two, quick, involuntary steps. "Yes. I'm Drew Campbell. Who is this? What do you want?"

"To talk, captain." The reply was measured.

"With respect to what?"

"Saigon, captain. October 17, 1970." The thick voice was gaining confidence and made no effort to disguise its sarcasm. "You do remember, don't you, captain?"

Drew Campbell was silent. The reference to Saigon jolted his mind, wiping out any lingering sleepiness.

"Saigon, captain, October 17, 1970, about midnight ..."

"I heard you!" he snapped. The hand holding the telephone jerked in rhythm with his stomach as an all too familiar image was recreated in his mind. For a terrifying moment he was back in the bombed city, racing mindlessly through a back alley. As on that distant night, his breath came now in irregular, frantic gasps. His heart pounded a warning.

"Well, captain ?" The uneven voice snickered in his ear. His caller was enjoying the fragmented interview.

This was a different nightmare. He struggled for control, placed his palm over the mouthpiece again and drew another deep breath. Stay cool, he admonished himself. And, think, dammit, think!

He backed to the bed and lowered himself to the edge of the mattress. He had to know who was on the line, and what the man knew how he knew! Was the man guessing? If he did know, what then?

"I don't know what you want, mister, but you have the wrong party." It was a thin pretense, but any plan was better than none just now.

The caller's response was immediate. "Well, I thought we might talk about the sergeant. But, if you're not interested, then why not just hang up, captain?" The voice was more confident now than ever.

Yes, why didn't he? It was an empty thought.

"Captain?" The thick voice again.

"Yes," he responded, his resignation clear. "What do you want?"

"Like I said, captain, to talk. But not now. Tomorrow night. Rousakis Plaza. Nine o'clock. Be there."

"How will I know ...?" But he was too late. The line was dead.

Drew eased the receiver into its cradle and looked at the clock. 2:45. He exhaled deliberately, eased onto his back and stared into the shadows, oblivious to his nakedness. He was exhausted, his body pleaded for sleep. But his mind was replaying once again the details of a decade-old nightmare. He was running in the Saigon darkness, the stench of the foul night air clogging his nostrils. He felt again the paralyzing fear, the oppressive crowds. Against his will, he forced himself to search through the frenzied memories for a face. Who was the caller? He replayed the scenes over and over, but his efforts revealed no more than the last replay. No one could possibly know! But someone did. That point was painfully clear. Tomorrow night. Nine o'clock.

As he had many times in the past year, he turned his head on the pillow, looked at the empty bed beside him, and longed for Ellen. He had never needed her in all the thirteen months since her death as he did at this moment. In the early months of his grief, her absence was a constant, stinging reality and he had wept often. His frequent tears had troubled him and he had sought counseling. More recently, he had done better with his grief.

Tonight, right now, he needed her. God only knew how much he needed her. For one of the few times since her death, he permitted his anger to surface and, suddenly, he expressed it.

"O God, you had no right to take her from me. No right to kill my beautiful Ellen! No right, damn you, no right! I needed her. I always needed her. I need her now!"

He knew instinctively his anger was both misdirected and therapeutic. If God was disappointed in him, he would just have to be disappointed. At the moment, he couldn't care less how God felt toward him. Except, he needed help and Drew suspected God was the only one who could give it.

He grabbed at the abandoned pillow. What he needed was to tell Ellen what he had never had the courage to tell her. Of the cancer in his soul, of everything that happened that disastrous night in Saigon. She would have understood; he needed her reassurance. With Ellen, he could think this thing through.

Think it through? What was there to discuss? It had been a night in hell and every day since an agonizing rending of conscience. He had borne it alone for all these years. Only Ellen's death had hurt more, but at least the grief of her absence had served to push aside the guilt. Now, in a single phone call, the grief and the guilt, twin tormentors, had returned with a vengeance, assaulting his memory, demanding an accounting.

If he could only crawl into Ellen's arms for a moment, maybe he could make sense of this madness. How many times had he come to her in distress, lingered in her quiet embrace, and found his spirit revived. And yes, oh yes! To regain his composure and make love to her. His body shuttered, remembering the savageness of their intimacy. They had shared a common lust for one another. He had never reconciled the two Ellens; one, a quiet, composed woman; the other, a woman of wonderful and surprising passion. He released the pillow. He had never felt so utterly alone.

Tomorrow night. Nine o'clock. Craziness.

Anxiety got the best of him. He sprang from the bed and stood before the large, rain lashed window of the upstairs bedroom, arms outstretched, palms planted against the dripping panes. Strobes of brilliant light shattered the darkness, etching short-lived colorless tattoos on his lithe naked body. In the fleeting bursts of light, each accenting his body in brief silhouettes, he observed the wind whipped waves crashing over the surface of the waters far below, but now felt no fear of the storm outside the window. It was the turmoil inside him that threatened to destroy him.

What if people discovered his crimes? What if they knew he had murdered not one, but two people? And his career ...! What if...?

"Stop it!" He screamed into the night. It's over, no one knows. Don't do this to yourself! But the panic did not ease until it had delivered him back in bed, helpless, dread sweeping over him in waves, swirling him deeper into a darkening emotional hole, to the bottom of a shadowy pit where, exhausted, he lay quietly. Eventually, he recognized the patter of runoff water tapping a soft rhythmic tone outside his window. The storm had abated. As the blessed quiet of the night claimed him, he closed his eyes and drifted into a fitful, shallow sleep. Tossing restlessly on the cool damp sheets, and dreaming just below the surface of consciousness, the Reverend Dr. Drew Campbell entered a familiar scene repeated over and over. A woman screamed in the dark. An explosion erupted. The screaming stopped abruptly. He crawled through a sea of blood, searching for the woman. She shrieked again. Another blast. Silence. Another sea of blood. Each time the details were the same. He could never find the woman before she began to scream again.

Chapter Two

The early rays of the Georgia morning sun streamed through the large windows, bathing his exposed skin with warm sunlight. He awakened slowly, seeing initially the bright fireball rising over the marshes. He remembered the innumerable times he had awakened to discover Ellen standing at the window of their upstairs bedroom, soaking in another brilliant morning on the Georgia coast. She had loved the island, cherished the marshes and the river. He would never fail to see her there in the early morning, her exquisite body revealed through her gown by the morning sun, though he suspected he might never be useful to himself or others until the vision no longer imprisoned him.

"Enough!" He spat the words into the empty room and raised himself to the side of the bed. Ellen's gone, he admonished himself with a force that surprised and steadied him. Sobbing over her memory will not bring her back, nor resolve this new dilemma. Someone has decided you, Drew Campbell, are expendable. Your future hangs on one ugly night of your past. Dredging up an old grief will paralyze you. This debilitating self-pity won't do.

He stood, drew a deep breath, and shuffled slowly across the bare oak floor to the bath. He splashed cold water on his face, pausing to search his face in the mirror. He toweled his face and looked again in the mirror. His eyes were red with fatigue. Was it guilt?

Fear? He tossed the towel in the corner. He needed coffee, he decided, and made his way down the wide hallway leading to the stairs. Moments later he was plugging in the coffee pot, the first constructive thing he had done in hours.

He carried his coffee to the spacious front porch which extended the length of the antebellum house overlooking Bluff Drive, a house much too large for a single person. Friends had suggested he sell and move off the island, even leave the city. They cited the obvious -- that living in a five bedroom house filled with painful memories was unnecessarily difficult for a young widower. They were right, but he had no intention of taking their advice, or ever leaving Isle of Hope, or the house.

The sun glared four feet above the horizon, a harsh, unwelcome trespass against his already wearied eyes. He positioned himself in a lounging chair behind one of the large columns supporting the upper porch, bearing the coffee cup in both hands and allowing the pillar to shield him from the increasing brilliance of the sun. This August day would be hotter than most. The humidity was rising steadily as saturated lawns fed their moisture into the heavy morning air. Scattered debris, washed loose by last night's storm, floated in the marshes of the unusually high first tide. Drew watched the ever-present gulls glide in apparent disorder over the brown, spindly grass, searching for vulnerable prey.

Overhead, the sky was thoroughly clear; a deep blue stretched to the distant horizon.

If there was any consolation for him, he theorized, it was being here on the Isle of Hope. He knew every inch of the small, Georgia Island, only six miles from Savannah's business district, and every charming detail of its history. On this, the east side of the island, Bluff Drive, a narrow lane bordering the steep bank, ran parallel to the waterway, the street bordered by a half dozen antebellum homes whose wide porches opened to the early morning sun. Beyond the intercoastal waterway, the marshes stretched endlessly until, finally, they gave way to the Atlantic Ocean.

What his friends did not appreciate about his island he could never adequately explain to any of them. He needed the strength the island offered. His spirit required the sense of belonging he received here each time he returned from the mainland. The island bore a quiet dignity, a stability which fed his often restless inner self. He loved this place, not so much for Ellen's felt presence as for his own reasons. In a manner of speaking, the island and the house controlled that part of him which regularly threatened to rebel against the orthodox expectations others placed on him. He would not entertain any thoughts of leaving the home that now was his only anchor. Isle of Hope was as much his life as his calling. Sometimes he wondered if this special place held his only real identity. He remembered coming onto the enchanting little island for the first time, crossing Moon River, the narrow stream immortalized by Johnny Mercer's song. When he first crossed the causeway onto Isle of Hope, he had passed the entrance to Wormsloe Plantation and, intrigued, he turned into the drive leading to the historic site. It was a majestic rural avenue, lined on either side by over 400 stately live oak trees, and emerging at the site of Georgia's oldest plantation. The 1.5 miles entrance to Wormsloe Historic Site in Savannah evokes a different era, turning back the hand of time to 18th-century Georgia. Wormsloe is the only standing architectural remnant in Savannah from the founding of Georgia, explained a Wormsloe's ranger. A State Historic Site, today Wormsloe is run by the Department of Natural Resources. The former home and plantation of Noble Jones, one of the original colonists who arrived in Savannah with General James Oglethorpe in 1773, Wormsloe offers a precious glimpse into the lives of Georgia's earliest European settlers. The Jones house was originally constructed of "tabby," a mixture of sand, water, lime and oyster shells. Much of the oyster shells used to build the house came from shell mounds left behind from ancient Indian settlements on the site thousands of years earlier. The tabby ruins of the original Jones house lies nestled within 822 acres of Georgia forest, sheltered by peaceful marshes to the east and the south. When the Jones family lived at Wormsloe in the mid-1700's, their home was strategically surrounded by eight-foot-tall tabby walls to protect Jones and him family from Spanish or Indian attack. An enormous stone monument and a wrought iron fence mark the first family burial site at Wormsloe. Noble Jones was buried at Wormsloe in 1775 alongside his wife Sarah and, later, their youngest son Indigo. In 1875, George Wymberley Jones DeRenne, a descendent of Noble and Sarah Jones, had Nobel Jones's remains moved to another cemetery and subsequently placed the monument "to save from oblivion the graves of his kindred." Wormsloe also features a Colonial Life Area, representing some of the typical outbuildings on the property and information about the gardens and crops grown at Wormsloe in the 18th century. Located on Skidaway Road on the Isle of Hope

  Remembering his first visit to Isle of hope he had wondered how the island got its name. He was told the answer was open to conjecture. Some say it originated with the Indians who first inhabited the picturesque island. Others say the French called it "L'Isle d'Esperance" -- Isle of Hope, but somewhere in time the name may have been lost. The more popular tradition, he was told, said the island was literally a 'place of hope' for Savannah families fleeing the yellow fever epidemic in the early seventeen hundreds. Many in the city did not escape the dreaded plague. When the island's first colonial residents inhabited the island, they gave the island back its former and more fitting name. It was 1733, the year General Oglethorpe founded the City of Savannah.

Drew was lost briefly in his thoughts of his beloved island. A blast of a motorist's horn startled him, and he came back quickly to the issue the telephone call that threatened to take from him all that was priceless in his life. His career. His commitment to honor Ellen's memory. A contemplated shot a politics. Maybe his home on this beloved island. Without warning, a shiver raced through his body, the cup shook in his hands. He stood and leaned against the protecting column for control.

Andrew Paul Campbell, son of a respected Presbyterian minister, was born on the waters of the Gulf Coast in a small, sleepy, Mississippi town that bordered one of countless dark water bayous. He was another in an endless line of ministers' children who enjoyed the privileges and endured the lack of privacy their fathers' vocation inevitably produced. It was not a childhood he had chosen, but somehow he had evaded the pitfalls of being the child of a minister. Countless other *PKs* had not been so fortunate.

One of five siblings, he had been the incurable romantic, often lost in daydreams which frustrated his parents and teachers. Later, upon maturing, he recognized the youthful fantasies were his means of escape from a confining, religious fundamentalism. His frequent, though usually private defiance of authority in any form was, he now understood, the manner in which he sought his freedom from a rigid 'do right' orthodoxy. It

-- the varied, consistent disregarding of authority -- explained the present unorthodoxy of his life, and his ministry. Early on, he sensed life was meant to be much more joyful than the "joy" imposed by a restraining adherence to religious rules. Someday, he confidently told his child-self, he would find his own faith, and live it, without unnecessary rules.

But his search was a mixed bag of successes and failures, as he later understood it was in any discovery of real freedom. The first real hint that his quest was not in vain came when he met and married Ellen, someone who loved him for what he was, not what he was expected to be. The exhilaration he experienced with her had rendered her death all the more intolerable. Now he fought daily for the courage to continue his search without her encouraging presence.

Nevertheless, he never denied that some of his most pleasant childhood memories were the hours he spent on the Mississippi bayous, paddling through the murky waters in the bulky old fishing boat he had inherited from his older brother. With a cane pole and a can of freshly dug worms, he entertained himself for hours, often forgetting the time much to the consternation of his parents who constantly warned him of the dangers of the dark bayou waters. But he had never been afraid of the foreboding waters, nor the swampy marshes. He knew them by heart, every mile. There, fishing the bayous on hot summer days, his dreams took him far from Mississippi.

His plans for his future had been muddled, at best. An ROTC scholarship offered a way out of the narrow, uncomfortable confines of Mississippi society. Soon after his high school graduation, his father put him on a train for South Carolina and a small Presbyterian college. He was graduated with a bachelor's degree in political science, received a commission, applied for the army's criminal investigative branch and was accepted. He trained at the FBI Academy in Quantico and was assigned in 1968 to a base near Saigon. Two years in Vietnam ended his obligation to the military, and his brief plans for a military career. He returned to the states in pursuit of an uncertain future.

That quest took several unorthodox turns. An extended conversation in an Atlanta bar with an off duty police officer led to a brief enrollment in a police academy, but he soon quit the school, realizing it would not lead him where he sensed he wanted to go. He entered night school at Georgia State University, intent on a masters' degree in political science. That venture also was unfruitful. Confused and angry, he joined a Vietnam veterans' support group, hoping to sort out the myriad of feelings competing within his psyche, but that effort only increased his growing depression. Like the majority of Nam vets, he was ignored, an outcast, at best an embarrassment to society. Finally, he found the courage to go home, to the sleepy town of his youth. There, alone with his parents, but mostly with himself, his life began to focus.

The help he needed came in the oppressive heat of a Mississippi midmorning as he paddled through the murky waters of his childhood in the small bayou bordering his parents' home. Early that morning he had awakened in the predawn hours, dressed and made his way to the still darkened and foreboding waters of the nearby narrow stream. As the sun peeked, and without any deliberate preparation, Drew slipped the narrow, aging fishing boat into the bayou and paddled into the slowly lifting mist.

Hours and miles of unconscious paddling later, he faced the question he knew he had to answer: what did he want from life? Further efforts to bury Nam and get on with living would be worthless, more to the point disastrous, if he could not answer that question. But that was just it! He wanted to bury the past, erase the damning memories of Vietnam, especially the last six months of that experience. Not the war, but his giving up on himself in his final months of that engagement, his headlong, foolish yes, suicidal behavior as his tour wound down.

Alone in the small boat he faced himself and did not like what he saw. Once principled and visionary, the man staring at him from the glassy, dark water had no cause. More damning, he had no integrity. He had tossed his self-respect into the gutters of Saigon and other equally wretched Vietnam cities, busting GIs of drug use, soldiers who were no guiltier than himself, holding them to a higher standard than he demanded of himself, and despairing of wasted lives while he screwed around with the whores of Saigon's back alleys. The guilt was an enormous burden, and Drew, though ready to get on with his life and make a contribution, felt his Calvinistic upbringing intensifying the sting of his offenses. There had to be a way out!

At midmorning, the sun bore down relentlessly on the bayou waters. With the oppressive air attacking his lungs, Drew stopped paddling and let the boat drift backwards toward the marshes. Moments later, the butt of the small skiff eased into the spindly grass and came to a stop. He sat motionlessly, not thinking, but listening. Nearby a mullet jumped. And jumped again. Within a few feet of the small craft, hundreds of fiddler crabs scurried into tiny holes in the mud. A crane, frantically flapping its wings, lifted its beautiful body with great effort over the marshes. The stately cypress trees stood unmoving. The pines swayed ever so slightly.

In the concert of activity, Drew saw a grace that swept him back to his youth, to a time of innocence when life was fun and hopeful. He recalled how in his youth he frequently blessed God for the bayous and its attending surroundings, its creatures great and small. The place of his heart had not changed, only grown more starkly beautiful. The grace, which many could not see would never see nor understand! Was more inspiring than ever.

Surely, he thought: if such grace is so constant over the years, if God cared so for it all, would not God still care for him? Could he not reclaim who he was? Who he was meant to be? What he was meant to be? Could he not give his ugly past, however brief yet burdensome, to that same God? The possibility immediately encouraged him. And Drew found himself praying. No words, but a prayer nonetheless, the truly honest kind.

Minutes later he found himself paddling hurriedly toward his parents' home. He had no clear plan for his life. What he had was a truth, a truth that frees. He had made two decisions. One, to trust his renewed sense of grace, and, two, to return to Atlanta. He would visit a friend who had called weeks ago urging Drew to join him in a speculative real estate venture. The deal might not be the answer and he doubted he had the resources to join it, but Atlanta was a place one had a chance to find himself. It was a place to begin again, a city rising like a new Atlantis. The next day Drew left for Georgia's capital city where the next good thing happened to him.

The deal his friend offered failed to materialize, as expected, but weeks later he met Ellen North, daughter of a wealthy Atlanta Realtor. Their relationship grew quickly and her widowed father, himself a maverick, approved of his daughter's new beau. Drew was offered an entrance position in North Enterprises.

Slowly, but perceptively, the brief fits of depression were quieted. With equal deliberation, Drew let go of

Nam and reached for respectability. The promising young man who had become a drug user and a hypocrite began a search for his personal integrity. Ellen -- friend as well as fiancé -- was a constant encouragement, and though she was aware of how Vietnam had broken him, she permitted him to keep his deeper secrets to himself. It was enough, at the time, that he had seemingly dealt with them. He thus ignored them. No need to worry Ellen. The past was that, passed.

In the fall of 1971 they were married, their joy cut short when Ellen's father died suddenly in 1972 and left her a considerable fortune, including controlling interest in North Enterprises. She sold the company within months of her father's death. In June, Drew and Ellen began a trip around the world that evolved into two and a half years of travel, taking them to most every continent. When they returned to Atlanta at Christmastide in 1974, Drew began in earnest a struggle to determine his future. The thirty four months of travel had been a glorious experience, but his need to accomplish something of his own occupied much of his thinking. Ellen sensed his inner conflict and encouraged him as she could. She had long realized Drew's healthy ego would not permit him to live off her resources indefinitely.

Consonant with the experiences of many ministers' children, yet inconsistent with so much of who he had been, Drew eventually faced the pull to study for the ministry. Though surprised and not a little anxious, Ellen supported his decision in mid1975 to enter

Columbia Theological Seminary in Atlanta in the fall of that year. It was, they both acknowledged, an experiment, maybe another temporary escape. Surprisingly, near the conclusion of his first year in seminary, the calling was affirmed for Drew, and to her added surprise, the four years of graduate study proved to be a deeply satisfying experience for her, too. She could not hide her pride when Drew was awarded the Doctor of Ministry degree. It was not her choice to be a pastor's wife, only Drew's wife. The latter choice overrode the first. She would play it out as far as it would go.

In June of 1979, the Reverend Doctor Andrew Campbell accepted the call of Grace Presbyterian Church of Savannah, Georgia, to be their pastor. His Vietnam past, though still a deeper part of him than Ellen suspected or he acknowledged, appeared no longer the threat it once was. If, indeed, it was a hazard of any proportions, Drew controlled it by throwing himself into his work.

Their life in Georgia's oldest city was full and happy, interrupted only occasionally by the expected petty conflicts in a church's life. Ellen's wealth enabled them to enjoy Savannah's endless pleasures and travel whenever Andrew's duties permitted.

The spring of 1981 burst upon Savannah in full color, impressing even her oldest residents with the richness of her new season. No one, least of all Drew and Ellen, expected it would be their last spring together.

What began as an uncommon weakness, given Ellen's ever abounding energy, led to successive broken bones. Their physician gave them their first warning. Early diagnosis indicated cancer. A three day stay at Emory University Hospital in Atlanta confirmed the worst: the cancer was in the bone and it was spreading rapidly. Within two months she was confined to bed, unable to care for herself. Then, almost two years to the day they had arrived in Savannah, Ellen Campbell died. It was June 16, 1981, six days before her thirtieth birthday. Drew buried his wife in Bonaventure Cemetery overlooking the Wilmington River. Drew Campbell was a thirty-two year old widower. A very wealthy widower.

    As he emerged from his grief, perhaps prematurely, it was apparent to the few who knew him well -- he and Ellen had intentionally limited their deeper relationships with others -- Drew was in a process of change. His eager smile, lost in Vietnam and regained when he met Ellen, now appeared infrequently. Slight annoyances, formerly taken in stride, were perceived as unnecessary interruptions and provoked him easily. He found less joy in his work, forcing himself on occasions to perform the simpler tasks of his calling. Deeper, and more foreboding, however, and only beginning to be recognized by himself, was a growing anger spawned by what seemed to him a gross injustice. He had fought within to find himself, to be a contributor, and following his introduction to Ellen and their subsequent marriage, he had changed. The change had been difficult, but he had made it. He had been determined to make up for wasted years, for his sins, and to commit his life to God's work. Even his embryonic political aspirations were intended to expand his capacity to help others. Now, with little warning, his Ellen had been taken from him. Still, loyal to her faith in him, he had determined to go on. It was becoming a losing battle. On occasions, when something or someone reminded him of her, the accompanying pain came unexpectedly, like a knife in the heart. He compelled himself to believe that life still held promise, bleak as it seemed, and he pushed himself relentlessly, refusing to give in, or quit. But the anger was real and soon, he was beginning to acknowledge, he might have to get some help, if not change vocations.

This was the Drew Campbell, fragile psyche and all, that had just received a different kind of threat. Should his early morning caller know what he pretended to know, the revelation would destroy him publicly, and the destruction would come on multiple fronts. Until now, he had safely locked away the night of October 17, 1970, a memory he had hated for years and still did, but had despised even more the manner in which he had dealt with it. By God, he determined, it's time I faced that, too, and dealt with it.

    Leaning against the column, he addressed an unseen presence. "Okay, Lord, so it's not enough that I lose Ellen! I must have more pain in my life. Is this to make me quit? Huh? Is it?"

He threw the half-filled coffee mug into the front yard and turned defiantly into the house.

"I'll be ready," he said to no one. But, he would not know what was required until tonight. Nine o'clock. Rousakis Plaza.

At midmorning, Drew backed the red Camaro out of the garage. He felt a special attraction for the car. It had been Ellen's, purchased in the fall of 1980, ten months before her death. He seldom drove anything else. It was a silly attachment, he knew, but an important one. He enjoyed a special bond with the Camaro.

The six mile drive to the center of the old city took him from the island by way of LaRoache Ave to Skidaway Road and on to Victory Drive where he turned left. A few blocks later he turned onto right Drayton Street and followed the one way street toward the riverfront until he reached Lafayette Square. The drive was completed in fifteen minutes. He parked in the small lot at the rear of the church near Lafayette Square and, on impulse, ignored the usual entrance and walked the busy street that ran the length of the large sanctuary. At the corner he paused and lit his pipe. The park fronting Grace Church was already crowded with tourists. He stepped into the square and took the nearest shaded bench. He had little enthusiasm for the demands awaiting him in the nearby office. Driving to the office, he had sorted through a myriad of feelings, rising to a determined defense, then falling as quickly to near-despair. Yet, the drive into the city paid a major dividend. He had accepted he clearly had a life threatening appointment in the evening, and facing that reality had helped.

    Drew hardly looked the part of pastor of one of Savannah's increasingly progressive churches. He seemed ordinary enough. The wisp of grey hair falling on his forehead shaded the soft brown eyes, belying his thirty-four years. The casual attire --dark blazer, khaki trousers, blue cotton shirt open at the collar effectively hid the one hundred and eighty pounds carried neatly on his six foot frame. The dress masked a hardened, lithe body. His physical condition was no accident.

    After Ellen's death he had turned his anguish upon himself with such fierceness he had become ill. His doctor advised strenuous exercise. Jogging helped burn off energy, but did little to cut the anger building within him. He needed to lash out, to fight, and to attack the grief.

    He heeded a friend's counsel and on an impulse, enrolled in a karate class. The decision proved therapeutic, providing a needed emotional outlet, and the workouts became an obsession for the grieving pastor. Three mornings a week he slipped quietly from his study at eleven o'clock, walked three blocks to a downtown health club and sharpened his skills in the art of barehanded fighting. Of course, he acknowledged: karate was not understood by most as a sport, and the training was incongruous for his role as a minister. The severe hardening of body extremities by repeatedly striking solid materials had transformed his hands and feet into dangerous weapons. He was more than capable of maiming an opponent. But that element of the training was the point of it all. Striking a post, a wall or a pile of sand permitted him to work out the anger that built within. At least it was better than cursing God. For Drew, it was a form of emotional survival. He trained with a passion others admired and opponents feared. Each session on the mats invigorated him, cleansed his mind and, he suspected, his soul. Returning to his office after sixty minutes of unrelenting physical exertion, he was always exhilarated. It was his secret, the only new activity he had allowed himself since Ellen's death. And it offered some control.

The pastor who occupied the park bench was fighting again for control. He tried to focus on his situation. What are my assets, he wondered? My liabilities? What could be the worst to come of this thing? It all seemed so utterly unreal. One moment he was a respected pastor trying to be responsible to his congregation and the community. The next, he was unwillingly being drawn back into an ugly experience he wanted forever buried. The darkness of a faraway place had come back to haunt him and he was, he acknowledged, vulnerable to its evil. If there was any consolation in Ellen's death, it was that she could not be hurt by this thing. But her memory could be hurt! That was the point. He must not let it happen, God help him! The thought jerked him upright on the bench.

He tried to focus his energies again on his predicament. His assets? Well, it had been more than ten years since he left the military's investigative agency, but surely he had not forgotten all his training. He could fight back, and he had friends. His liabilities? They were clear enough. He was guilty. His accusers were nameless and faceless. His ministry could be destroyed, and his now waning political ambitions, too. He had so little information. But this he knew: the threat was real.

The paranoia he recognized in himself troubled him. He was thinking 'they', but what if it was only 'he'? That would change things, wouldn't it?

Go over it again.

The caller's demand would include blackmail; he was sure of it. Drew Campbell was a rich man, albeit it was his late wife's fortune he possessed. He had promised her to spend it wisely, and to share it generously. A blackmailer, ironically, might fit both conditions, but it broke the spirit of the promise. Still, given the situation, he might pay a reasonable demand. If such a compromise preserved his life and prevented a nasty revelation, well, he might agree to it.

Drew left the bench and made his way again to the rear door of the church. Jackie Starling greeted him with her ever-present smile. She had served as his secretary since his arrival in Savannah, and he honestly did not know what he would have done without her.

"Good morning, Dr. Campbell," she offered with mocking cheerfulness. "You missed your early appointment," she offered without any hint of judgment. "I re-scheduled Mrs. Porter for next week, same time. Okay with you?"

"Sure, Jackie. Thanks. And, hold my calls for a while, if you please."

She nodded, handed him his appointment schedule for the remainder of the day and left him at the door to his study.

The large office was divided smartly into two areas by floor-to-ceiling bookshelves which extended across two thirds of the width of the room, separating a smaller, formal reception area from the larger, more casual study. In the formal space were placed handsome, leather chairs surrounding an oval dark oak coffee table on which rested a large ashtray and several ivory carvings. He had purchased the pieces when he and Ellen were in Kenya.

The inner, larger portion of the room was less tidy, but nonetheless inviting. An enormous desk at the far end dominated the room. It was, Drew thought, much too pretentious, but it had been an expense a wealthy man could afford.

In the smaller reception area where he greeted his more formal visitors, the books were lined neatly on the shelves. There were no visible papers. The names of prominent and influential authors competed for space on several shelves. Karl Barth, Dietrich Bonhoeffer, John Calvin, Martin Luther King, Reinhold Niebuhr, and other recognizable names were on the spines of the many volumes. An entire collection of Ernest Hemingway novels filled a shelf. A dozen translations of the Bible, including Hebrew and Greek versions, occupied another.

But, in his larger study area, nothing seemed in place but a large, imposing desk. Books were scattered about the floor beside and behind his high-backed chair. Endless piles of papers competed for the limited space on his desk. An old wooden filing cabinet, once belonging to his father, was the only other furniture of distinctive note in that portion of the room. Each of the four large drawers in the file was ajar, except one, the last. It was padlocked. A door in one corner led to a conference room; another to his private bath. The working office was a comfortable setting where only his secretary and select friends were welcomed.

Drew moved to the file cabinet to retrieve a folder and reached for the handle on the top drawer, much as his father had previously through many years. He was poised for the hard pull when his eyes fell on the padlock securing the bottom drawer. He backtracked to his desk and found the key hidden in the back of the center drawer. Returning to the file drawer, he inserted the key in the small Yale lock on the bottom drawer and opened the fastener. With quickened breath, Drew knelt before the drawer and pulled. It moved reluctantly. He pulled repeatedly, inching the reluctant drawer open. Pausing briefly to stare into the receptacle, he then withdrew an oblong package wrapped in brown paper. A nylon string secured the heavy parcel. Inside the wrapping was an oiled cloth. Deliberately, he turned the layers of cloth aside. And there it was, its blue steel unmistakable in the filtered rays coming from an overhead skylight.

He stared for several long moments at the military-issue weapon, designated in the Vietnam era as a .45 caliber M1911A1 automatic. He had brought the fearsome weapon from Nam. Eight years had passed since he had wrapped the large handgun and stored it from sight at Ellen's request.

The last time the .45 had been fired two people had died. Why he had smuggled the gun from Nam he did not know, but he suspected it was the guilt, and the .45 would serve to remind him of it. Drew squeezed his eyes tightly and pushed away a recurring nightmare. The gesture helped, and he looked again at the gun, ran a finger along the length of the barrel and began the process of returning it to its hiding place. Finally, he put the weapon away and dropped his suddenly weary body in the comfortable leather chair beside his desk.

A foreboding closed around him, pushing him deeper in the chair. One brief telephone call had radically altered his life, leaving him with few options. He found little comfort in remembering how, years ago, he had killed without thinking and that at the moment he, a minister, was ready to do so again. And that awareness, so incongruous with who and what he was, only served to spawn a new fear -- himself.

His most treasured possessions were threatened: his memories of Ellen and his ordination. Both demanded his loyalty, and both condemned the old Drew who was surfacing, a man without principle or loyalty. He could not just resign the threat he had created for himself. Nor could he allow some faceless voice to steal his life so easily. The only person he knew who could possibly extricate him was the man he was more than ten years ago. Maybe another way would emerge, but until it did, he was slowing welcoming his old self back to life, just in case.

Chapter Three

Two thousand miles southwest of Savannah on a small, sparsely inhabited island in the Caribbean a man much older than his years hunched over the keyboard of a large mainframe computer. His chair was pushed closely to the table and the wheels of the chair locked firmly in place to prevent its movement. His right hand rested lifelessly in his blanket-covered lap, the crippled fingers curled into a claw. His right shoulder slumped. Half-glasses hung perilously on the tip of his nose. With the working fingers of his left hand he tapped the keyboard slowly, precisely.

    The man had sat in this position, undisturbed per his instructions, for over two hours. The work was laboriously slow, but he was a patient man. His most ambitious project would soon pay handsomely. Not in dollars, however. He had enough money, for the present. It was not dollars he was seeking, but death. With any luck at all, two men, maybe three would die. An FBI agent. A senator. Perhaps, a preacher, too.

    He already regretted the preacher's death. But the mission was more important than any single life. Quite possibly, the preacher would, by his death, save more lives than he had ever saved souls.

Chapter Four

Drew scratched a final note on the draft of a report and pushed aside the papers, weary of the afternoon of aimless paper shuffling. His small staff had left for the day and taken with them the constant chatter of volunteers. The solitude was appreciated. He moved to the window overlooking the busy square and studied the steady flow of tourists crisscrossing the manicured park below, one of dozens of oases in the old city. It was a peaceful scene, and a startling contrast to the apprehension building steadily within him. He tried to ask some faith questions of himself. Where was his trust now? In the old Drew who did not give a damn about much of anything? In the old Drew who had killed? In Drew the caring pastor? Or a new Drew created overnight by a surreal nightmare? And what about God? What did he have to do with this ... this thing?

Whom can I talk to, he wondered. If only Ellen ....

Ellen's name produced a flood of memories. He recalled their first visit to Savannah, a visit more perfunctory than official. He had come with little intention of pursuing a ministry with no viable future. The inner city church lagged far behind the city's marvelous restoration, and the congregation's demise was all but certain, as was true with most mainline protestant denominations. He and Ellen arrived in the cool of a summer evening, a week prior to the scheduled interview, preferring to drive rather than fly the two-hundred-fifty miles from Atlanta. It was an intentional thing, a gift to themselves following final examinations at the seminary. Later, they recalled how little they talked during their first hours in Savannah. Only afterward did they realize how quickly the old world atmosphere had seduced and silenced them. By the time they met the search committee, they had fallen in love with the queen of Georgia's cities.

Now, barely three years later, Ellen was gone. What he wanted least was to leave Savannah. What he wanted most, more so by the moment, was to get whomever it was that threatened his thin line of sanity. That thought unnerved him, the recognition that he was becoming comfortable with the Drew who exited Vietnam. A mean, cynical man he had endeavored to bury, a man who could kill and not think twice about it. A shudder rippled from head to foot as he recollected his former self.

He was remembering when a more comforting idea surfaced. He checked his watch. Seven o'clock. Two hours until his appointment in Rousakis Plaza. He exited the church by the rear door and backed the sports car from the parking space. Pausing at the next intersection, he steered the car between an imposing church and a row of small shops lining the other side of the narrow street. The Camaro's tires rippled as they rolled over the old brick paved alley. Soft illumination from the gaslights fought off the gathering darkness. The city was settling quietly now, the streets almost emptied.

The lull of activity would be short-lived, however, for soon the tourists would claim the streets again. But this was a special time of day in Savannah, the interlude between the working day and the night life. The squares were now places of solitude, if only for a brief period.

Entering the next square, the Camaro melted into the flow of thinning traffic and turned right at the first corner. At the second intersection he steered left and maneuvered into the only vacant parking spot on the car lined street. Stepping from the car, he locked the doors, paused to permit a small foreign car to pass slowly, and crossed the street. Down the darkening alley the small car slowed noticeably, turned left and drove away. Drew began a walk down the sidewalk fronting the line of row houses bordering both sides of the street. He stepped to one of the myriad of colorful doors and knocked.

"Drew! Now nice! Come in, please." The smile from the beautiful young black woman reinforced the welcome. She opened the door wide, and embraced him as he entered.

"Hello, Mary," Drew responded, accepting her gesture of affection. "Hope I'm not intruding."

"Intruding? Are you kidding? Of course not. Bobby and I were just talking about you. Haven't seen you in days. He'll be delighted to see you." She led him into the tiny sitting room and called for her husband.

Mary and Bobby Taylor were a remarkable couple. Transplanted from the northeast where both were educated and Bobby worked for a major newspaper, they had moved to Savannah the same month as the Campbells. Bobby joined the staff of the Savannah Morning News, and Mary immediately involved herself in community projects. Things that mattered. People things. Where people hurt and people suffered injustices. She quickly gained a reputation as an activist, suspected naturally, but respected.

Southern towns do not accept outsiders easily, but Mary Taylor cared for people too deeply to be discouraged and, too, she was hard to dislike. She possessed a heart like a velvet covered brick. Hard on the outside and soft inside. Drew readily admired her firm resolve that hid a truly sweet spirit. And the soul of Mary Taylor was genuine. She mirrored integrity and others sensed it instantly.

Their friendship was authored during the early stages of Drew's grief. He and Mary met while Ellen was working as a volunteer in the community's shelter for abused women. The unlikely association deepened quickly when Mary introduced him to her husband. The mutual interests of the three the music of Neil Diamond, quiet evenings discussing local and world issues surprised and pleased them. They acknowledged the differences in their lifestyles and their vastly different positions in society, but seldom spoke of them. A willingness to enjoy an accepting relationship, one the community probably frowned upon, marked their fellowship.

Bobby quickly made a reputation for himself as an investigative reporter, a position he negotiated when the Morning News had first approached him about becoming its city editor. Managing news was not his idea of a newspaper career; cutting to the heart of stories was.

Mary Taylor not only gave Bobby the anchor he needed. She had personal interests she pursued with a passion and which Bobby applauded, and Drew admired. It was Mary who inspired the affluent women of Savannah to give more of themselves to the women's shelter than a few cursory hours of volunteer service. "These women need you," Mary offered to anyone who would listen. "They need people who see them as real people, human beings who deserve our help, who are not more numbers to add to our volunteer resumes." Many had felt their intentions scorned, but Mary's challenge had been a turning point for scores of people. Association with Mary Taylor soon became the socially rewarding thing to pursue.

"Drew!"

Bobby greeted his friend with a bear hug. "Where have you been? We've missed you."

Drew forced a smile. More than anything, he wanted to pour out his heart to these valued friends. Instead, he forced a laugh, and looked into Bobby's large brown eyes, which were as sympathetic as ever. The heavy lips hid a lurking smile. "I've been here. Sorry. Several crises, you know. Deaths, the like," Drew offered weakly, and dropped into a Boston rocker.

Mary interrupted with a welcomed inquiry, "Wine, anyone?" She asked, and was soon returning with a bottle of medium-priced Merlot.

Two hours passed slowly. Each time the lurking appointment came to mind, which was often, Drew sank more deeply into the comfortable chair. At half past eight Drew bid his friends goodbye and stood to leave. Mary embraced him warmly and left the two men to say goodnight. Bobby took his arm and led him to the front steps. He paused to glance down the narrow street, and turned worried eyes toward his companion. "Let's walk," he said, taking Drew's arm again and starting slowly down the sidewalk.

Savannah was alive now. Faint echoes of the city's heart could be heard in the increasingly humid night air. Bobby squeezed Drew's arm and spoke deliberately. The gestures made their point.

"Drew," he started, "you know that series we've been running on the drug trade? Well, I've gotten some threatening calls. It's not the first time, of course, but there's something different about these recent calls. I have to take the threats seriously. I'm trying to get Mary to visit her aunt, but she won't have any of it. She's not only beautiful, she's stubborn, as you know."

"What's so different this time? You've been threatened before." Drew remembered the series of articles on political corruption.

"We're getting close to some powerful people. Local people, political people. It stinks, Drew, it really does. And I'm worried about Mary. But again, well, I may be overreacting. What do you think?"

Drew turned and pointed to the Camaro parked across the street. "Here's my car." His friend needed to talk, he knew that, but this was not the time, not for him. He shrugged his shoulders, tossed a cursory response and recognized immediately he was disregarding his friend. "I don't know, Bobby. Better safe than sorry, I suppose."

"Yeah, I think you're right. I'll get Mary out of town soon. Maybe this weekend. It's her aunt's birthday. She knows she ought to go."

Drew was in a hurry to end this conversation. "Keep me posted, Bobby," he said over his shoulder and stepped toward the Camaro. "She's sure worth it," he ventured over the top of the car.

"Goodnight Drew." Bobby turned and started toward the apartment. Strange, he mused, he had just been dismissed by his best friend. Drew had never done that before.

In the Camaro, Drew turned the key and the powerful engine roared to life. As he turned the wheel and pulled from the parking spot, bright headlights from behind appeared. He braked suddenly, surprised, because he had not seen the car approaching. He glanced in his rear mirror and saw the second car pull from a spot less than fifty feet behind his own. Obviously in a hurry, the driver squealed the tires and swept past Drew. The abrupt, unexpected maneuver angered Drew, but his anger quickly turned to puzzlement as the car roared past. Unless he was badly mistaken, the car was the same one that had driven by so deliberately an hour or so before. A silver Toyota. No, there was no mistake. It was the same car. And why was the driver in such a hurry now? Drew watched the small car negotiate the next turn and disappear.

      Did the incident have anything to do with him? He shook his head. He didn't understand, but that was it entirely! He didn't know anything. Too many things he didn't know, many of them imagined, possibly. He studied his watch: eight-thirty-five. Well, if he was being watched, he could do something about that. He stepped on the accelerator and the car leaped from the curb. Turning left he drove away from the riverfront where the meeting was to be, then right onto a one-way street heading south. Suddenly he braked, steered quickly into one of Savannah's countless lanes that ran behind the many rows of homes. On either side of the alley, trash cans lined the passageway and back porch lights illumined the narrow passage. Drew asked the Camaro for more speed and roared down the alley. If he was being followed, his pursuer would have to follow him down the lane or race around the block to pick up his trail again. At the end of the lane, he slowed briefly, checked the traffic, and then sped across the street and into the next alley. He repeated the maneuver several times until he was a half dozen blocks from the Taylor's apartment. Anyone trying to tail him would have to speed through several traffic lights, stopping at each intersection to see if he continued his alley race or turned onto a main street.

Approaching the end of the next lane, he turned sharply onto East Broad Street and raced several blocks toward the riverfront. Satisfied he was not followed how could they have kept up? He slowed and blended into the stream of evening traffic approaching Bay Street. The street ran the length of the extended park overlooking the river. With several cars ahead of him, he turned into the parking lot of the Pirate's House, a favorite restaurant of locals and tourists alike. Good, the trade was heavy tonight. He parked in the back lot and made his way toward the entrance of the restaurant. Near the door, he paused in the shadows, and waited. Moments later, a taxi pulled to the entrance and deposited its fare. Drew moved quickly. Before the door of the taxi closed, he grabbed it, thanked the last rider and entered. "Riverfront," he instructed and settled into the shadows of the back seat.

Three blocks later, the driver slowed to enter one of the steep entrances to the riverfront. "Not here," Drew said, "by the next stairs." The driver obeyed and merged into the line of cars edging its way along Bay Street, stopping after another a hundred feet. Drew compensated the driver for the abbreviated fare and walked quickly toward a nearby metal stairway leading to the riverfront and Rousakis Plaza.

The stairs were steep. He kept close to the wall of the narrow stairway, completed his descent onto the plaza and checked the time.

8:58. Two minutes.

A jazz band occupied the center of the plaza, playing heartily to an appreciative gathering. Good, he thought. An enthusiastic crowd meant less chance of running into friends. He came safely onto River Street and loitered on the edge of the streams of tourists crowding the steamy riverfront.

Every storefront was congested as the throng of tourists stopped at each doorway to peek into the interior of the tourist trap. Drew thought briefly of the member of his congregation who had designed the restored riverfront. Together with the countless squares which highlighted the old town, the riverfront was a source of great pride for the locals. Between the old storefronts and the many tugboats and an occasional sloop moored on the river, the masterfully designed plaza offered countless gathering areas where those strolling the riverfront could find respite from the mauling crowds.

At the far eastern edge of the plaza, the 'Waving Girl' anchored the riverfront. She was captured in a beautifully crafted granite stature commemorating the young girl who daily had climbed up to her favorite perch to watch and wait for ships to return from the sea. It remains one of Savannah's favorite stories involving the life of Florence Martus who died in 1943. She was the daughter of a sergeant stationed at Fort Pulaski. Life was lonely for Florence whose closest companion was her devoted collie. At an early age, she developed a close affinity with the passing ships and welcomed each one with a wave of her handkerchief. Sailors began returning her greeting by waving back or with a blast of the ship's horn. Eventually Florence started greeting the ships arriving in the dark by waving a lantern.

    A sudden blast from a ship's horn roared above the din and echoed off the walls of the storefronts. Drew peered through the soft light of the nineteenth century lamps. A giant freighter bellowed its arrival, moving effortlessly up a seductively quiet river, sliding silently through the ever moving waters of the Savannah. A Japanese flag hung limply from its mast. Curious eyes stared from the ship and the shore. An occasional wave from shore was returned from crewmen gathered at the huge ship's railing. Drew returned his gaze to the crowd. He had little interest just now in maritime industry. Instead, he searched the faces about him for any hint of his caller.

    He pushed his way toward the edge of the plaza proper. His foot was on the first step when someone grasped his elbow firmly. He stopped abruptly. Before he could turn a voice said quietly, "Just keep walking, captain toward the water." Drew stiffened, but kept walking, the hand firmly holding his elbow. Nearing the dark waters of the Savannah River, he slowed his pace.

    "Okay." the voice said moments later, "far enough. Let's talk."

Drew turned to face a man four inches shorter than he, and many pounds heavier. The bill of an Atlanta Braves cap hid the man's eyes. Jet black hair protruded over his small ears. A week's growth of uneven beard marked his face, drawing attention to his shadowed eyes. The man wore a black T-shirt -- the words I AM GOOD boldly stamped across its front -- and dirty running shoes.

The man smiled. "Well, captain, it's been awhile, wouldn't you say?"

Drew stiffened, and spit out his question. "Who are you?"

The man leaned back on the railing fronting the river, studying the taller pastor. His smile became a sneer. "It doesn't matter who I am, captain, but it matters that I know who you are. In fact, I know more about you than you want known. That's what we're here to talk about, preacherman."

Drew sensed his intimidator was much smarter than he appeared. "What do you want?"

"A little cooperation, captain, that's all."

"With what …?" Drew asked, fearing the answer.

"A small business venture."

"You're not making sense!" Drew glanced about as he raised his voice. They were standing midpoint between two lamp posts and the dim light was welcomed. Drew stared into the eyes of the little man.

"Well, let me put it to you straight, `captain,'" the man said, deliberately stressing Drew's previous military rank each time he addressed his captive. "We know about your, uh, activities, shall we say, on the evening of October 17, 1970. I'm sure you remember the night. The back room of a Saigon shanty. The girl, the sergeant? You do remember, don't you, captain? Great sex, huh? Of course you remember, you couldn't forget such fun, huh? And neither could I."

Drew stared at the man in disbelief.

"Oh, yes. I was there, captain. Came with my sergeant. Surely you remember him. The one you wasted, remember? Ah, yes, I was there. Right there in the room, but you didn't have time to notice. I saw it all, captain. My sergeant's face blown off. And the girl, too. And you," the man laughed, "running like a scared rabbit, bare ass and all, your britches in your hand! I was there, captain, and I saw it all." He let his words trail off, their shock value complete.

Drew's stomach retched. Oh, gracious God! He hadn't permitted himself to really believe it could be this bad. Bile rose in his throat as he turned to face the river.

The man stepped closer. "No one has to know, captain. All we need is just a little assistance from you. After that, your secret will be safe with us. We'll have no need of you then."

Drew could not speak. But he could think, and to think they would have 'no need of him then' did not compute. His secret would never be safe. They would kill him, of course.

"Do we have your cooperation, captain?"

"What do I have to do?" he asked, still thinking.

"Now, that's more like it," the man said, adjusting his cap and moving inches closer as he lit a cigarette. "Day after tomorrow you'll take your boat out to the ten mile buoy at the head of the channel. You know the one, captain. You've fished it many times. During the afternoon you'll fish. At dark, you'll tie up at the beacon and await the arrival of a freighter."

Drew stared at the man, trying to comprehend the instructions.

"Got me so far, captain?"

Drew nodded.

"During the night, sometime near twelve midnight, a freighter will pass within a hundred yards or so. A discreet flashing light will alert you. You'll be standing ready, motor running. A package will be thrown into the water. You'll retrieve it and bring it in the next morning."

What will be in the package, he wondered, and asked.

"It's not for you to know, captain."

Not hard to figure out, Drew thought. "What do I do with the package once I'm home?"

"Hold on to it. You'll receive instructions."

"And if I refuse?"

"Oh, you won't refuse, captain," the man said, turning to leave, his eyes searching the milling crowd. Drew had more questions, but his mind was frozen.

"Wait." It was all he could think to say.

The man was still searching the faces of the crowd and Drew stared at the little man, hating him more by the second.

The man turned to Drew again. "One more thing, captain.
Not a word to anyone. No one. Got that?"

"I haven't decided anything," Drew responded in desperation.

"Oh, but you will. Enjoy your evening, pastor." The man turned and walked from the water's edge. Two men appeared to join him as he disappeared into the crowd.

Drew watched until the boisterous company of people absorbed the man and his companions in its midst. He turned back to face the river, processing what he had heard. Just accepting the last few minutes was difficult enough; calming the rage building within him was near impossible. And the fear. He took an uncertain step from the railing. He was sure of one thing: he could abandon all hope of extraditing himself from this nightmare easily.

Instinctively, he walked toward the steps leading to the upper level of Factor's Walk. It didn't matter if he was being observed. Nothing mattered at the moment but getting out of the city and home on his island. Home, where he could think, and perhaps, pull himself together and come up with a plan.

He walked the several blocks to the old Pirates House restaurant to find the Camaro. He pulled out onto

Bay Street and then, driving deliberately from the waterfront, white knuckled hands gripping the wheel, he sensed company -- the Drew Campbell of Vietnam. The "presence" was not unwelcomed.

Chapter Five

A full Georgia moon reflected from the quiet waters below Isle of Hope's Bluff Drive. The stately old homes lining the narrow frontage stood as silent darkened sentinels over the waterway, offering encouragement to one of their own. A dozen private docks jutted from the shoreline, eerie fingers stretching into the darkened, threatening waters. They, too, were symbols, reminders that even stately Bluff Drive was vulnerable.

A pensive Drew sat in a darkened corner of the side porch. His circumstances appeared bleak, to say the least. He had calculated every possibility and entertained every plausible escape, even some ridiculous options. No hopeful answers emerged from his frantic mental games. He would have to cooperate, at least until he could come up with a workable solution. He had little time to concoct a plan.

It was surreal. One day he was caring for stricken people, assisting others with problems, showing them a better way while living himself with a stricken spirit. The next, unbelievably, he was slipping through the night, playing a reckless game of Guess Who. Maddening, yes! But, for a moment, he acknowledged a strange exhilaration, a feeling he suspected he needed to draw him out of the debilitating, vacillating moods he was experiencing until now. At the least, he was discovering, he was not altogether dead inside. He could think, and he could feel something other than near dysfunction.

What he was thinking was not clear, to be sure, but that would come with time, if he had enough time. What he was feeling was a rising fury, and it caused him to feel more alive than at any time in months.

He thought again of the little man who fronted him at Rousakis Plaza. The sniveling little bastard! He thinks his prey is helpless, and he can use me as he wishes. Well, think again, you son-of-a-bitch! I may be a pastor, but I am not helpless. You can shake this cobra's basket, but you have made a big, big mistake. You put your hand in the Cobra' nest!

His anger produced a surge of adrenalin, and for precious seconds he was in control, anxious for his next encounter with the little man. But, just as quickly, he faltered as he remembered: blackmailer or not, *he was guilty*!

He returned to the wearying task of dredging the past, searching faces submerged in his memory. What he kept coming back to there was no escaping it was that one dark, insane night in Saigon. And, tonight, more insanity. Only recently he had preached with conviction of another man snared in his past – the biblical character Jacob, son of Isaac, mired on the banks of the Jabbok River, enduring an anguished night of the soul. The Old Testament patriarch had wrestled with God. Or was it an angel? His conscience? Did it matter? The point: Jacob had reckoned with his past. Coming to meet him at the dawn was his enraged brother, Esau, and Jacob could do nothing but pray and prepare. Esau was Jacob's fourteen year old past the cheated brother, the sibling bent on revenge. If only, thought Drew, I was facing an angry brother!

Does everyone's past come back an apparition as had his? Drew's trained theological mind thought not, and he was certain his trek through the Jabbok would not end as neatly as did Jacob's, in his brother's arms in a tearful reunion. Yet, he could learn from Jacob. He, too, could prepare. In a measure of fragile faith, Drew recalled the words of the Genesis story. "And Jacob got up and crossed the Jabbok, and behold, Esau was coming." Tomorrow, Drew reasoned, so help me God, I'll cross the river and face my past. Then, a subtle doubt: maybe God doesn't care.

In the emerging morning, Drew sat at the familiar kitchen table and studied the cup in his hands. During a restless night, he had come to a conclusion that offered hope: there was only one person with whom he could immediately discuss his dilemma. He would call Bobby. Then, perhaps, if matters got worse, he would ask an old friend to help. Rod Gray had been his trusted companion in Nam where they worked together in the army's Criminal Investigative Division. They had been a team on many CID assignments; in fact, Rod had worked with him on a final investigation before they shipped out of Nam.

Okay. One step at a time. He reached for the phone, thought about his phone being tapped, and said, "To hell with it," and dialed.

"I need to talk with you, Bobby." Drew left no doubt of his anxiety.

"What's up, Drew? Trouble?"

"Yes, but I can't talk about it now. Can you get away?"

"Sure. What's this all about, anyway?"

"Later. For now you must trust me. And listen," Drew said, "I need to talk alone, unobserved."

"Okay. Where?"

"You suggest the place." "Bobby was silent for a moment. Then, "There's a small print shop behind the newspaper offices. The owner is a friend of mine. The shop has a rear entrance that opens into the lane. I'll go there after lunch and."

"I can't wait that long."

"Right. I'll meet you at, say, ten? We'll not be disturbed. Will you be okay? ?"

Drew reassured him. "I'll be there."

Drew called Jackie. She was not to expect him, he related. He might be in later in the morning.

Follow your routine, Drew reminded himself as he drove from the bluff, and did exactly that. He took the shortest route to Candler Hospital, Skidaway Road, turning left on E DeRenne, then a right onto Reynolds. He parked the Camaro in the area reserved for clergy and entered the massive complex. None of his parishioners were hospitalized, so he lingered at the information desk longer than usual, pretending to scan the list of patients. He could walk through the hospital corridors, he reasoned, and left the desk. The men's restroom provided another stop.

After an agonizing half-hour, he returned to the parking area. The early morning air was oppressive. Shimmering heat waves rose from the asphalt pavement and trickles of sweat rolled down his face and inside his shirt. The interior of the car welcomed him like a furnace. He roared the engine, switched on the air-conditioning and waited in earnest for the blast of cooler air.

9:29. He steered the car from the hospital grounds, guiding it east on a narrow lane leading to Drayton Street, a heavily traveled one-way avenue leading to the heart of the city. The Camaro was quickly absorbed into the thick of traffic.

At Bay Street Drew ignored a red light, turned right, swept into the line of cars, slowed the Camaro as it neared City Hall and turned into the entrance of the Hyatt Regency Hotel. Without pausing, he drove into the parking garage and followed signs to the second floor. He sat in the parking slot for several minutes, watching the entrance ramp. As far as he could tell, no one had followed him. He glanced at his wristwatch. No hurry, he thought. He drew a deep breath and tried to relax.

As he exited the Camaro, he saw it. The small foreign car of the night before, parked on the far side of

Bay Street. He squinted through the mix of haze and brilliant sun. Someone was sitting in the car. No, two persons, but he couldn't see either face distinctly. Now he was sure he was being watched, and they didn't care that he knew it. Of course! That was the point. He was to know. It was a kind of weapon, a signal of their intent, a reminder to follow instructions.

Drew was sure the occupants of the small car could not see him. They were waiting for him to leave the single exit from the parking garage. Simple enough. He had to come their way eventually. He watched the small car a moment more and an idea presented itself. With some luck, it would work.

He hurried down the ramp and through a side entrance to the hotel. He wished he had taken one last look at the small car, but it was too late now. He made his way cautiously down the stairs until he came to a door marked 'LOBBY' and stopped. No, he decided, not in the lobby, and started up the stairs again until he reached a door lettered 'SECOND LEVEL'. He entered and started briskly down the long corridor, his pulse racing. He saw what he was looking for, a housekeeping cart positioned at the door to one of the rooms. So far, so good. He entered the room quickly and encountered a maid dusting a small oak desk.

"Police officer," he said firmly. "I have to make a telephone call. Step outside, please."

The maid's look was a question.

"Now!" He said in a commanding voice, startling the maid. She left the room quickly and closed the door.

He stepped to the telephone, and searched the desk drawer for a telephone directory. He dialed the number and waited, stealing a moment to peek out the window. The small car was still there. Now he could see the two men clearly. Good. The desk sergeant answered.

"Officer, I am a visitor to Savannah and I want to register a complaint."

"Your name, sir?"

Drew paused. Then, "Berry. John Berry."

"Your location, sir?"

"Uh , the Hyatt."

"Room number?'

"What the hell does that matter?"

"What's your concern, sir?"

Drew tried to sound agitated, and it was easy to do. "My daughter and I are staying at the Hyatt, officer, and we just came from a walk and we were standing at the corner of Drayton and Bay Streets waiting for the light to change. A man sitting in a car at the corner made an obscene remark to my six-year-old daughter, and she's very upset, and I am, too, officer."

"Where did this happen, sir?"

"At the corner of Bull and Bay Streets."

"The man made an obscene remark to your daughter?"

"Yes."

"When did this happen, sir?"

"Just now."

"Well, sir, would you like to come to the station and file a complaint?"

It wasn't working, Drew thought. "Dammit, officer, I don't need to file a complaint. I just want you to do something about the man. I'm not taking my daughter from this hotel until that man is removed!"

"Is he still there, sir?"

"Yes, he's still there! He's sitting in a small foreign car, a silver Toyota , no, there are two men in the car. What kind of city is this where men can talk to kids that way? And there's another dad here who is pretty pissed off, too. If you can't do something about it, we can."

"Easy, sir," the officer said. "I'll have an officer check it out right away. We will need you to come to the station when we bring them in for questioning. And, you'll need to file a complaint, Mr. Berry."

"Of course. I'll be there in ten minutes." Drew hung up the receiver.

He stepped to the window to watch. Shortly, a patrol car eased up behind the small car and two uniformed officers approached the men from either side of the vehicle. Drew watched as the two men stepped from the car and began talking with the officers. He recognized his visitor in the plaza from the night before. Drew paused to enjoy the scene for another moment and then hurried to the corridor door and down the stairway.

In the lobby, he looked quickly and saw a door marked OFFICE EMPLOYEES ONLY' and bolted for it.

Drew made a left turn and ran down a hallway to a door leading to a small park. Outside, the trees and flower beds rushed by, the colors a blur. He stopped at the edge of Bay Street and glanced down the street. The two men from the small car were being placed under protest in the squad car.

Drew sprang forward again, across Bay Street, past the main entrance to the Savannah Morning News and turned into a small alley at the far end of the block. Another half block and he ran down the lane behind the newspaper offices.

He saw the small sign over the door: BULLDOG PRINT SHOP. He knocked once, and waited. The door opened and Bobby's welcomed face appeared.

Drew looked quickly in both directions and stepped into the half darkened room. Bobby closed the door behind him and took stock of his friend's appearance. Drew was breathing heavily; his shirt was drenched with perspiration.

"Man! What's going on with you? You look like you've been racing with the devil!"

Drew selected a large box and sat, trying to catch his breath. He was surprised at his heavy breathing, considering the almost daily workouts in the gym. He would have to do something about his poor lung power.

Bobby stared down at his friend. Finally, their eyes locked. Bobby's demanded an explanation. Drew nodded.

"Can we talk here? I mean, is it safe?"

"Yes. To both questions. I've used this place for private interviews many times. The owner is a friend. His name is Jake, a confidant. He knows more about what's going on around town than anybody, and I trust him implicitly. He's confirmed much of what I suspected, hears it on the streets. He's my deep throat, of sorts."

Bobby paused. "What the hell is this all about, Drew?" he asked, taking a seat nearby.

Drew held up a hand. "I'll tell you everything," he said. He drew a deep breath, pushed himself to the edge of the large box and stretched to relieve the tension. He looked at his friend sympathetically, wishing he had other, less serious information to share, and began his story.

"Vietnam," Drew said deliberately, "it starts in Nam, and it's not a pretty story. I mean I'm not proud of it." He shifted positions on the box and continued. "Toward the end of my tour, the last six months, I was busting guys who were into drugs. CID. Heavy traffic, the drugs, I mean. The hypocrisy of it all, Bobby, was that I was into the stuff, too. Not as heavy as most, but I did my share of coke. When I wasn't working on a bust, I rode shotgun on convoys. It was something to do, and I didn't care whether I lived or not. Half the time I was too high to care, I guess. On convoy, we shot up everything that moved."

Drew paused. The remembering was easy, telling it wasn't. "I remember one ride, it was dusk, and we were bone tired. One vehicle had been wiped out, six guys wasted. We were angry, and we wanted the Cong to show himself. As we turned a bend in the road, a man suddenly stepped out of the bush. A little, old man. Somebody hollered and somebody opened up. Cut the little guy in half. That night I did what I often did. Went into Saigon, got sloppy drunk and got a woman. It happened a lot in those last six months."

Bobby was silent. He had escaped the draft by joining a reserve unit.

"After one big, dirty operation, our last bust, I was wiped out. It tore me up to nail those guys. Not the pushers, mind you, but the kids who got caught up in that stuff. Even though I was doing it, it really got to me."

Drew stopped again, looking to Bobby for understanding.

"After that last bust, I went into the city again. I was determined to forget everything. I paid a few bucks for an evening with a Vietnamese woman, and got stinking drunk. I'm not proud of that, it's to my shame, but it happened. I used her, it's as simple as that. She took me to a back room in an alley and I remembered making it with her, or trying to . I'm not real sure what happened. I was so smashed I don't know if I performed or not."

He looked again at Bobby. His friend was not judging him. He was grateful for that. "But that's not the worst part of it," Drew said, and drew a deep breath. "Sometime in the night, maybe it was early morning, I don't know. It was still dark, actually, I remember that much. I was awakened by the woman's screaming. Awful screams, really. She was crying, begging. I remember trying to get my head together because I was still smashed. In the near darkness I could hear these terrible screams and for a moment or so, I couldn't decide where the screams were coming from. Then, finally, my senses returned, I guess, and I could make out this huge guy literally raping the girl."

Drew paused, and wiped away beads of sweat.

"I yelled at the guy, I think. But he just laughed and kept screwing her. She was crying and I knew, sooner or later he might kill her. But it was her terrible screaming that freaked me out! I started searching for my .45 and remember thinking, I'll scare the hell out of him. I could hardly sit up, much less stand steady. I found the gun and waved it in his direction and told him to get the hell out of there. He laughed and kept at the girl and she was still screaming. I couldn't understand a thing she was saying, but it was clear she was being brutalized. I shouted some command, something stupid, and the bastard cussed me. Then ."

Drew stood, and faced Bobby.

"The .45 exploded. The noise was like a cannon, but the screaming stopped. I managed to crawl to the man and rolled him off the girl. His face was gone. I mean, just gone! I blew his face away! And I could read the lapel insignia, even in the darkness. U.S. Army. Bobby! I killed an American soldier! And to this day, I don't even know his name."

Bobby let out a low whistle.

"That's not all," Drew continued. "The girl started screaming again. I couldn't believe the sounds she was making. She was really crazed, and I just went berserk. I starting screaming, and ... shooting. She caught one of the ... damn! In cold blood, I just wasted her! I grabbed my clothes and ran like a crazy man, half naked, into the alley. All I could think about was getting out of there. I remember running all night, it seemed, and somehow I got back to base."

"No investigation?" Bobby asked, quietly.

"No. Not that I know of." Drew's answer was a whisper.

Then he told of the call from the stranger at two in the morning and the meeting in Rousakis Square. "They, he was there! In the room. That what he says. Says the man I shot was his sergeant. He was there, and he saw the whole damn thing! Now I cooperate by delivering the package or he exposes me. Everything I stand for, everything I love will be ruined. Ellen's memory. My ministry, which, by the way, I've been considering giving up. The church's reputation. Any hope for politics. Everything!"

Bobby had listened in silence, seldom taking his eyes from his pastor friend. His face bore an incredulous stare. "How can I help?" he asked.

They sat in the dim light and talked over all the questions haunting Drew for the last thirty-six hours. They agreed the most likely contents of the package would be drugs. There was little doubt on that score. Bobby tried to put things in perspective.

"Drew, a lot of guys did things in Nam they aren't proud of. You were not the worst, though that's not saying much. You've had your personal hell for it, and I think you have tried to make up for it. So, I don't judge you. Somebody else has to do that."

He stood, stretched. "Now, as I see it, you've got several options. One, you can go along with the blackmail. If you do," he said, drawing himself up, "many people get hurt. It won't be Bibles for your Sunday school in that package. We're probably talking a major cache of cocaine, probably worth millions in street value. And if you go along with it you will be participating in the misery and the deaths of hundreds -- who knows, maybe thousands. You'll be the conduit that will introduce untold numbers of kids to a life of crime, because once they need the stuff, they'll steal, kill their mother to get it. In the process, you'll save your ass, although that's not guaranteed, but you'll leave many lives in the gutter."

"You don't have to tell me that, Bobby."

"Well, I needed to be sure. There are other options. For one, you could go to the authorities; for another, you could try handle things yourself, but how, I'm not sure. But if you choose to report this to the authorities, I can tell you, confidentially, it better be the right authorities."

Bobby paused to look at Drew. "Let me tell you what I mean. The story I've been working on for months has led me to some interesting connections between the drug traffic in this area and our local law enforcement, specifically the sheriff's department. Another day or two and I could be writing some very interesting stories, the kind of stuff that explodes and keeps on exploding for months. My editor is hounding me to give him something real soon, because we know the Atlanta papers are working on a similar story. And my editor will have my ass if they break it before we do. But, the point is, you have to be very careful, Drew, and I mean, 'very', if you go to the authorities. You might do better to choose the feds. The state guys, well, I don't know who you can trust there, either."

"If, on the other hand, you choose to go it alone, I think they'll bury you in a wink. They need you right now, but you're not indispensable. What they have planned for you is pretty obvious, I think: they are going to have you bring the stuff in for them, deliver it, and keep on using you until you are no longer useful. When they are through with you, they won't expose you; they'll drop you next to your favorite buoy. And, if you expose them, they'll kill you without a second thought."

Drew had been listening quietly. Bobby had said nothing new, nothing he hadn't thought of, except the part about local law officials. He had created his own particular hell and there seemed no way out without everything precious to him being destroyed. But, he realized at the moment, what was really important to him would be destroyed anyway! Then, another thought occurred to him.

"What about the story you're working on`?" he asked. "If I could hold them off for a while, could the media attention scare them off?"

"I doubt it. You said they indicated they planned something soon. Right?"

Drew's face fell. "Yeah. Tomorrow."

Bobby related something else. "Drew, there may be some local figures other than law enforcement people involved in Chatham County's drug trade. It looks like at least one major county official is also connected. Which means, of course, there may be others. The net we hope to throw might catch some big time fish. Meaning, too, you have got to be, not just smart, my man, but very, very careful."

"And," Drew reminded Bobby, "I don't have much time."

Drew stood again and walked about the shadowed room. "If I can keep the stuff from hitting the streets --

72

well, I want a shot at it." He turned to Bobby, his face set with determination. "I want that, Bobby. As this thing grows, I want it more and more. I want to face that little bastard again. No, I want to know who's behind this operation. And I think I know where I can get some help, at least some expertise. I have a friend, an old friend from Nam. We served together in narcotics investigations. Busted a lot of GIs together, I'm sorry to say. I haven't seen him in a couple of years, but we've kept in touch. His name is Rod Gray. He went with the FBI after coming home from Nam, and I believe I can trust him. At least, he could tell me what to do. He owes me that much. I wouldn't expect him to get involved on my part, but he could help direct me." He looked at Bobby. "Can I tell him the information you shared with me, you know, about local authorities, etc.?"

Bobby stood quickly. "No, Drew. I'd lose the story in a second. They'd take everything I have and lock it up and I'd have nothing, except one angry editor after my head. Not now, Drew. And, I mean that, understand?"

Drew nodded.

Bobby held out his hand to Drew. "What I will do is this: I'll be a friend, and I'll give you any information I get that I think might help, without jeopardizing my story. Okay?"

"Sure," Drew said, taking his friend's hand. He felt a bit betrayed, but remembered he had done the same thing to his friend the night before. Still, he trusted Bobby.

"Drew," the reporter said, "You are out of your league, my friend, no matter what you do. I know you have been a mean S.O.B. in the past, and I know you are one strong man, physically. One thing you haven't considered is getting out of here. You're a wealthy man, Drew. You could just run, run like hell and never come back."

Drew was speechless. He had never thought of running. And, he knew this for sure, he wouldn't think of it again. Whatever he did, it would not include trying to save his skin by skipping out. His hand was on the door. "Thanks, Bobby, but running is not an option, not even a remote possibility. I'll keep in touch."

A very tired pastor opened the door slightly and peered out. He nodded at his friend and closed the door behind him.

Drew spent the rest of the day routinely, forcing himself to attend to office matters and some afternoon appointments. The worst was a conversation with Mrs. Guerney who wanted to talk about shrubbery to be planted in the new memory garden. In the early evening he took his meal in a small French restaurant near Johnson square. The food disagreed with him. At home by eight o'clock, he tried working on his sermon for Sunday morning. The effort was futile. He would use an old sermon from his files.

He resorted to reading Dietrich Bonhoeffer's *Letters and Papers from Prison*, written from a Nazi concentration camp decades ago. Bonhoeffer was a

Lutheran pastor who participated in the assassination attempt on Adolf Hitler. The attempt failed and Bonhoeffer was arrested. Later, he and several others were marched out into a courtyard and hanged...by wire. Three days later the Nazi concentration camp was liberated.

Recalling the Bonhoeffer story helped, although he could not say how; he just felt better hearing a fellow sufferer think through the pains of imprisonment. Not all prisons, Drew thought, require bars. Then, another thought: at some point he would have to make his peace with God and though he was certain of God's sympathy, he was also convinced peace would not come without a price.

Finally it was late enough to assume Rod Gray might be home, and alone. He found the number in a ragged telephone book. He couldn't chance another call from his home telephone, so he drove to the nearest public telephone located outside the Kroger store on LaRoache. The drive took less than five minutes. As he stepped into the booth and began dialing the Washington number, his hand, he noticed with dismay, was shaking. What if Rod couldn't come, wouldn't come?

"Hello."
"Rod, this is Drew Campbell."
"Drew! Hey, this is great. Where are you? D.C.?"
"No, Savannah. Can you talk a minute?"
"Sure. What's up?"
Drew paused. "I'm in trouble, Rod," he replied.

"Trouble? Made the deacons mad, did you?" Rod laughed.

"No, nothing like that. It's much more serious."

"What is it, Drew?"

The two men had been close, really close for a time, years ago. That closeness was not a certainty now, but Drew was trying to reclaim what remained of it.

"Can you come to Savannah for a couple of days? I need your help, Rod. I mean, I really need it."

"Sure. When do you want me?"

"Right away. How soon can you leave?"

"I'll catch the next plane. Want to meet me at the airport, or do I come to the church?"

"Neither. Rod, please understand: I can't be seen with you. It is that serious. I'm taking a chance talking over the phone, but I can tell you this much: I'm being blackmailed and it has to do with the work you and I did in Nam. Understand?"

The agent was silent. Then, "Okay. Where do I meet you?"

"There's an art show in Johnson Square tomorrow. I'll meet you there at twelve twenty. A lot of folk will be on lunch break then and there will be a crowd in the square. Can you make it that soon?"

"I'll be there. And I'll find you. Look for a concession stand."

"That's good. But, Rod, remember, we can't be seen talking, not like we knew each other, okay?"

"I understand, Drew."

"Thanks, Rod," Drew said quietly and replaced the receiver. As he did so he noticed his hand was no longer shaking. Maybe, just maybe, God did care. Maybe things were going to work out after all. He drove back to the bluff and, after a steaming shower, was asleep within minutes.

In Washington, Rod Gray replaced the receiver slowly, and measured the conversation with his friend, Drew Campbell. The two of them had been close in Nam, and had stayed in touch since, though infrequently. An occasional call had been the extent of it. Drew's call had been the first he had received from the clergyman since a few weeks after Ellen's death. Rod had never met the reportedly beautiful Ellen North, and the agent had not known of her death until Rod had called late one evening, as he had done tonight. Friends, but not close friends.

Rod considered the call carefully, and decided things were going very well, very well indeed.

Chapter Six

"What do you mean, I have to leave now?" the woman demanded and sat upright in the middle of the bed, making no effort to hide her nakedness. "I just got here," she pouted. "And what about dinner, huh? Don't I at least get to eat?"

"Sorry, baby, but that call means I've got to catch a plane, real soon." Rod Gray replaced the telephone and without a glance in the woman's direction, entered the bathroom. There would be other times for sex with Betsy. There always were. For Rod, Betsy Connors was sex, now days his only sex, by choice.

"You're sorry? Well, I'm hungry."

He stepped out of the bath and repeated his explanation. He punctuated his reasoning with pointed finger. "I told you: I have to go. I'm sorry, Betsy. Okay? Real sorry."

"Screw you!" she retorted. "Maybe next time you call I won't be available either. I'm tired of you leaving just when we get started," she shouted, and threw a pillow at Gray. "And, I'm tired of leaving hungry. I don't even ask you to pay!"

Betsy Conners slid to the side of the bed and reached for her panties. "You're going to be sorry one of these days, Rod Gray. I mean, you're really going to regret the way you treat me. If you think you can just call when you want," she pouted, her eyes moistening, "and get your jollies off with me, you've got another thought coming! I won't be treated like a whore, you hear me!" It was the best she could do, because she did not mean a word of it. She crossed her arms defiantly across her large breasts.

"But you are a whore, my dear, and a very good one," he said, wrapping a towel about his waist as he approached her. He reached for her arm and she jerked it away. "Don't touch me! I don't need you, Rod Gray." She stepped away from him.

He grabbed her arm again. "Sit down, Betsy."
"No!"
"I said, sit down!" He forced her to the edge of the bed and put his arm about her bare shoulders. She struggled weakly, and then submitted to his firm hold. When she started to cry in earnest, he pulled her to him. In a strange kind of way, he loved Betsy, he knew that, and he knew, too, that his love was selfish and often abusive. Yet, he could not count the times she had come to him when he needed her. Of all the women he had ever made love to, she was not only the best, but also the most willing not to meddle in his affairs. She asked little of him, except to be near him when his company was available. Still, she was expendable, and they both knew it.

The agent met Betsy at a retirement party for another agent and had been taken immediately with her easy beauty, unaware initially she served many influential men of Washington for a price. He had inquired discreetly about her, surprised and not a little excited to learn she was one of Washington's most often requested prostitutes. In a perverse kind of way, given her less than advantageous origins, she had made the most of her assets.

When she had come to his apartment the first time to deliver her services, he had thought of her like any one of many Washington prostitutes he had enjoyed: she was good at what she did and she kept her mouth shut. After employing her rites of sex on several occasions, he not only found himself enjoying her companionship, he missed her when an assignment took him from Washington. He gave her a key to his apartment, but she never used it except to bring in groceries and prepare the apartment for his arrival. She was always part of that preparation, and that made her feel wanted, needed, something no other man offered her. In return, she gave Rod everything he wanted, and more. Betsy Conners was a professional, the best of her kind in D.C. In time, to Rod's limited circle of friends, she became "Rod Gray's girl". The relationship was approaching two years in length.

The pattern of their time together had changed little over the last months. He would call from the airport of another city and give his anticipated arrival time. She would go by the apartment, check the refrigerator and cabinets, Then, shopping list in hand, pretending to be dutiful housewife, she shopped. Back in the apartment, she put the stock away and prepared the bedroom by pulling the covers down, opening the curtains and putting out his favorite slacks and cotton shirt. If it promised to be a cold evening, she would light the gas logs in the living area. She always chilled his favorite Chardonnay. All chores done, she would shower and prepare for his arrival. The preparation invariably included new and sensuous lingerie.

For Betsy, the routine was the only real meaning in her life. She had discovered what pleased the man, and it pleased her to be appreciated. The scene was repeated mostly on weekends. Only occasionally did he call her to the apartment on a week night, and then it seldom included anything but sex. She asked little of him, because he took care of her the rent on her tiny flat, spending money, a few presents, things to make her life a bit more comfortable. Once a regular in the beds of some of Washington's more prominent personages, now she turned tricks only when bored or she needed a few extra dollars. Rod never asked her about time she spent with other men, only that she be careful. "Careful for whom, me or you?" she had asked. He never answered, and she did not push. She needed Rod Gray, and she knew he needed her; he had said as much and she remembered how good that made her feel. Deep inside, she suspected it would all end one day without explanation. Until then, she had decided, she would enjoy the arrangement. It was almost like being married, she had convinced herself, without the bother of marriage.

But the arrangement had its drawbacks. Like tonight, and so many other nights he suddenly announced he had to leave, or she had to leave. What did he do that required so abrupt an end to a wonderful evening on so many occasions? It had to be important and dangerous, too, for she had overheard some telephone conversations that made her think so, and she had seen the gun he frequently wore beneath his coat. But she did not ask about his work. She had even stopped wondering about it. Rod wanted it that way, and she wanted to please him. It was true, she was frightened of him at times, but there was no reason to give up the good thing she had going. Most of her friends envied her arrangement.

Nevertheless, nights like this one, interrupted just when they were really getting into it, she really hated these nights. She had worked hard to get this night ready for him, for them, and now it was over. Just like that. "When will I see you again?" she asked, sniffling her tears, and standing to pull over her head the loosely fitting silk dress she had bought for this night.

"Betsy, you know I'll call you just as soon as I know myself. Now get your things together. I have to get to the airport after I make some calls."

She nodded a reluctant understand. "I'm sorry for throwing a fit. But, I miss you. I needed to make love tonight. I needed you. But," she added quickly, "I know, whatever it is, it's important." She slipped into her sandals and went to the kitchen to put away the early makings of dinner. He followed her.

"Forget that. The maid will get to it in the morning." He took her shoulders and looked her in the eyes. It was a sympathetic manner. "Betsy, I'm really sorry, but I have to go. Now please, get your things and go home."

She brushed past him. Locating her purse, she swung it over her shoulder and reached for the door. "Maybe I won't go home, not just yet."

She opened the door and walked out, stopped and turned back to face him at the doorway. Without speaking, she kissed him on the lips, turned again and left.

Rod stood at the door, watching her descend the wide stairway until she disappeared at the second landing. He shook his head. It wasn't fair for her to be treated like this, not after all she did for him with little or no expectation. He would have to make it up to her. Yes, an expensive gift. Betsy wasn't difficult to pacify.

He closed the door and went straight to the telephone. He had several calls to make and little time to complete them. He lifted the receiver and touched an automatic dial button. Shortly, the connection was made.

"Wendell speaking," the voice replied.

"Rod Gray here."

"Yes, Mr. Gray?"

"I need two seats on a flight to Savannah, Georgia, as soon as possible, for agent Moore and myself. Then, inform the chairman of my departure. I'll be in contact with you tomorrow, the next day at the latest."

"I'll take care of it, Mr. Gray. Give me a few minutes."

"Right," Rod replied, and replaced the receiver and moved to the bedroom. There, he retrieved his familiar travel bag.

The telephone rang once and he touched the hands free answering button. "Rod Gray." He continued his well rehearsed routine of packing.

"Mr. Gray, your reservations are complete. Flight 430 at ten-forty-seven. You'll have to hurry. Your tickets will be waiting for you at the Delta ticket counter. With your permission, I will delay calling the chairman until morning. He has dinner guests this evening and asked not to be disturbed."

"Yes, that's fine. Thanks for your help."

"Not at all, sir. It's my job. Have a good trip."

"Thanks," Rod responded, and disconnected the call. He moved his finger down the list of automatic dial buttons and touched the next to last in the row. On the fourth ring a woman answered.

"Hello."

"Doña? Rod here. Meet me at National in an hour. Delta ticket counter. We'll be gone several days. I'll give you the details on the plane." Then, "By the way, it's hot in Savannah. You might remember that when you're packing."

"Savannah?" she asked.

"That a problem?"

"No problem," the woman said firmly. "Anything else?"

"No." Rod answered and returned to his packing, completing the simple task in ten minutes. He placed his bag at the door and returned to his bedside. He had to make another call.

He entered the unlisted numbers and listened for the ring. The response was immediate. "Yes?" a man's voice asked.

"It's begun," he said quietly. "I'm on my way to Savannah with agent Moore. I should know something by tomorrow evening."

"So fast, huh?" The Deep South accent was heavy, and clearly deliberate. "Then, I'll await your report."

Gray smiled. Senator James Alexander Maxwell, junior senator from Georgia, was a pompous ass, playing beautifully a role he enjoyed to a fault. The senator worked very hard at his public image. Only this morning the Washington Post had carried a page one story on the senator's antidrug stance. The story was accompanied by a picture of the desk pounding senator in a tirade against illegal drug trafficking. Though the senator was good at projecting control, Rod knew what lay beneath the facade: a sniffling coward who would sell his mother to the highest bidder. Rod detested the man, but, on the other hand, he was useful. Too, there was no denying the man knew how to wield the considerable power at his disposal. At the right time, and it might be sooner than expected,+ Rod would deal with him. For the present, it was necessary to permit Maxwell to think what he wished.

"Any instructions for me?" Rod asked, biting his lip.

"None. Keep me informed."

"Right. I'll be in touch."

Rod Gray, special agent for the F.B.I. joined the agency shortly after returning from Vietnam. His background -- eight years in the army's investigative branch, most of them in drug enforcement, led him to the Bureau. It was a natural career progression and, not incidentally, a perfect cover.

For the last five years, he had been assigned to the President's Council on Drugs. The assignment was more than he could have hoped for, considering his loathing of the routine. The President's Council was, like so countless other legislated groups, a vocal but powerless advisory group composed of well-heeled appointees charged with making the President -- or somebody -- look good. It was, in fact, a do-nothing group and everyone knew it.

What it provided Rod was a bit more substantial. His assignment to the council meant, among other things, he did not have to report to the Bureau on his activities, only to the Chairman of the Council, a business tycoon who actually spent little time on the Council's tasks. The great latitude it offered a special agent was enormous. He enjoyed a nearly unlimited expense account. When he was directed by the chairman to investigate a lead, he could take his time about it. Really, it was the legal counsel employed by the Council who directed the activities of staff, including Rod's. Too, by custom, self-directed investigations could be pursued by the agent, if he determined such activity necessary. His jaunt to Savannah fell in this category.

Doña Moore was the junior agent assigned to the Council, working under Rod's direction and supervision. She was a black haired, Mexican American beauty who Rod surmised early would never cut it with the agency. But she had surprised him. She quickly established herself as a hardworking, insightful agent, and a credit to the Bureau.

Rod wanted her with him in Savannah for several reasons, not the least of which was the calming influence she might have on an overly excited pastor; that quality would prove helpful when they talked with Drew.

Rod completed his packing and walked across the room to deposit his bag near the door. He returned to the table beside his bed and withdrew his service revolver and identification from the drawer. Satisfied with his hurried preparations, he left the apartment and made his way to the garage.

The drive to National Airport took twenty-five minutes, enough time to recall the brief conversation with Drew. Their friendship had begun in earnest in Vietnam when both were assigned to CID. Initially, Drew had been a capable and dependable military officer, even brilliant at times. Later in their tour something had happened to his friend, the thing that happened to many GIs. Drew turned mean and nasty, and Rod was certain Drew was doing drugs, but never confronted him with his suspicions.

Rod never had been comfortable with Drew's early, keen sense of ethics. Ethics were for the good guys, those who sought to cure every social ill. Rod saw his duty in black and white: find the pushers and bust their asses. Drew would agree, but he would not let it go at that, at least early on. He worried over the poor bastards who got caught up in the poison. Often, for no good cause, reasoned Rod, his friend sought out the addicts, counseled with them, and pled for them before military courts.   Rod was not overly surprised when, following his friend's emotional withdrawal from the war, Drew informed him that he had decided on the ministry.

But that was in the beginning. Then Drew himself, driven perhaps by despair, had changed. In the last months of their tour, he stopped doing his good deeds. His attitude turned destructively cynical. He got his work done, though it was average at best. Much of the time he spent in the back alleys of Saigon. Rod tried to warn him once, and a fierce argument ensued. Rod let it go after that incident. Yet, they remained friends.

In Nam, Rod always felt he could count on Drew when lines might be drawn. The one time his conviction was tested it was proved. Their ride, an UH60 Huey, caught fire on approach and crashed. Rod was rendered unconscious on impact and it was Drew who pulled him from the wreckage before the chopper exploded. They were the only survivors.

The agent parked the government's Crown Vic and moved, bag in hand, to the Delta counter. Doña was waiting several steps from the counter.

"I have the tickets. We've just time to make the flight." She handed Rod the airline folder containing his tickets and fell in stride with the older agent. She did not ask questions; details would be shared in due time. They entered the stream of pedestrians moving toward their flight. Within minutes they were comfortably seated at the rear of the aircraft as the Boeing 727200 lifted from the runway. Doña watched the lights of the capital city fade as the jet streaked into the night.

She turned to Rod. "I've not been to Savannah." It was a simple enough request for information.

"Nor I," he responded, "and I wish my first visit were for a different reason. A friend of mine seems to be in trouble. We're going to see if we can help."

He told her of the scant conversation with Drew. She listened without questioning. When he finished, Rod reclined his seat and closed his eyes. Doña accepted the dismissal. She looked out the small window and wondered about the Reverend Andrew Campbell. She chanced a wondering glance at Rod and shifted uncomfortably in her seat.

Senator Maxwell stood at the door of his Washington home, bidding his dinner guests goodbye. He detested the small, meaningless tasks his public role thrust upon him, almost as much as he despised the people who insisted he meet their every need. Selfish crybabies, that's what they were. Well, he had more important things to do at the moment. His thoughts had been elsewhere during the inane table conversation. He was not a trusting man, barely trusting himself, and for longer than he cared to remember, he had suspected Rod Gray was planning to betray him. No real evidence for his suspicions, just gut feelings, such as the tone of Rod's voice when he updated the senator on their operations, and, too, what the senator suspected he was not told. He knew he was at Rod's mercy; the agent directed everything, knew everything. What the senator did not know bothered him more than Rod's reports. "Just trust me,
Senator," was Gray's standard retort. Now, years into the operation, the admonition was growing thin. Rod could ruin him with one telephone call. It was time, Maxwell had decided, to insure his own future.

   He had thought about it for months. The only sure answer was to rid himself of Gray, take the man out of the picture altogether. Isolating him, or simply ending their association would not be sufficient. As long as Rod lived, Maxwell would be vulnerable. And, there was little doubt in the senator's mind -- Rod was a calculating, devious man. The truth was, trust was not a word found in Gray's or the senator's vocabulary.

There was only one man with more to lose than the senator, and settling into a large leather chair in his library, he placed the call on his safe line, the first he had ever made to his more powerful accomplice.

A woman's voice answered the international call.
"Si."
"The Man, please."
"Who's calling?"
"Capitol Hill."
"Uno momento."

An interminable minute passed. Then, a voice he had not heard in several years. Maxwell shivered when he heard it.

"Eagle One."

"Engineer is not to be trusted. You and I have the most to lose, and I think it's time to rid ourselves of the problem."

An extended pause. Then, "One question: you're sure?"

"Sure enough. If he decides to cut, you and I are unprotected. Sooner or later, if he skips or if he doesn't, he'll demand more. You could survive, given your isolation, but your operation wouldn't. I don't have that luxury. We have to act."

"I believe you may be right. I will take care of it. But we need that package first. It's too much to ignore. Don't you agree?"

"I've got enough."

"Well, Capitol Hill, I don't. You'll have to cooperate a bit longer. Then, in the final transactions, which I understand will occur soon, our 'friend' will die. Do we agree?"

Maxwell had no choice. "As you say. It's agreed. Make it clean. I don't want any linkage."

"We are always neat, Capitol Hill. Now, forget it. We'll take care of everything."

The line disconnected.

The senator leaned back in his chair. Again, a shiver ran through his body. Just talking to The Man scared the hell out of him. But, he reassured himself, it was done. In a few days he would be perfectly safe.

There was a light tap on the library door, and it opened slowly. Mrs. James Maxwell entered and came directly to her husband's chair.

Morgan Ann Hunnington. Maxwell's loveliness belied her fifty years. Teeming with southern charm, she was the consummate senator's wife, able to gain from the most antagonistic opponent of her husband's ideas no less than a sympathetic response. Her subtle sensuality seldom went unnoticed by either sex. The men desired her, almost openly, much to the chagrin of their ladies.

She usually got what the senator needed, and what she wanted.

Morgan Ann knelt between her husband's knees and leaned into his chest, producing the inevitable stirring in his groin. "A successful evening, don't you think?" she asked in a whisper.

Maxwell stroked his wife's hair, lifting the heavy waves of blond tresses from her back and permitting them to fall lightly. "You were grand, as usual," he offered. His hands drifted down her back and cupped her buttocks.

"You won't give them your vote, will you?"

"No. They'll have to offer more. But that will come in time. It usually does."

"I know. You're too good for them, darling."

He lifted her face. "He wanted you, baby."

"Who ?" she asked, knowing exactly whom he referred to.

But he played the game. "The Secretary."

"Well," she said, rolling her large eyes, "it didn't hurt the cause, did it? Just doing my job, darling, just like you taught me." She put her full lips to his. "Want to take what the Secretary wanted?" she purred.

Following his wife quietly up the stairs to their bedroom so as not to wake their teenage daughters, the senator had two options. Enjoy his wife's body, or revel in the thought of being rid of Rod. He was unbuttoning his shirt as they reached the bedroom door. The Man would insure the disposal of the erstwhile agent.

Chapter Seven

Drew maintained a lively step and tried to think about the Savannah he knew so well. His Savannah, as he liked to think of the city, replete with fantasies of the past and ample conveniences of the present, where nostalgia is preserved and blended smoothly with the contemporary. His Savannah, nestled in disarming quiet against the river, waiting to wrap her embrace about an unsuspecting visitor.

He listed in his mind the city's myriad of images. Three Savannah's actually. The old historic district, the Victorian district and the newer plastic and concrete of south Savannah. Then, there were the beaches of Tybee Island. Yet, the historic old city was his very favorite. Wherever he looked he saw porticos of old mansions. Solemn stares from carved faces of original leaders. A backdrop of magnolia, azalea and wrought iron fences. Flowered gardens in quaint corners. The scent of boiling shrimp. Whispered voices, and party laughter. Fountains splashing in the distance. Art shows and sidewalk sales. The distinctive, mellow sound of a freighter's horn. Quaint shops. Colors of every hue. And in the spring the absolutely awesome Azaleas!

Savannah was a city being discovered anew daily, waiting, and ready to weave her mystic spell. He never tired of the city, positioned as a gateway to the coastal empire and a string of engaging islands. Coastal

Georgia, one hundred twenty miles of ocean shore, marsh and sand dunes.

Drew distanced himself from the church as he walked toward Johnson Square. All Saturdays should be as this one, he thought. Bright, and hopeful. Yesterday had taken its toll; today would be different, he reasoned, and instinctively knew his newly found hope resulted from his call to Rod Gray. The anger had receded a bit, replaced at the moment by a fierce determination to end this thing. Still, he recognized the 'old' Drew lurking in the shadows.

As he had hoped, the park was crowded. He was sure the art show would draw hundreds and chose the noon hour because many employees would frequent the city's most popular square on their lunch hour. Art lovers also swelled the numbers milling about the common. Good, the more the better, he reasoned, and entered the circular flow of walkers. He strolled as casually as possible while searching the crowd for a concession stand. Rod was here, he sensed it. And, he was sure his friend had spotted him. Drew kept a watchful eye for any familiar face he might recognize. He must avoid them all, especially today.

A face stopped him abruptly. Twenty feet to his right. There was no mistaking him, but Drew took a second look to confirm it. Yes, the same black hair protruding from under the cap. The same small ears and growth of beard. Drew floundered for a moment. As he did, the man from the riverfront caught his eye, touched the bill of his cap, smiled, and looked away. Drew could feel the surprise register on his face, and chastised himself. He should have expected the man; he had told himself that much. Find the elusive concession stand. Give Rod some clue, warn him.

He pushed his way past gathered conversations and reached the nearest drink counter. He paid for a coke, accepted change and was about to turn from the vendor when a voice whispered clearly, deliberately over his shoulder.

"Be cool," the voice instructed.

Rod! Thank God.

Drew turned, his insides churning.

"Borrow a light, mister?" the man asked

Drew complied, searching his shirt pocket for matches. Had he not known the voice from his past with certainty he would have needed a second glance at the face. Dark, reflecting shades hid the familiar, penetrating eyes. A visor was pulled firmly over his forehead. But, there was no mistaking the powerful shoulders and the strong chin.

Drew patted his pockets, located the matches and concentrated on striking a match. Holding it to Rod's cigarette, he whispered, "Trouble, nearby."

"I know," Rod said through closed lips. Then, "Walk."

Drew obeyed without looking back.

Rod called after him, "Thanks for the light, buddy."

Drew's eyes swept the immediate crowd about the concession stand. He was sure his caller was in close proximity. He would have to let Rod take the lead.

Suddenly, from his right, not thirty feet away, a woman's angry shout broke above the noise of the milling hundreds. Drew jerked his head in the direction of the scream.

"Take your hands off me!" the woman shouted, directing her demand to a man wearing a black T-shirt. A man with small ears and a week's growth of beard. "What do you think you're doing?" she yelled again at the man, now stepping closer to him as he retreated in disbelief. "Animal!" she continued. "Someone arrest this man! Somebody put this crud where he belongs." The woman's voice rose as she gestured toward the man trying to disengage himself from an embarrassing situation. The crowd closed in on the two central players.

Drew stood frozen for several moments, unsure, when Rod suddenly took a firm hold on his elbow, then released the grip. A command followed.

"Wesley Hotel, room 337."

Drew turned to see his friend moving away from the still shouting woman. A split-second later, Rod disappeared into the crowd. Drew stared after the older agent, then jerked his head in the direction of the woman who was screaming louder than ever. Two men had come to her aid and had the accused man in tow. Finally, Drew bolted into action, following his friend from the crowd drawn by the woman's screams. He pushed against the flow of people, breaking free from the outer circle of curious onlookers. Within seconds he was racing down a side street bordering Christ Church. The Wesley was two blocks away.

He ran harder now, bumping without regard into anyone in his way, pounding his feet toward the old hotel. Another block and he slowed his pace. Rod was nowhere to be seen.

Drew reached the side door of the hotel and entered quickly, walking to the elevator which stood open and waiting. Moments later, he stepped off on the third floor, oriented himself to the numbering of the rooms and found 337. He took a deep breath, and knocked once, then again. He tried to calm his heaving breath. The pounding heartbeat would settle to normalcy in moments. Rod opened the door and motioned him inside, closing the door quickly, locking it.

"Hey, buddy!" It's good to see you!" Rod exclaimed, and grabbed Drew in a bear hug. "And you executed beautifully. Just like old times, huh?"

"Yeah, except I'm a bit rusty, I'm afraid," Drew said. "Rod, thanks for coming. I really mean it. Thanks."

"No problem, Drew," Rod responded, and motioned to two chairs near the window.

Drew dropped in a chair and drew a prolonged breath. "I was worried; I was followed to the square. Guess I should have expected it, but it shook me anyway. Thank God for the woman. That was a Godsend."

"I'll take credit for that, my friend. The woman is with us, Drew."

Drew stared in disbelief. "What do you mean, 'with us'?

"I brought her with me. Figured we might need a woman's touch along the way; that is, if things are as bad as you say."

"But ."

"I trust her completely, Drew. She's awfully good. I've worked with her for some months now. I think she can help. You'll like her, and you, well, you'll see for yourself. She ought to be here any minute."

"Rod," Drew explained feebly, "I don't need , I mean, I don't want anybody else in on this. I just need you to hear me out, suggest some alternatives. How could she help, anyway?"

"Well, she already has, hasn't she?"

"But how did you know, she know ?"

"It's our business to know, Drew."

Drew's shoulders slumped. "I don't know, Rod, this whole thing is so unreal. I ." He stopped and looked at his old friend.

"Now, tell me," said Rod, "what's this trouble you're in?" He got up from his chair and walked to the window. Drew followed him with his eyes, and was glad for the familiar confidence in Rod's step. His friend had a way of calming him, always did, in fact. He studied Rod at the window. The same strong frame, compact and coiled, ready to spring. Only the streaks of gray in the cropped, light brown hair betrayed his age. That, and the tiny lines creeping about his eyes. Otherwise, Rod was the same youthful friend of years ago.

"Rod, let's talk about the girl ."

"Later, Drew, after you've met her, okay? She only knows a friend of mine is in trouble, and that's only a little less than I know. She is here at my request and will ask no questions. If you feel uncomfortable after you've met her, she'll leave. No questions asked. If you decide otherwise, she stays. Hell, I don't even know what this is all about, Drew. Now, do you fill me in, or not?"

"Yeah, all right." Drew rested his hands on his knees. "Okay. This is all going to sound totally absurd, but it's not. I mean, it's real, Rod. I don't know how deep it goes; all I know is it appears I'm in one hell of a bind."

"Start from the first."

Drew looked at his friend for reassurance. It was there, in Rod's eyes, his posture. "Well," Drew continued, "do you remember the last big bust we made in Nam?"

"Yeah, in mid or late summer, wasn't it. 1970."

"October, actually. We wrapped it up and we took a day of R and R in Saigon. We split in the afternoon if you recall, and ."

His recital was interrupted by a quiet knock at the door.

"That's Doña," Rod said, moving to the door quickly.

Rod admitted the woman, took a quick look down the hall, and closed the door behind her. He followed the girl as she approached Drew with outstretched hand.

"Hi," she said, "I'm Doña."

"Drew," Rod offered, "this is my colleague, agent Doña Moore. Doña, meet the Reverend Dr. Drew Campbell."

"Just Drew, please", he said, and accepted her outstretched hand, surprised by its warmth. He studied her quickly. The distinctive Latin American features were dominant. "I think I owe you a 'thank you'," Drew said. "That was some performance out there. You convinced me, at least."

"Work is work," she responded, running her fingers through the neck length strands of thick, black hair. She added, "Who is the greasy little bastard, anyway?"

"Good work, Doña," Rod offered. Then he added: "She's going to be one of our best, Drew. Maybe we can use her. What do you think?" He put his arm about Doña's shoulders, the exaggerated gesture of a proud supervisor. Doña moved from under Rod's condescending display.

"While you two decide my fate," she forced a smile, "I'll wash some of this heat off my face," and moved to the bath, closing the door behind her.

Drew watched her disappear and turned to Rod. "What's her background?" he asked.

"Latin American. Her mother was from the Caribbean, I believe. She came to the agency several years ago. She's thirty-four. A master's degree in criminal justice. Her father was Deputy Director of the agency before he left the bureau. It was a shame, too, because he was one of the few who had the confidence of all the bureau people. Doña was assigned to the President's Council because I worked with her father for several years and my chief thought I could help her through some things. Her mother died when she was very young, I think. She never talks much about it. Her father, David Moore, reared her from the time she was five. Never married her mother, though."

"Her father? What happened to him?"

"Took early retirement."

Rod looked toward the bath. "Anyway," he offered, "she's been a fine agent. Below that smile is one tough girl. She gives no quarter, and expects none. I can count on her, but you've seen that for yourself. So what do you say? Is she in ?"

"Yeah," Drew answered, "she's in."

"Good. Now, soon as Doña is ready, let's get on with your story."

Doña returned from the bath. Drew was stunned by the change effected so quickly. She was a pretty woman, he thought. Actually, she was beautiful. Not the cover girl type, but lovely. No need for extensive makeup. Her beauty was subtle, natural. The light brown skin was clear, her dark eyes sensuous. He had known a woman like her once, he thought to himself, but that woman was dead. The recall disturbed him. This woman was alive, and the thought made him angry. Quickly, he buried the attraction.

Doña turned to Rod as if waiting for instructions.

"Drew says you're in, and he's about to fill us in on his situation," Rod said, and looked to Drew who was standing at the foot of the bed occupied by his friend. "Start from the beginning, Drew."

"Yes," Drew responded with uncertainty. He realized the woman's presence widened the circle of those who would know what he had hidden for years. "From the beginning ." He pulled a chair from the writing table.

"Viet Nam ...," Drew began, relating for the second time in less than twenty-four hours the sordid details of that night in Saigon. He omitted the story of his last six months in Nam, but was careful to relate as much detail as he could remember about the night in question. When he finished his story, he told of his call from the stranger at two in the morning. "They, he was there! In the room. That's what he says. Says the man I shot was his sergeant. He was there, Rod, and he saw the whole thing! Now I cooperate by delivering the package or he spills everything!"

"Let's rest," said Rod, noting Drew's posture, "I'll get us something to eat," and left the hotel room. Doña excused herself and entered the bath.

Drew walked to a window of the old hotel room, the ray of hope peeking through his ravaged spirit growing brighter. The agents were experienced; they'd know what to do. God knows he had tried to resolve this thing alone and had gotten nowhere. He would follow Rod's lead; he could trust Rod. The man would know what to do. Doña? He hoped so.

Doña came from the bathroom, toweling her hair. The faded jeans and sweatshirt had been exchanged for a cotton skirt and blouse. She stopped the toweling for a moment and looked at Drew sympathetically. Instinctively, she had decided, she liked the man; his manner was refreshing. She suspected that below the humility and the obvious pain laid a firm, vigorous spirit, and she liked the feelings the suspicion produced. She had known a priest like him several years ago and the resulting unworkable relationship, though brief, had been a mistake. But this man was Protestant, not wedded to the church, and he was a widow. Abruptly, the fantasy became uncomfortable. Nevertheless, she smiled, and returned to drying her hair.

"You want to talk?" she asked from under the towel. "Rod ought to be back with lunch shortly." She started toward the bath, stopped at the door of the bath and turned to Drew.

"No," he responded.

She stepped into the bath. "I'm a good listener."

He did want to talk. He walked to the entrance to the bath and leaned on the frame of the door. "Doña, I want to thank you for coming. I just hope it's not a waste of your time."

"Hey, I'm glad to be here, and it's good to meet Rod's friend. And, by the way, and I really mean this: I'm sorry about your wife. It must have been terribly hard on you. Rod said she was a terrific girl; he likes, uh , liked you both a lot."

Drew was silent.

Doña was combing her wet hair and paused to look at Drew. "Did I say the wrong thing?"

"No," he said. "I guess it's just ." He walked back to the window.

She came to his side, put out her hand and touched his. A momentary contact. Feelings. She withdrew her hand and intentionally avoided his eyes.

"I think I understand," she said softly, "a bit at least. My mother and I were really close. Of course, I was only five when she died, but I remember so many wonderful times with her. Now, every time I see a child and its mother, it , well, it hurts."

"And your father?"

She threw a momentary stare at Drew and looked away. "I don't talk about my father," and returned to the bathroom.

He did like the woman. She reminded him of Mary Taylor. Sympathetic, resolved, and candid. A no-

nonsense kind of person, except when foolishness was appropriate play.

"Tell me about Savannah while I finish my hair," she asked, returning to the bath.

"Some other time, okay?"

The door to the hall opened and Rod entered with a large brown sack under each arm.

"Food, I hope," Doña called from the bath. "I'm starving."

They ate in silence. Ten minutes later, Rod took a final bite of his sandwich and another sip of beer.

"I see only one plausible option," he said. "I want to suggest it to you, Drew, and get your reaction."

Drew laid an unfinished lunch aside, and nodded.

Rod continued. "If you, I should say, we, try to extract you from this situation by contesting the blackmail, people are going to be hurt. There is only the slightest possibility that they would simply expose you and leave it at that. I don't think you are willing to let that happen, if I hear you right, Drew. The other possibility is they would expose you and believe me, they can and will do this. They would take revenge. They've obviously gone to some trouble to set this thing up, and I doubt they will be willing if you cause them trouble. They will hurt your ministry and be satisfied with that."

Rod turned to Doña. "You agree?"

She nodded.

"Another option would be to go to the authorities, but the results would be much the same, and besides, we lose all opportunity to find out who's behind the threat and the drugs , if that is what is involved, which I think we all agree is the case. Right?"

Rod did not wait for agreement.

"So, the only plausible option, as I said, is the one I offer now." He leaned forward again, opening his palms; the gesture indicated his best judgment was open to question. "I suggest that you follow instructions. Bring the package in. Deliver it as told."

"And ?" Drew asked.

"Just that. You make the delivery and they get their stuff. We let the shipment go, but we get some faces, some leads. We don't involve the state drug people, if we can avoid it. It may not be that significant a shipment to let through, comparatively speaking, provided we make some IDs. The faces might match some others we have been interested in. And, listen, conceivably it's all they will want from you. Surely they know they can't push you too far. Using you more than once is risky; they won't do that. Drew, it's not a sure thing, but it seems to me the best plan, the only viable plan we have. And, if we get the IDs, then we'll put a hell of a scare into some of the little people, get some more leads and, if necessary, provide you protection."

"I agree," Doña offered, looking to Drew.

Drew shook his head, and stood to walk across the worn carpet. It sounded much too easy, and voiced his uneasiness with the plan. "They know my background. So I'm a pastor, but I'm not without experience in a world of violence and drugs. They know that, too." He walked back to Rod. "I'm supposed to believe they need me for just one more delivery, that the operation is getting too risky for them and they only want one more shipment? Bullshit, Rod! These people are scum, worse than scum! I'm just realizing, they'll get rid of me the moment I'm no longer useful or I'm any kind of threat."

"It's happened before," Rod said solemnly.

"What's happened?"

"The blackmailers -- they disappear after getting what they want."

The pastor studied his old friend. He had to trust somebody, and Rod was his best and only hope if he did not want to go it alone. He resisted raising the dozen questions forming quickly in his mind. He was tired of questions. He wanted to do something, to act. He rubbed his eyes. "Okay. Right now I don't have much choice. Maybe something will change. So, what do I do now?"

Rod sat back in his chair and clasped his hands over his chest. "Wait. Until they contact you. Do as they say. We'll stay close, you keep us informed. In the meantime, you go about your business as usual and I will take care of some other matters in Atlanta to justify our time in Georgia. I'll leave Doña in Savannah to wait for your signal. If they make contact, you must get in touch with her immediately, preferably without using the telephone. Now, how can we do that?"

Drew thought a moment. He had a suggestion. "There is an old mail slot on the rear corner of the church next to the alley that runs the length of the building. There used to be a door there that led to the original office entrance. The church bricked up the door years ago and changed the entrance to the offices to the one used presently at the opposite side of the building. There is an air-conditioning unit with a fence around it which hides the old entrance and the mail slot. Many people use that alley to get through the block without walking around the church, so the traffic is fairly heavy at times. The mail slot is just inside the fence. I can reach it easily from within the basement without being seen. If I need to get word to Doña, I can tape a note to the underside of the metal cover of the mail slot."

Drew looked at the younger agent. "You could check the cover regularly. And if you need to get word to me, you can drop a note through the slot. It will fall behind some old storage boxes and furniture and no one will see it. I'll check it morning, noon and night, from the inside."

Drew waited for Rod's evaluation. Suddenly, the idea sounded a bit juvenile, but Rod's face brightened. "It'll work," Rod said. "Fine. Now, Drew, you get out of here without being seen and get on with your routine. Doña, I'll be in touch several times a day, calling until I catch you in. If they make contact with Drew, it will probably mean they are ready for him to make a pickup.

I'll get back in time for the delivery. But you must not act without me present. I need to be here. Understood?"

"Yes."

"If you must leave for an extended period, like three hours or so, I will take that as a sign to get back here. Leave me a message behind that picture," he instructed and pointed to a faded print of the Talmadge Bridge which hung over the bed. "And pay in advance for this room, say, five days."

"Drew," he said, turning to his friend. "If there is, by some chance, an emergency, ring Doña's room once and hang up when she answers. It will signal her to check the mail slot right away. Of course, you must hear her answer before you hang up. Don't do that unless there is a real emergency. Understood?"

Drew nodded. Then, "Rod, there's one thing." He looked squarely at the two agents. "You're both putting your careers on the line for me, I know that. Will it mean trouble for you?"

Rod stood. "We can handle it, this one time, and that's all I am going to say about it. Now, are we ready?"

Drew nodded, and started for the door. He knew there was something he needed to say, and so he tried as best he could to say it clearly. "You guys , well, I thank you. I was afraid you might dismiss me as some kind of nut. You didn't, and I am deeply grateful." He reached for the doorknob. The old Drew had withdrawn a bit more.

110

Rod stepped closer. "Drew, you seemed to have forgotten something. You saved my ass in Nam. He turned to Doña as he continued. "Drew pulled me from a Huey just before it exploded. I would not be standing here if it weren't for that man," he said, pointing to Drew. Then, back to Drew, he said firmly, "I owe you this, my friend. So, no more sad apologies or thanks, okay?" He slapped his minister friend on the shoulder.

"Yeah, right," Drew replied, and glanced at Doña who was standing at the window across the room. "And thanks to you, too."

She crossed the well-worn carpet and extended her hand to Drew. "Glad to be a part of this. Let's hope it turns out right for you," she said, and added, "And for us." Her hands covered his, and applied pressure. A message?

"Right." Drew said, withdrawing his hand. He opened the door, looked in each direction. He nodded to the agents and left quickly.

Doña awoke in midafternoon. She tried to focus on the earlier meeting, on the conversations, the plans, on Drew, but the brief nap had left her groggy. In the bath, she splashed cool water on her face and added a subtle touch of eyeliner. Returning to the bed, she slipped into a pair of jeans and chose a light blouse. She ran a brush quickly through her hair and slipped a sun visor over her black tresses. Satisfied, she opened her small hand bag and checked its contents: a woman's essentials, her bureau identification and her service revolver. Satisfied again, she left the Wesley. She quickly mingled with the ever-present pedestrians and started the several blocks to Grace Church

Five minutes later she entered the alley behind the old buildings and saw the fence surrounding the air-conditioning units. She eased her pace to let an elderly couple pass, then took a hurried look behind the fence. She saw it, the rusted cover of the mail slot. Good. She continued toward the square.

She relaxed her stride. Now, she determined, I can enjoy the old city a bit. Nothing is going to happen immediately, she reasoned, and walked into the park fronting the church.

Drew was satisfied he had left the Wesley unnoticed. He checked with his secretary. There were no calls requiring a return call. Mr. Foster was gravely ill again, however, so he completed a quick visit to St. Joseph's Hospital, and then spent the bulk of the afternoon paying obligatory visits. At dusk he guided the Camaro along Bluff Drive and into the garage. He was reaching for the back door when a now familiar voice called from the shadows.

"Just a moment, captain ."

Drew retreated from the steps. He could see vaguely the face of his riverfront acquaintance. A rage swept up within him, and the old Drew returning with a vengeance. Take the man out right now, no trouble! The man moved out of the deeper shadows. He was showing no weapon.

Drew stepped closer until he was only two feet from killing the detestable little bastard. His finger twitched, itching to lash out and break the man's face. He could do it, he wanted to do it. One stiffened hand to the throat would incapacitate the enemy. He gathered his strength silently, ready to strike.

"Don't do something foolish, captain," the man said slowly. Drew could not see the sneer, but he knew it was there. He released the valve on his intent; the old Drew receded ever so slightly.

"Okay, captain, that's good. Now, listen up," the little man commanded. "Tomorrow afternoon you are to take your boat out into the channel and fish. Be at the ten mile buoy as night falls. Then, in darkness, tie up to the buoy and wait for a freighter that will pass within a hundred yards at about one o'clock in the morning."

"I don't fish that far out in the channel by myself," he interrupted.

"You will tomorrow night, captain, and you fish alone, got it?"

"Yes."

"Good. Listen carefully now. You will know it's the freighter you want by a signal from the stern, a flashing light. It will blink three times, and then ten seconds later, two blinks. Then one. At the moment of the last blink of light, a package will be thrown overboard in the direction of the buoy to which you are tied. The sea is supposed to be calm tomorrow night. Nothing more than the swells you are familiar with. The package, of course, will float. It will be your responsibility to find it, but you'll have some help. It will be wrapped in reflector tape so that any side up will reflect light. Sweep your flashlight in the direction you think the package will have floated. Watch the tide. Retrieve it, captain, or you're in real trouble. You understand me so far?"

"I'm listening."

"Store the package in your boat. The next morning you will fish until about noon, then return to the marina, dock your boat in the slip."

Drew did not respond; he was thinking: what kind of questions Rod would want him to ask.

"Captain ?"

"So, where do I deliver it?"

"Very good, captain. Now, listen carefully. Go straight to your car and drive to the dock. Load the package in the trunk of your car. Then drive to the parking garage on the west side of Johnson Square. You know the place, right?"

"Yes," Drew replied.

"Good. Park your car on the third level and leave it there. Walk to your office and stay there for one hour. Then you can get your car and we'll be out of your hair, captain."

"I understand."

"Good. And remember, we'll be watching every step," the familiar voice said.

"And if I can't find the package at sea?"

"Oh, you'll find it, or you're a dead man. But you're not stupid, captain. Do the job and we're through with you."

"I don't believe you."

"You don't have a choice, captain." The little man stepped closer. Their faces were now inches apart. "Don't mess up, captain." Then he stepped back into the shadows and was gone. Drew held his wrist up to the moonlight and checked the time. 8:26. He returned to the house. There he wrote out a terse note to Doña outlining the instructions his visitor had given, then drove to the church. In the basement he taped the message to the inside of the cover of the designated old mail slot. In his secretary's office, he telephoned Doña's room at the Wesley as he had been instructed. After one ring, she answered and he replaced the receiver. He scribbled a quick note to his secretary to the effect that he would be out of town for a couple days and to call the pastor at White Bluff Presbyterian Church, requesting he cover for him should a pastoral emergency arise.

He would return to the marina by midmorning, the note to Doña had said, and he would make the delivery soon thereafter. He asked them to contact him if he was not to follow their agreed-on plans, and he hoped to see them, he noted, when the assignment was complete. If not, he would get in touch with them as soon thereafter as possible.

Drew pushed the Camaro through the severe curves on the north side of the island, hurrying back to his house. He had work to do. His gear had to be gathered for the 'fishing' trip, and the boat prepared.

He worked into the night, double checking every detail. On occasions, he felt his heart racing. It was almost over, he reminded himself repeatedly. The reminders kept him in a feverish pitch. Finally, there was nothing more to do, but wait.

Doña wiped the perspiration from her forehead, drawing the handkerchief across the back of her neck before she returned it to her purse. The humidity was especially oppressive, even at this late hour, and she promised herself a cool shower upon return to the Wesley. Later, while waiting for Rod's return, she would enjoy dinner at the Pirate's House.

Without realizing it, she had reached the designated corner of the church. She was abreast of the fence surrounding the old mail slot when she stopped, looked about. She checked the alley; no one. Quickly, she stepped to the slot and lifted the cover. The envelope released easily into her hand and she slipped it into her pocket. She returned to the sidewalk and continued through the alley, retracing her steps to the Wesley. Within minutes she was back in her hotel room and tearing open the envelope. She read the note, reread it and tore it into small pieces. Rod would call within the hour. She left the room and found a public telephone in the corner of the lobby, dialed an international number and waited. A woman's voice answered on the second ring.

"Si."

"Eaglet here. Put him on."

"Si."

There was a moment of silence. Presently, a man's deep voice came on the line. "Eagle One. Go ahead."

"The pickup is tomorrow."

"Good. Anything else?"

"No."

"Okay. Proceed as planned. And be careful."

"Yes, I will."

Doña replaced the receiver and returned to her room. She stretched out on the bed and waited.

Chapter Eight

Drew left his study by a rear door reserved for a quiet exit. In the basement threaded his way through discarded furniture and boxes of financial statements many years old until he came to the green four-drawer file cabinet pushed against the outside wall. For the second time in days, he moved the file and gained access to the old mail slot. The note was gone. Nothing from Doña, however.

He moved the filing cabinet back into position and returned to his study to make final arrangements for the Sunday morning worship service. His preparations lacked spiritual energy, more perfunctory than ever. He was caring less and less for the duties of his calling. Less than an hour from service time he paced slowly in his study, occasionally peering out the window. At least the weather would be agreeable for his "fishing" trip.

Bobby Taylor had slept poorly. With the advent of morning filtering through the bedroom window, he slipped his feet quietly to the floor and stood at the side of the bed. Mary was sleeping easily. He rejoiced again in the tranquil beauty of the woman he loved. Her ebony face rested peacefully on the satin cover of her pillow, the distinctive profile etched cleanly against the white background. He recalled with a shudder their unrelenting lovemaking the previous evening. He considered returning to the bed, waking her tenderly, and taking her into his arms again. Quickly he reconsidered, kissed her softly on the forehead and quietly left the room.

Shortly, the Mr. Coffee initiated its gurgling pitch. Bobby placed his briefcase on the kitchen table and spread stacks of notes and papers. He arranged them in an order he had sketched in his mind, separating them into various predetermined piles. One stack held information he had confirmed; the other batch contained tips and unsubstantiated data.

Satisfied with his preparations, he poured a mug of coffee and sat at the table. For the next hour he wrote furiously, filling pages of a legal pad with accumulated information and suspicions. Then, he wrote a one page letter. Finally, the work completed, he tore the pages from the pad and put them in a large manila envelope, sealed the inch thick binder and wrote a single name in the upper right corner: Drew.

Two and a half hours later, Bobby was sitting at his desk at the Savannah Morning News. He typed furiously on the word processor; the story was beginning to jell. He glanced at the clock in the newsroom. 10:17. He picked up the phone dialed a number and waited patiently. Within moments Drew answered his call. "Grace Presbyterian Church. Drew Campbell speaking."

"Drew," he said quietly, "we're breaking the story tomorrow morning. I thought you ought to know."

"I understand," Drew responded. "I'm going fishing this afternoon after church and will return tomorrow. I'll call you then, okay?"

"Agreed."

"Thanks."

Drew replaced the telephone and dropped into the large chair next to his desk. His efforts to pray were of no avail, and he found himself thinking of Ellen. Or, was it Doña? Neither face would come clear in his labored fantasy.

Following the worship service, he greeted parishioners who spoke perfunctorily of the sermon. He was not sure what he had said to his people, but at least he had maintained his composure and concluded the service without incident. Later, he reasoned, he would make it up to them for living a lie. And, to God.

Half an hour later he was leaving his office, but stopped at the door and returned to the old filing cabinet near his desk. He unlocked the file and pulled open the bottom drawer. He took the .45 from the drawer and unwrapped it. With a terry cloth hand towel from his bath, he wiped the oil from the weapon. If he remembered correctly, the barrel bushing often slipped from its proper position. He checked it and was satisfied with its alignment. He operated the firing mechanism. It worked perfectly. From a small box in the rear of the drawer he selected a handful of .45 ACP cartridges, placed the gun and shells in his briefcase and left the church.

He spent the early part of the afternoon preparing The North Star, a sleek, twenty-six foot StarCraft, capable of sleeping four comfortably in spacious forward berths. Powered by a three-hundred-fifty cubic inch Chrysler marine engine, she was more than adequate to ride the seas of Savannah's coast line.

Finally, he was ready and slowly edged The North Star from its slip. The powerful engine purred. He nosed the boat into the waterway and started for the mouth of the Savannah River. It was midafternoon.

The North Star slid effortlessly through the channel. Soon, the boat entered the channel leading from the mouth of the river. Drew increased the engine's speed and settled The North Star into a rhythmic pounding over the two foot swells.

Early Sunday evening, Bobby Taylor gunned the Chevy Monte Carlo over the bridge spanning the intercostal waterway, speeding toward Tybee Island. The caller had given him thirty minutes; no more, no less. Only nineteen minutes remained. He had spoken with Mary briefly to let her know he had been summoned from his desk. No need to give her details.

He had started from the office in a hurry when a thought had struck him at the door. This might be risky; what if something happened to him? He had returned to his desk and taken the manila envelope from his briefcase and given it to a young reporter. His instructions had been clear: if he was not in the office by seven in the morning, the young man was to deliver the envelope per his instructions. The young reporter was pleased; the man he admired and considered the best reporter at the newspaper obviously trusted him.

Now Bobby was pushing the time limit the mysterious caller had given. The man had been insistent: Bobby must come alone and he must come immediately, if he wanted the information the caller possessed. Bobby tried to recall the man's exact words. "I can give you what you're missing."

"And what am I missing?" Bobby had asked, bothered by the call which interrupted the piecing together of the final story. He had a two hour deadline for the Monday edition of the Morning News; otherwise his story would have to wait another twenty-four hours.

The caller had replied coldly, "The name of the man who directs the business you're investigating."

He had Bobby's attention. "How do I get that name?"

"I will meet you at the dunes on Ninth Street on Tybee Island in thirty minutes. You'll get the name then."

"How do I know you're not some sort of crazy?" The information had a price; nobody gives that kind of information for free.

"I want him dead," the caller said, "but I can't do that, of course. But I can put him in jail, or you can. To prove I know what I'm talking about, I'll give you a name you will recognize. The man is in your story, that is, if you are half as good as they say you are." He spoke the name. Senator James Maxwell.

Bobby hesitated no longer. "I'll be there. Thirty minutes."

"You've only got twenty-eight left."

Tybee Island is seventeen miles from Savannah, one of a series of island stretching the length of the Georgia coast. Its eastern shore faces the Atlantic and, on a clear night, one can see the lights of the ten mile buoy from the Tybee shoreline. Highway 82 connects the mainland and the Island over a flat, marsh lined series of inlets and auxiliary roads leading to occasional marinas and vacation homes.

Time was running out. It had taken only a minute to call Mary. Another two minutes to give the envelope to the young reporter, and three minutes to race to his car and speed from the parking garage onto Abercorn. Two minutes later, he turned east on Highway 82 in the direction of Tybee Island.

Bobby pressed down the accelerator until the Chevrolet was speeding well above the limit. The sun eased down behind the far horizon as he passed the midpoint of the drive to Tybee. He switched on the car's headlights.

Exactly twenty-seven minutes had passed since he had hung up the telephone. He guided the car around the sweeping right turn onto the road dividing the beachfront property. One minute later he slowed, turned left onto Ninth Street. In this direction the street was only several blocks long and dead-ended where the beach fell away to the water. Ahead, he could make out an automobile parked on the right hand side of the street. He steered to a stop behind the car and stepped from his vehicle. The door on the driver's side of a silver Toyota opened and a man got out of the car and spoke quietly.

"Get in. We can talk here."

Bobby obeyed, and got in on the passenger's side. "Okay," he asked impatiently, when the man reentered the car. "What have you got for me? I've got about twenty minutes to talk. Twenty minutes, max."

The man turned as if to speak, and leveled a pistol at Bobby's stomach. "Don't move; don't make a sound."

"What the !" Bobby nearly shouted. "Who are you? What the hell do you think you're doing with that gun? Put that thing away, man, or I'll have you arrested!" Bobby opened his door and was nearly out of the car when two strong hands gripped his neck from behind and jerked his head up violently. He tried to twist away, out of the vicelike grip, but his assailant's grip tightened, squeezing his throat. He fought for consciousness, but the hands about his neck would not release. It was useless to try to speak or scream. He gasped for breath, flailing his arms in all directions. The clamp on his neck tightened and Bobby, desperate for air, made one final, but feeble twist of his body to free himself of the grip on his windpipe. It was of no avail. He felt himself sinking, falling into a bottomless pit. Then, suddenly, his head was jerked violently to the right. A nasty cracking noise shattered the quiet of Ninth Street. A violent pain seared Bobby's brain. He lost consciousness.

As his body went limp, the hands about his throat released and grabbed the falling reporter, pulling him from the door of the Toyota. The driver joined the assailant and opened the trunk. Together, they lifted the reporter's lifeless body and laid it in the empty compartment. The lid was slammed shut and the men quickly got in the front seats. The Toyota's engine started and the driver wheeled the small foreign car about and turned right. Soon, the Toyota was headed toward Savannah, rolling at an acceptable speed. Its occupants did not want to attract attention. Bobby's parked car would not be questioned until late the next day.

It had taken longer than anticipated for the North Star to reach the area of the ten mile buoy. There were other boats in the area, but none near the buoy. He threw out an anchor and waited until it caught. He pretended to fish until the evening began to gather. As darkness approached Drew guided The North Star to the side of the buoy, careful not to bang its bulkhead against the steel girders connecting the main towers. The swells had deepened and, although he was wearing a life jacket as he knelt at the bow of the small yacht, he was sure he would be thrown into the dark waters. Eventually he secured the lines and settled back into the boat's safer quarters.

The light atop the tall buoy swept methodically around in constant circles, throwing a blast of its magnificent horn with every turn of the search light. The swells broke against the boat, then the steel girders, lashing the starboard side of The North Star with sprays of salt water.

He tried to sleep. The alarm clock over the galley was set for midnight. But he could not sleep. When the clock bellowed at twelfth hour, he was still awake. He made coffee in the two cup percolator, willing the water to boil. When he had emptied the pot, he glanced at the clock. It was twelve ten. He went up the cabin steps, took his binoculars from the case and swept his eyes over the horizon.

Several miles out, in the mild moonlight, he spotted the dark shape of a freighter on the horizon. Ten minutes passed before he could make out the red and green lights on the bow which told him the ship was headed straight for the buoy to which he was secured. It's time, he thought, rescued the anchor and retrieved the grappling pole fastened to the side of The North Star. He went below to test the powerful portable light. He decided it was too strong, too easily noticed, and exchanged it for the lesser beam of a smaller flashlight. Now, he would wait.

Eventually, the freighter moved within a quarter mile of the buoy beckoning the ship to Savannah. Drew kept in the shadows as the menacing vessel passed within a few hundred feet of the buoy. Drew waited, searching for the expected quick beams of light. Then he saw them. Just as a deafening shriek of the ship's horn was sounded, Drew saw three brief flashes of light at the stern. So far, so good, if you dared call a drug drop good. He held his breath. Then, two more quick flashes. Finally, one. He listened for the sound of something hitting the water. Nothing he could distinguish from the continuous sound of the waves. He made his way quickly to the bow and released the lines securing The North Star to the buoy. The craft floated free as Drew carefully made his way back to the security of the cabin. He started the engine, backed away a safe distance from the giant structure and guided the boat toward the area just vacated by the great ship. Leaning out the side of the cabin, he swept his light over the water, careful to keep his beam on the side of The North Star opposite the ship.

"Damn! Where is it?" he muttered, seeing nothing. He was feeling a bit of panic when the beam he was sending across the water reflected off something less than forty feet from The North Star. He lost it, then recovered the reflection. The package -- no doubt about it. He kept the beam of light on the package as accurately as he could and steered The North Star toward it. When he had the package against the side of the boat, he could see well enough in the moon light to extinguish his light and reach for the grappling pole. The package slid down the side of the boat and drifted away. He swung The North Star around and made another pass.

This time he cast deftly, but as he tried to lift it in the boat, the package was unmanageable. He led it with the pole toward the lower sides of the rear of the boat and tried again to haul it in. It was simply too heavy. He took a chance and let it drift away from the stern of The North Star while he hurriedly fastened a rope about his waist and attached the other end to a metal eyelet. Careful to keep an eye on the floating treasure, he swung the boat around once more and made a pass at the package. With the carton maneuvered to the rear of the craft, he leaned far over the stern and grasped the package with both hands. He drew a deep breath and heaved with all his strength. The package rose to the top of the stern where Drew held it firmly. With a final pull, he fell back into the boat. The package crashed on top of him and rolled to the side.

Drew struggled to his feet, his breath coming in giant gulps. He was soaked with salt water, but the package was in the boat. He looked at it in the available light. It was wrapped with interior flotation, and was approximately twenty-four inches long, more than a foot thick. The little man was right; Drew guessed its weight at a hundred pounds.

He looked about; he had drifted with the engine in neutral nearly a quarter of a mile from the buoy. He slipped the engine into forward and headed in the direction of Hilton Head Island, South Carolina, steering in the direction of the glow of lights from the popular resort. Well out of the channel, he cut the engine and released the anchor. Soon The North Star strained to a stop as the anchor caught and held. Though exhausted, he prepared for the remainder of the almost spent night, securing the package in a large cooler brought on board earlier. At the first sign of light, he could begin the agonizingly deliberate ride to Isle of Hope Marina.

In the belly of The North Star lay the stuff of death.

Chapter Nine

The sun was nearing its peak as Drew maneuvered The North Star into slip 47 at the marina. He had slept poorly during the remainder of the night and, given the tension of the last several days, he longed to crash in his bed and sleep. But there could be no sleeping now, not until he contacted Rod and Doña and, hopefully, rid himself of the evil riding in The North Star.

The ride inland had gone smoothly. The seas were as calm as he had encountered them in months, but the three hour trip had not been as easy on his emotions. Each mile, it seemed, presented another question for his already weary mind.

The last hour had been the most difficult, for he had searched his experience for any and every alternative to delivering the package. Again, he had considered taking what he was sure was drugs to the local authorities. Bobby's cautioning cancelled that option. Dump the stuff and run? That, too, was an option. He was wealthy enough to run until hell froze over. The idea was quickly shelved. It was too late to say he simply wouldn't cooperate. Rod's plan appeared the only plausible one. And if an F.B.I. agent thought it was best, what reason did he have to question it? Besides, panicked as he had been when talking with Rod, he had drawn his friend into a conspiracy of their own. Now he was responsible for the possibility of Rod and Doña's scheme getting them in serious trouble. The fact was, he had no other option. He secured the boat to the dock and, in as normal a routine as possible, took his leave of the North Star. He would collect his car keys and position the Camaro to make the instructed transfer.

It was an exceptionally bright day as he plodded methodically up the walk to the front door and he took it as a good omen, especially following the fretful night. Halfway up the walk he picked up the morning newspaper and, in the kitchen to get a cold Pepsi, he tossed it on the table. Popping the top of the soda, he spread the newspaper on the kitchen table and leaned over to peruse the front page. The tranquil morning was shattered by the half *inch type headline.*

REPORTER MURDERED, WIFE MISSING

Drew bolted upright. He read the headline a second time and started on the lead paragraph.

The Chatham County Police Department discovered the body of a Savannah Morning News investigative reporter last evening in the marshes on Highway 80 midway between Tybee Island and the mainland. Bobby Taylor, 32, respected journalist who had been following a story of drug trafficking in the coastal region, was killed Sunday evening, initial investigations showed ...."

Drew stared with disbelief at the story. Bobby! Oh, my God! He could not make sense of what he was reading. He dropped into the chair and struggled to understand.

Mary Taylor, 31, the murdered man's wife, is reported missing by authorities. She was last heard from when her husband was overheard talking with her by phone in midafternoon. No clues to her whereabouts have been reported by the police ..."

Drew's hands shook uncontrollably. Again he looked at the story. It could not be true! Oh, God in heaven! How could this have happened? Who could have? He roared a curse and suddenly, his and swept across the table in one great motion that sent the newspaper flying in all directions.

Where was Mary? Was she alive? In the name of God what was going on? He raced out of the kitchen and up the stairs. Within minutes, he was dressed and out the back door. The door banged against the wall as he rushed through it. Halfway to the garage he bolted to a stop, suddenly remembering the package in the bowels of The North Star. He hesitated, his rage disordering his power to reason, then, deciding, dashed the last few steps to the garage.

He roared the Camaro from the car shed and drove quickly to a point on Bluff Drive directly above the boating dock. Disregarding any concern for someone who might be observing his frantic behavior, he raced to slip of The North Star and leaped into its fore deck, made his way along the hand rail to the deep well at the rear and dropped to the cabin door. His hands trembled uncontrollably as he tore at the lock. Flinging the door open he entered the cabin and pulled the large ice chest into the cabin walkway. He lifted the ominous package from the chest and, with surprising strength, raised it to his shoulders. Leaving The North Star unlocked and vulnerable to theft, he struggled up the steep dock steps to the Camaro and deposited the container in the trunk of the sports car.

Again, the Camaro stormed to life. Drew chose the quickest route to the Taylors' home. The reckless ten minutes required for the five mile drive were thoughtless, but charged with conflicting emotions.

Drew braked to a stop near the Taylor's house. Several police cars, blue lights flashing, blocked any effort to get nearer than half a block to the scene. He jumped from the car and ran down the sidewalk. As he bolted up the steps an officer grabbed him by the sleeve.

"Hold on, mister. No one's allowed in the house."

Drew glared at him. "The Taylors are my best friends. I just heard about the murder. I have to go in there!" he shouted.

The officer looked him over. "Stay here. I'll talk to the detective in charge." Soon he returned and waved Drew inside where he was met by a burly man who identified himself as Detective Mosely. Drew explained his relationship to the Taylors as he looked about the living room where they were standing. The place was a mess. Except the sofa, every piece of furniture was overturned. Papers were scattered across the floor. Cushioned ripped open.

"He was working on a story about the drug trade in this area," Drew said. "He called me day before yesterday and told me the story was breaking soon. That's all I know. Is there any word of Mary?" he asked.

"Nothing yet. We'll find her, though." The man stopped, and considered Drew. "She may be dead, too, you know."

Drew nodded and walked past the officer into the kitchen. It was no different than the living room. A total wreck. Each room resembled the last. Nothing had been left in its original place. What were the assailants looking for? It really did not matter at the moment. He thanked the officer, asked that he be kept informed and promised to be on call if needed.

As he walked toward his car, the tears came without warning. He stopped at the hood of his vehicle and turned in the direction of Bobby's house, staring at the chaotic scene. He leaned over the still warm hood of the car and buried his head in his hands. Bobby gone! He could not grasp it; his mind denied it. He stood erect, looked at his hands and remembered the firm hold his dead friend had taken on them only two days ago. He leaned limply against the car, trying to decide what to do next, but his thoughts were jumbled. One moment he was enraged, the next, stricken. Abruptly, another feeling came, a foreboding that sent shivers rippling through his body. Was there a connection between his midnight caller and Bobby's death, between the package he delivered and the story Bobby was pursuing?

He took another look toward the Taylors' home and entered the Camaro. Backing the car from the barricaded block, he drove slowly, aimlessly, from the scene. There was no reason to hurry now.

Three blocks from his murdered friend's house, he braked, paused at an intersection, and suddenly wheeled the Camaro in the direction of Grace Church. Within minutes he steered the car into the reserved parking spot and sat, staring into the darkness. In the next few minutes he experienced a composure he had not felt in years, and Drew Campbell made decisions that would undoubtedly and might forever change his life.

During most of his years, he had sought a level of engagement with life that made sense, and offered a reason for his living. The protracted search had led through a young life on the bayous, through college, Vietnam and the empty months following the war. On two occasions he thought his search had ended. When he met Ellen, and when he chose the ministry. Now, those causes for living were, for all practical purposes, gone.

Since Ellen's death he had been an emotional wimp, living on the edge of a psychological disaster. He saw himself the pitiful one he was, despite efforts to convince himself and others that he was handling it all perfectly well. Now he saw clearly the difference between keeping a cherished memory and being imprisoned by it. It was time to put Ellen's memory were it belonged -- in a special place in his heart, forever locked and unexamined. In the space of several quiet minutes he made that choice.

The decision freed him to think of Bobby's death and Mary's disappearance. If his friend's murder was not connected to his blackmailers, it was, nevertheless, linked to the gutter mentality of the drug lords. But, it was quite possible, he acknowledged, that Bobby was dead and Mary in peril precisely because his blackmailers knew of his meeting with Bobby and decided the reporter was a threat. If that were so, 'they' might have decided to hold Mary as a further reason for Drew to cooperate.

Whatever the fitting scenario was, his ministry, at least that of a pastor, would not survive. Not primarily because of exposure, but because his spirit would not survive. Something had been resurrected within him, something strange yet hauntingly familiar, something he knew, as he sat there in the dark, that would not go away easily, if ever.

The decisions came rapidly.

The bastards would not get their damnable package!

He would leave Grace Church, and the ministry.

He was a rich man, and he would use his wealth, and any other resource he possessed, first to find Mary, and second, to find Bobby's killers.

He carried the waterproofed package to the church's basement and concealed it behind the large boiler and a dozen cardboard boxes. The task was completed in less than twenty minutes. That would do, he reassured himself, until he decided how to dispose of the deadly stuff.

There was something else he needed to do. He entered the church and approached the sanctuary. The heavy doors opened reluctantly at his push. He walked slowly to the front center pew and sat. He looked up and studied the huge symbol hanging silently overhead. He wasn't sure what he wanted to say, or expected to experience. He dropped his hands in his lap and closed his eyes. He sensed no overwhelming peace such as he had frequently promised from the pulpit. He would not label the composure that marked his spirit religious, but in a strange sort of way, he sensed God was as angry as he at his faceless enemy. The decision to leave the ministry did not include a decision to leave God. So, he tried to pray, starting several times to mouth words he thought appropriate. Each time he began, he stopped, the last time in midsentence. The words were meaningless, forced phrases and he recognized how equally meaningless they must sound to worshipers on a Sunday morning. Did it matter to God how they sounded? Isn't it the yearning of the heart that God desires? Didn't the Spirit promise to pray for us "with sighs too deep for words"? So he began again, permitting the words to escape his lips in a whisper, not stopping to analyze them or endeavoring to wrap them in a labored holiness.

He prayed, without shame, for God's help. He was less sure than ever how the Almighty's help might come, yet he prayed for it nevertheless. He thanked God for Bobby's friendship, and prayed for Mary's safety.

Then, in a whisper, "Lord, I tried to be your priest. You know I tried, but I can't do it without Ellen. So, here --," he held out his hands, palms up. "I forfeit my calling. I won't stop loving you, God, but I have to find out who murdered Bobby. I have to stop the bastards who ruined my life!"

The thought of Bobby burned a place in his heart near to his memory of Ellen. And the anger returned with a vengeance. He rose from the pew and spoke a final word to his God: "Forgive me --," then, as he stood, " -- even if I do know what I'm doing."

As he walked out of the massive sanctuary he was glad it was not night. The nights were the hardest of all.

He went to his study. There he sorted through what he knew, did not know, yet suspected. Yes, there was some connection between his callers and Bobby's death. At this point details did not matter. On the surface of things, it was difficult to ignore the possibilities. And, yes, Bobby's death was related to the story he was preparing. Too, he was at least partly responsible for Bobby's death. But how? Had 'they' found out about their meeting at the print shop? Then it occurred to him: they killed him to insure the delivery. They didn't have to know of the meeting, because they knew about the story Bobby was writing. It didn't matter how they knew, they knew! That's it, of course. What's a life worth compared to millions? Drew's fear for Mary increased and he wondered where her body would be found.

The telephone rang.

"Reverend Campbell?" The voice was calm, controlled. He recognized the voice of a local funeral director.

"Yes."

"Reverend, this is Robert Jackson."

"Yes."

"I've received a call from the editor of the Morning News. They want to have a memorial service for the young reporter that was found dead last night. You know of the death, do you not?"

Drew assured him he did.

"Well, sir, the family is coming to Savannah to receive the body when it's released by the coroner. Autopsy, all that, you know."

"I assumed that, yes, please."

Mr. Jackson continued. "The editor doesn't want to wait until the autopsy is concluded. They want some kind of service for their employees since most of them will not be able to travel to Boston where the family wishes to have the service and committal. Would you do the memorial service, Reverend? The paper requested I ask you. They understand you were friends of the Taylors."

"Of course," Drew responded, and thought how appropriate his last service would be for Bobby.

They discussed arrangements. Nine, tomorrow morning. The sanctuary of Grace Church. Employees of the paper only. Drew thanked the funeral director for his call and replaced the receiver and began composing in his mind what he would say about Bobby. Then he thought of Mary, and suspected he would conduct one more service. Mary's.

    Drew spent the remainder of the afternoon walking mindlessly through the busy squares filled with tourists. He returned to his office when he knew his small staff had departed the facilities. Not knowing what to do next without talking to Rod, he left the church offices for his car and then headed the Camaro toward Isle of Hope, certain he would hear from the agents. He had not followed Rod's plan and was sure Rod would be more than a little disappointed.

    By the time he arrived on Bluff Drive, the evening had deepened over the marshes of the intercoastal waterway, gradually turning the bluff into a half mile stretch of eerie shadows. It would rain tonight, he decided; the air was heavy, a sure sign. He studied the shadows from the darkness of the upstairs bedroom window. He loved these cool evenings. They often brought rain, and if tonight a minor storm, all the better.

    He was turning from the opened window when he saw a figure move quickly across the front lawn. A man. Drew strained to see the direction the man took, but the figure just as quickly disappeared. The shadows were too deep, and too heavy. Then, another man, looking up at the house, standing beside the magnolia tree at the end of the sidewalk. Drew stepped quickly from the window, keeping the second figure in view.

He did not have to wonder what they wanted. He smiled. It had not taken them long to come after him.

He stepped quietly to his closet, located his sneakers, slipped them on and moved carefully down the stairs. Halfway down the steps, he reasoned: I can't just walk outside. They'll be waiting. And I can't wait inside. He retreated to the hallway outside his bedroom and slipped as cautiously as he could into the rear bedroom. It was darker here, but the room was empty, except for three large boxes in a far corner which contained some things of Ellen's, things he had not been able to give away. He unlocked and raised the window leading out onto a short slanted roof. Sitting on the window sill, he lowered his hips to the roof and inched his way to the edge of the overhang and held his position. He could not hear any movement, nor see any. He decided to take a chance. He studied the ground below, trying to remember the terrain accurately. It was a drop of ten feet to the lawn. He launched himself quietly over the side. Hitting the ground, he rolled as he had been taught years before in his military training. Even so, the ground met him with such a force his knees pounded into his chest. He lay as still as possible, catching his breath and evaluating his position.

He was slightly stunned by the effect of the fall, but he was okay. Nothing broken. Good. He looked around quickly for any sign of the men he had spotted just minutes before. Nothing. On hands and knees, he eased back into the thickness of shrubbery bordering the house and was still. His breathing returned to normal.

The light off the waterway illumined the spaces along the side of the house and the walkway to the garage. He could see enough, he thought. The garage! The .45 was there, in the glove compartment of the Camaro.

Then, he froze. There was a movement to his left. Forget the gun. He looked down the side of the house. A figure was moving slowly toward the rear. He peered through the shadows, trying to size up the man whose movement would bring him only a few feet from Drew's position. Where was the other man? He glanced quickly in the other direction. Nothing. Well, one thing at a time, he thought, and pulled his feet under him for the spring. Remember make the chop clean, he admonished himself. Explode your energy precisely. Don't hesitate! When you move, move! The man was coming closer. Drew could see his face now, though dimly. It was not a face he recognized. No matter.

Wait, he told himself, until the right moment. The man moved directly in front of Drew and passed him. His pulse raced with abandon. Now! Drew tensed his body and sprang as a single unit, his right hand poised high above his head. The man started to turn at the sound of Drew's vault. It was too late. Drew brought the hardened edge of his hand down on the man's neck, concentrating the energy of his body into the blow. His strike was on target, slamming into the man's neck with a dull thud. An involuntary rush of wind escaped the man's throat and his body crashed to the ground. Drew rolled to a crouch, prepared to strike again if necessary. There was no need.

Drew looked around quickly. Had the other man heard the scuffle? Apparently not; there was no immediate reaction. Quickly Drew pulled the man into the bushes and positioned himself again.

Several minutes passed. No sign of the other man. Drew crept from his hiding place and edged along the rear of the house. His foot touched something. Keeping his eye on the corner of the house, he stooped and felt for the object. It was a long stick, three inches thick at its base and about two feet long. He picked it up, gripped it like a club and stood again, continuing toward the garage. Still no sign of the other man.

Reaching the garage, he stepped across the path and into the doorway leading to the Camaro. From here he could see in both directions. His position was secure. But Drew noticed for the first time the pain in his hand that raced up into his wrist. He could worry about that later. Watch for the other man, he reminded himself.

He saw the burst of light before he felt the pain of the blow.

A blackness covered his senses and he felt himself falling. His last memory was the sensation of wet grass on his face. That, and his leg was jerking.

Drew sat at the kitchen table and pressed the ice pack to the back of his head. He figured he had been on the ground less than thirty minutes. The house was in shambles; every room rifled. Did they think he was stupid enough to hide the package in his home?

He sipped a glass of cold water and tried to organize his thoughts. Where was Mary? Being held? Dead? What to do with the hundred pounds of cocaine? Did he wait for 'them' to get in touch with him? And what to do about his relationship with the church, and when?

He needed to find Rod and Doña and get their counsel before deciding.

Chapter Ten

The sun crept inch by inch above the roof of a nearby building. Finally it was in full bloom and streamed brightly into the single window of room 337 of the Capital Hotel. Drew turned his head to avoid the glare and was looking straight into Doña's eyes. There he found sympathy in her warm gaze, but she did not speak. Outside the window he could hear the hiss of an early morning street-sweeping machine. He glanced at his watch. Rod should arrive any moment.

Drew had slept only a couple hours, waking shortly after mid-night to the realization he had to talk with Doña who he hoped could contact Rod and secure his immediate return from Atlanta. His head throbbed incessantly and the three aspirin Doña had given him had not even slowed the palpitation in his temple. He had gulped coffee constantly since he had awakened. The caffeine abuse was playing havoc with his nerves. If he closed his eyes and stayed absolutely still, the throbbing seemed to abate, if only slightly. Any relief was a blessing.

Drew suspected Rod would be disappointed in his failure to execute the plan they had designed, probably as frustrated by not getting a 'make' on the dealers as he was in Drew's botching of the strategy. But Rod's friend had not been brutally murdered, nor another friend abducted, if not also killed. At the moment Drew had two greater concerns than Rod's probable disappointment:

find Mary and his assailants, and dispose of the cocaine. He turned to Doña, still sitting quietly, facing Drew. She had listened carefully to each detail of his account of the last twenty-four hours.

"I guess I screwed things up, huh?"

Doña shrugged her shoulders. She had learned not to second guess Rod Gray, nor to surmise anything from an operation's diversions.

He rose to stretch when the door opened suddenly and Rod entered with a rush. Doña had given him scant details when she had made contact and urged him to return to Savannah as soon as possible. All the senior agent knew was that things had not gone as planned.

Rod's clothes were disheveled and he obviously had not shaven since the morning before. He dropped his overnight bag just inside the door and, ignoring Doña, directed his question to Drew.

"What the hell happened?"

"They killed Bobby," Drew said, then remembered he had not disclosed his conversation with his black friend, but his reference to Bobby made no impression on Rod.

"And the drugs?" the agent asked with a sense of urgency.

Drew looked at Rod, then at Doña. He thought he understood the stress underlining the inquiry. The two agents had put their careers on the line for him and he had now put those same careers in jeopardy. He had not seriously considered that before now. The earnestness of Rod's question brought the issue into focus. He made a decision. He lied.

"I got rid of the stuff. This morning, before I contacted Doña."

Rod's face went blank.

"You destroyed eight million dollars of evidence?" Rod spun around as if shot. "Son of a bitch, man! What were you thinking about? Without the drugs we don't have anything. And your ass is mud! They'll cut you up into little pieces and we can't protect you without disclosing our duplicity." He threw a glance at Doña and started for the bathroom, stopping to stare at Drew, then continuing into the bath and jerking the door closed. Drew's stomach wretched. Doña still had not moved.

"Okay," Rod said, coming from the bath, his composure regained. He took control of the crisis. "Give it to me quickly," he instructed and sat on the edge of the bed facing Drew.

Drew carefully recounted the details of the last day for the second time, this time adding the lie. "What was I supposed to do?" he asked. "I was exhausted. I find out my best friend has been murdered and his wife missing!" He sighed. "So, I screwed up. But the drugs are gone. That's worth something, isn't it? And the two of you can get out of here. It's up to me now." He glanced at Doña, then at Rod. To hell with it, he thought. I don't need another guilt trip.

Rod rubbed the back of his neck and studied Drew carefully. He turned to Doña. "He's right. We've been cut out. If we try to help further, call for protection for Drew, anything like that, we'll be cited, no, charged with code violations. And canned!"

Doña's eyes narrowed as she received Rod's evaluation. She asked the question neither man had raised. "What about Mary?"

A prolonged silence hung between the three, broken only when Rod stood and walked to the window, passing Drew who watched the two agents in silence. Rod was the first to speak.

"If she's still alive, they'll kill her as soon as they discover the drugs have been dumped. Either way, dead or alive, it doesn't matter." He turned to Drew. "That's how you screwed up." His response was cold. "I'm sorry," he said, but his words carried little sympathy. "The police will be looking for her, and I suggest you cooperate with them to whatever extent you can without implicating yourself, or us." He looked at Doña. "I think we get the hell out of here." Then, "Drew, I wish it had turned out differently."

Drew was thinking, planning ahead. He was sure the blackmailers would contact him, and when they did, he would make a deal for Mary's life. His only plan.

Ready?" Rod asked Doña.

"As I'll ever be," she said and stood. She began retrieving her gear while Rod and Drew said their uncomfortable goodbyes.

"I am grateful to you both," Drew said stiffly, but he meant it. He extended his hand to Doña who ignored the gesture and put her cheek to his in a light embrace. "Careful," she whispered in his ear and stepped back. He looked at her curiously, surprised by the deft warning. "What --?" his eyes asked, but received only an almost imperceptible shake of her head. Their eyes met for an extended second before she looked away and picked up her bag.

Rod excused himself during the stopover in the Atlanta airport. "God to find a men's room."

"I'd like to freshen up, too," Doña said. "Meet you in that lounge," she asked, pointing to the nearest bar.

"Sure."

They parted. Their flight was scheduled to board in less than an hour.

Doña walked past the first restroom until she stopped at a telephone. She dialed the familiar number and waited.

The same woman's voice. "Si."

"Eaglet. The Man, please, and hurry."

"Si."

Another wait.

"Eagle One."

"Problems. We're on our way back to D.C."

"Damn!" Then, after a moment of silence, "Okay. We'll talk soon. Be careful."

"I will."

The Man said, "I love you."

"I love you, too, Papa."

In another booth, Rod spoke quietly. "The think the bastard's lying and he's got the stuff. We'll know shortly when Charlie makes contact. Then we'll take our time."

"Very good," the Senator replied. "When do we get the money?"

Rod ignored the greed. "We took out the reporter."

"You what --?"

"He was making waves; your name surfaced. We had no choice. We've bought so time, that's all, enough to make final delivery and split the take. Then it may be necessary to get out."

"What do you mean, 'out'?" The man was shouting.

"It's time. I told you there was a risk, remember?"

"Yes, but --, well, I can't just run."

"You do what you want."

"There's no connection with me."

"You don't know that for sure."

"Damn you!"

"Yeah, that may be, but not yet. Now, listen carefully."

The senator started to argue a point, but Rod cut him off. "Just sit quietly. The reporter probably left some notes. We looked for them last night. Nothing. We'll keep looking. If we find them, we're clear. If not, then, well senator, we'll all have some running to do."

"I want out, right now. I'm out."

"No, senator, you're not. Now, stay cool. I'll keep you informed. If he still has the coke, we'll make a deal."

"Keep me out of it!"

"Too late for that. But, remember: maybe we'll all walk clean."

"I have to trust you."

"Yes, that's true."

Senator James Maxwell laid the receiver in the cradle. It was happening, just as he had suspected. His call to The Man was entirely justified. Prudent, to say the least. Well, Mr. Know-It-All Agent -- he smiled at the thought of Rod's demise -- we'll see who's really in charge. When he thought of The Man again, he shivered.

Chapter Eleven

Something was nibbling at his brain, but he couldn't get hold of it. Something Bobby said, but he could not even remember where or when he said it. He went over every moment he was last with his friend since this 'thing' had begun. At his home, with Mary. At the print shop. Nothing.

He was wasting time. Mary's time.

Why hadn't 'they' called? Had he miscalculated? Was she dead? Then why was her house ransacked, and his? Why hadn't her body been found? If he was right and she was alive, they would contact him, demand the cocaine as ransom, and he would demand, in turn, some evidence that she was not dead.

Then, the nibbling became a bite. Her house! Ransacked. Of course, notes! Bobby had left her notes! But, he told me, remembered Drew -- "I haven't told Mary about this story. Too dangerous."

But there were notes! Yes, by God! And the notes could help him, direct him -- somewhere, surely. That's what the two men were after at his house, and why Mary's home was torn apart. Had they found what they were looking for? No, because Mary would be dead. He stood and began pacing, trying to recall anything that might give him some direction. The effort was of no avail.

He called the SPD again. No new word about Mary, but they had an entire homicide team on it, given her husband's death. If nothing turned up, they would list it a kidnapping and request help from the F.B.I.

Drew fought the panic that threatened to mess up his mind even more than it was already. He had always preferred being alone until he met Ellen. With her gone, he had drifted back into social isolation except for the Taylors. He had done his work with people, but retreated to Isle of Hope whenever possible. Now the solitude he coveted was becoming a new enemy. He was in this thing alone. And he was Mary's only hope.

Whom might Bobby have given his notes to? The only associate he had ever mentioned was his editor. Yes! He grabbed his car keys and ran out the back door. Fifteen minutes later he parked in the alley behind the Savannah Morning News building. Getting out of the Camaro, he saw the small sign over a back door on the opposite side of the alley and the faded words BULLDOG PRINTSHOP and remembered his last moments with Bobby.

The editor of the News was not expected in until late afternoon. No, he didn't want the man to call him. He'd come back later. He returned dejectedly to the Camaro. Opening the driver's door he noticed again the worn letters over the rear entrance to the print shop.

It hit him like a jackhammer. Jake! "I trust him explicitly." Bobby had said. "He's confirmed much of what I suspected, hears it on the streets."

Drew bolted around the corner and entered the small outer office. So much depended on what the shop owner told him, or did not tell him. If he drew a blank, he still had the editor to consult. Or, again, he could do nothing, and try to live with his conscience. But, he knew instinctively now: the old Drew he had become again would never permit the latter.

The owner of the shop was not a pleasant man, but Drew ignored his disagreeable manner and tried to gain his confidence. "You don't know me, Mr. Harrison," Drew began.

"The name's Jake," the older man replied with a near sneer. His shirt was smeared with ink and barely missed covering the belly lapping over his beltless tan slacks.

"I was a friend of Bobby's," Drew continued.

"So what?" Jake retorted.

"Yes, well, I was hoping, since you were a friend of Bobby's, that you could tell me something about Bobby."

"Like what?"

"Well, I don't know, really. Maybe anything he told you an important story he was working on when he died."

"You mean, when he was murdered," Jake reminded him, spitting an accumulation of tobacco juice into a trash can. The man wiped his mouth with the back of his hand, then the hand on the leg of his pants.

"Yes, when he was murdered," Drew continued.

Jake studied Drew's face. "You're the preacher, right?"

"Yes." Drew shifted, more impatient by the second.

"Wait here," Jake replied and left Drew standing at the front counter. Shortly, he returned with a large manila envelope. Jake handed it to Drew.

"Wondered when you'd come for it." Jake's face was expressionless.

"What do you mean?"

Jake spit again. "Bobby said if you came you'd have it figured out."

"I don't have anything figured out."

"You will, son," Jake said and started for the rear of the shop. He stopped, and looked at Drew.

"They'll burn in hell for what they did!" he said, and disappeared through a door. Drew stared at the envelope. His hands were trembling.

Chapter Twelve

Drew sat on the wide porch and opened the manila envelope, withdrew the several pages, the top of which was a short note.

> *Drew, my friend,*
>
> *If you're reading this, something has happened to me. I have purposefully not given these notes to Mary because I don't want her involved if I'm not there to protect her ...*

Drew sighed. *Mary, where was she?*

> *... but someone has to have this information and given your present predicament, maybe it will help you."   Thanks. Bobby.*

A fear declared itself in Drew's belly. He stood and walked to the door, then through the first floor of the house. He forced himself to return to the materials.

> *Eight months ago, I began following a lead to a major drug link to Savannah/Chatham County. In fact, it links Savannah, Atlanta and Washington, and God only knows where the story leads.*
>
> *This is what I know: a major drug shipment arrives in Savannah monthly via the port. A South American freighter carries approximately 100 - 200 pounds of cocaine valued at more than five million dollars into port. Prearrangements have been bought to insure the entry and transfer are ignored*

locally. A county police officer takes over transfer of the drugs when the shipment is on shore. Most of those involved are of small consequence. But, the names get bigger: the chief of the county police department is connected, as are several other local officials and some lesser heads. Their job is to insure safe transfer of the shipment each month, get it to the drop area. The payoffs for local help are made at that point and place. Then the drug lords take over. My information came from a dock hand who was on the take, but had a sting of conscience when his thirteen year old son overdosed. The informant's wife left him recently and took their only other child, a daughter, with her. The man took his life three days ago.

Drew remembered seeing the story of the young man's death.

I cannot confirm the following, but I have enough pieces of the puzzle to believe I am on the right track. The drug ring is directed by a D.C. connection, a man of low profile but great positioning. Maybe a government official or at least connected with some agency under whose shadow he can operate. The street operation is guided by a former Nam buddy. The only name I have is Charlie which may not be his real name. Another 'partner' will cause you pause: the junior senator from Georgia. The three men were together in Nam and ran a drug ring among the

GIs. Before returning to the states, the three men designed a drug trafficking scheme to be operated once they were positioned at home. They left Nam and split with the scheme in place. Eight years passed and the D.C. figure initiated contact with the other two. Since 1980, the small, tightly controlled group has been responsible for bringing into the states shipments of cocaine worth untold millions, primarily through the Savannah port. Two weeks ago, the operation appeared to stop cold. I was told the group planned one more shipment and then the operation would be shut down permanently. Shortly after that, my source died of a heart attack.

I have decided to write the story as I know it, but my editor thinks I'm purely guessing and refused to give his approval. I hope to change his mind when he sees my final copy.

Please see that my Mary is cared for.
Bobby.

Drew laid the pages on the floor and leaned back in his chair. What kind of madness was he into?

Chapter Thirteen

Mr. Taylor's body is not prepared for viewing, Reverend," the funeral director, informed him quietly.

Drew was not understanding. "I am leaving for Washington as soon as the memorial service is concluded. I would appreciate it if you would allow me to see my friend. It would mean a lot to me. I've seen bodies in much worse shape than Mr. Taylor's, I assure you."

Mr. Jackson studied Drew's face.

"Nam," Drew said soberly.

The man smiled. "Of course. Come with me, please, but only for a moment. We have to ship the body to Boston later this morning."

Drew followed the funeral director to a preparation room at the rear of the facility.

They stepped into a sterile room that smelled of embalming fluid. Bobby Taylor's body lay on a stainless steel table under a green surgical sheet. Mr. Jackson drew the sheet and Drew looked into the expressionless face of his friend. He forced himself to the side of the table, and glanced at the director. He spoke in a near whisper.

"Please leave me with the body."

"Of course," Mr. Jackson replied. "I'll just step outside."

Drew stared at Bobby's face. The telltale signs of the autopsy were evident. The neat incisions told all.

There was something Drew had to do for himself. He reached under the sheet and took Bobby's hand. The last time he had held that hand, it was warm and expressive. Now it was cold, stiff, and unresponsive. But Drew held it, a final gesture of their friendship. Tears swelled in Drew's eyes. He needed to say something, but the words would not come. What did come was rage, a madness so ugly it scared him.

Mr. Jackson entered the room quietly. Silently, Drew placed Bobby's hand under the sheet, and left the room without speaking.

At precisely nine o'clock Drew walked into the sanctuary. He wore his black Genevan robe. A white stole hung about his neck and his Bible was carried at chest level. His eyes were red with grief. Several dozen employees of the Morning News were seated in the center pews. He nodded to them as he mounted the chancel steps and walked to the pulpit.

"My friends, we are here to remember our friend and colleague, Bobby Taylor, and to give God thanks for all that was good and kind and loving in his life."

Drew led the liturgy by memory, but when he got to the personal comments regarding Bobby's life, he pulled from his Bible the notes he had written in longhand. Pausing throughout the reading to check his emotions, Drew spoke of Bobby's devotion to the priorities of his life as Drew knew them: his marriage, his work, and the causes in which he believed. The service lasted less than fifteen minutes.

Shortly before noon, Drew caught a Delta flight to Washington. The sky was a dull, uninteresting gray, so he leaned back in his rear window seat and closed his eyes. The flight had a layover in Atlanta. He was due to arrive in Washington late afternoon. The answers he needed to break the gridlock were in Washington. If he was lucky, Mary might still have a chance. For all the grief he had caused so many people, he was beginning to give himself little chance at anything good.

Rod accompanied Charlie to the door, pausing with his hand on the knob before opening it to dismiss the little man.

"Okay," he said, an unmistakable tone of resignation in his voice, "everything's going to be all right. Maybe we made a mistake taking out the reporter, but still, I'm telling you, Charlie, don't worry. The preacher has the coke or he wouldn't be in Washington so fast. He doesn't know anything. No notes, no linkage. He's fishing in D. C., Charlie, because he doesn't know what else to do."

"But, you forget," Charlie said, the frustration evident in his voice, "the guy's not dumb, and he'll mess things up if we don't stop him. Let me take care of him."

"I tell you, Charlie, he's no problem."

"Then, what's he doing in Washington?"

"Like I said, he's fishing," Rod responded. "Nothing to worry about, Charlie. Just do your job. We'll get the package soon."

"And when might that be?" the little man asked.

"In a few days, Charlie. Just be sure everyone is ready when I give the signal."

Charlie nodded.

"And Charlie, don't come here again. Got that? Never again!"

"Yeah, I hear you," and left the house.

Drew used a pay phone at the airport to call the senator's office and was told the senator was unavailable. His schedule was very tight, the receptionist said, but she would be happy to get an aide on the phone who would be glad to talk with him. "The senator certainly wants to accommodate his constituency." Drew declined.

He hung up without responding and considered his options. He needed to get to the senator personally, to see his response to a startling accusation, but that seemed out of the question. Who ? He tried to dig deeper into his mind. Then he remembered: he had met the senator's wife several months before when she substituted for her husband at a Savannah conference on domestic violence. Drew had sat next to Mrs. Maxwell on the dais; he to offer the invocation, she to address the assembly. She had been friendly enough, and had offered to be of any help she might could give. The consummate politician's wife. He returned to the pay phone and dialed the senator's residence.

Near noon he had located the senator's Washington residence in Arlington. He stepped to the front door of the brownstone and knocked. Seconds later a housekeeper greeted him.

"May I help you, sir?"

"I'm Andrew Campbell, from Savannah. I have an appointment with the senator's wife."

"Please, do come in, Dr. Campbell. Mrs. Maxwell is expecting you."

The maid led him to the library and left to inform Mrs. Maxwell of Drew's arrival. Shortly, Morgan Ann Huntington Maxwell appeared and greeted Drew warmly.

"Dr. Campbell! I'm delighted to see you again. I had hoped you might call on us. This is a wonderful surprise." She offered her hand. "Please, do be seated, and tell me, right now, what is this urgent matter that brings you here. We certainly want to be of any help we might can offer."

Drew eased himself onto the oversized sofa, using the moment to survey the spacious, predictable room. A wall dominated by shelves, another by a large portrait of Thomas Jefferson. Two high-backed leather chairs and side tables complimented the sofa on which Drew sat. As expected, a large globe occupied a far corner of the room. On the coffee table lay a single volume: The Strategy of Southern Politics, by James Maxwell, U. S. Senator.

Morgan Ann Huntington Maxwell chose the chair normally occupied by her husband. She crossed her legs slowly and politely tugged at the hem of her dress. Her eyes met Drew's and held them.

"Now, how can we help, Dr. Campbell," she asked evenly, her best effort at charm underscoring each word. She smiled broadly. Her sensuousness was not lost of Drew; he had heard rumors of her reputation.

He was working hard to restrain the fury lying just below the smile he returned briefly. What did the woman know? How much did she know? He had not planned his approach to Mrs. Maxwell. Should he go straight to the hell of it, or ease around a corner or two, probing, hoping for a clue, testing her? He chose a compromise of the two. Start up front, but not directly.

"Mrs. Maxwell," Drew began, "I have access to information which could spell ruin for your husband and you. I wanted to give the senator the information first hand, but he's unavailable and I will leave Washington soon. I thought I should come to you with it."

Morgan Ann Huntington Maxwell's eyes narrowed. The smile lingered, but was obviously strained. "Dr. Campbell, what on earth could you be talking about -- ruin for me and my husband? I'm afraid I'm at a loss to ..., if this has to do with the vicious rumors of another woman in my husband's life, I can assure you there is no validity to the rumors whatsoever. James and I have a wonderful marriage."

"It has nothing to do with rumors, Mrs. Maxwell, or with the senator's fidelity to you. Or, at least, not in so far as other women is concerned."

"Then what ?" she demanded, her southern charm lost in the exchange.

Drew leaned forward. "I have reliable information about an operation which smuggles drugs into the states through Savannah and God only knows the implications of that operation. My best friend is dead, murdered, because my friend was about to expose the operation. And, my friend's wife has been abducted. I fear for her life, too."

"What you're telling me is unbelievable, Dr. Campbell."

"Murder is easily believable, Mrs. Maxwell, when you see the corpse, when you see my friend's house wrecked, when his wife is missing."

"Dr. Campbell, I am shocked at this. What can we do to help? Have you contacted law enforcement ...?"

"No. Because, there is something far more disturbing." He lied, "Your husband has been seen in the company of some drug dealers --."

Mrs. Maxwell sat up straight. "Dr. Campbell, my husband is on the President's Council on Drugs," she said indignantly. "He works with F.B.I. What you are suggesting is preposterous!"

"Possibly," Drew responded, "and for your sake, let's hope that's the case." He had said enough. Mrs.

Maxwell, he was convinced, did not know of her husband's involvement with the drug operation. If she did, she was the complete actress.

Drew stood. "Mrs. Maxwell, I have taken enough of your time. I hope I have not caused you unnecessary worry. I just thought your husband should know his name has been linked in such a manner. I suggest you inform him as soon as possible." Then, another lie: "I'm going to the police soon with what I know, and what I suspect. I will not mention the senator's name, but I am confident the authorities will come upon it. Perhaps the senator can ward off any problems that might cause. I do thank you for your time."

Drew left the Maxwell residence and a stunned Mrs. Maxwell and with no additional information. The best he could hope for was that the senator's wife would relate his visit and the content of their discussion. That alone might flush the senator out.

He drove the rental car away with no idea where to do or what to do next. He had determined before he left Savannah not to contact Rod Gray or Doña Moore. He had put them in jeopardy enough, as it was. If he did approach either of them they would have to report it, and then the 'problem' would be taken out of his control. But he had no control, that was the point. Where did he turn now? Time was running out -- for himself and, more importantly, for Mary. He would have to return to

Savannah soon, and if he returned empty-handed, he would have no choice but to go to the police with what he knew. What he knew included his crimes of a decade ago. Too, going to the police would probably signal the end of Mary's life. The blackmailers would kill her and run. There were other sources of cocaine besides the hundred pounds hidden at the moment in the base of Grace Church.

He banged his fist on the steering wheel. "O God, I deserve whatever chastisement you decide. My ministry's gone. Ellen's gone. Bobby's gone. I can't bring back the hurt I've inflicted. But, for Mary's sake, help me!"

Help came in the form of a skinny thought. A remembered whisper, "Careful." A barely noticeable movement of the head. A split-second eye contact. Doña! Had he read it wrong, imagined it? He had been sure, at the moment, but now --? Even if he was wrong, if it had been an innocent enough admonition, a woman might be more sympathetic with another woman's plight. It was worth a chance.

She answered on the third ring. Sure, she'd be delighted to have dinner with him. Yes, she could be ready in half an hour. And yes, she knew some place quiet. Hers, in D.C.

When Senator James Maxwell returned to his home in Washington, his wife met him at the door. Within minutes, she had told him of Drew's visit. The senator was visibly shaken and his wife demanded the truth. He told her all of it. She listened without speaking, intent on hearing every detail.

"How much money do you have in Switzerland?"

"Several million."

She leaned toward him. Her lips neared his. Suddenly, she withdrew and whipped her opened hand across his face. "You fool!"

Stunned, his eyes teared.

She slapped him again, harder than before. "You absolute, complete, utter fool!" She stood and started for the door.

"Morgan Ann! What are you going to do?" It's being taken care of, I ...."

She whirled at the door. "The only thing I can do; I'm going to try to save us!"

Chapter Fourteen

He had enjoyed the evening more than any he could recall in the last year. They had avoided the subject of Drew's troubles which had introduced them. She wanted to know about the war, but he had changed the conversation politely to her life in the bureau. She, in turn, asked about the ministry. They laughed at the verbal maneuvering and agreed not to talk about anything ponderous during dinner.

As she refilled his wine glass, he studied her face, as he had studied her all evening. The coal black hair, the light brown skin and the dark eyes inherited from her mother, obviously. But her father's Caucasian influence was equally evident. The sharply defined nose and thin lips, both given her by the American who thirty-three years before had slept with Maria, the woman from the Caribbean.

She lifted her wine glass and smiled. "To a very nice evening." They touched glasses lightly. Their eyes met briefly as she stood and began clearing the table. Drew studied the slender fingers taking the dishes from the table, the effortless poise, and considered the contrasts of the business-like agent he had met in Savannah and the beautiful woman whose presence he was enjoying more by the moment. Drew forgot momentarily why he had made the date with Doña.

"Take your glass to the sofa, why don't you, while I clear the table."

"May I help?"

"Thank you, but no. Make yourself comfortable. I'll just be a moment."

Drew relaxed on the three piece sofa surrounding the glass topped table in the center of the sitting area. He rested his head on the back of the sofa and closed his eyes. We have to talk, he reminded himself.

Presently she joined him, pulling her legs up beneath her in a chair across the small room. "Still regrouping?" she asked sympathetically.

He opened his eyes and looked at her. There was a profound softness about her he had not seen in Savannah, a kindness that pulled at him, and frightened him. He often had been attracted to other women since Ellen's death, but largely the attractions had been sexual, something he could identify and which so far he had managed to avoid, not necessarily out of disinterest. But this woman was drawing from him a different response, though he would not give it a name. The physical attraction was strong, too, he admitted, but it was the warmth of her person, the easy connection they had established that was now building his confidence.

Could he trust her? He decided at that moment he had no choice. Mary's time was wasting, if indeed she had any time at all. He had to trust someone. He had to have at least one plausible, trustworthy piece of the puzzle, or return to Savannah empty-handed, which he was sure would spell disaster.

"Can we talk business?" he asked.

"If you wish," she answered, and her tone was immediately professional.

He uncrossed his legs and leaned forward. "I lied to you and Rod."

Doña's eyebrows rose, but she said nothing.

Drew continued. "The package is hidden. I didn't destroy the cocaine."

"I suspected as much," she said, holding his eyes with her own. "What do you plan to do with it?"

"That's just it. I don't know what to do, so I came to you. Mary's life is in the balance, if she's not already dead. I wanted a chance to save her, if I could, but I'm stymied. I do have new information."

"Oh?" Her response was offered evenly and hid no hint of surprise.

"Bobby, my reporter friend -- he left me some notes. He was working on a major story about trafficking coming through the Savannah port. I have some names, but I can't get anywhere with what little I know. I need your help, Doña. I didn't want to ask, you or Rod -- but I have to now."

She looked at him, examining his face, and thinking.

"If you won't -- can't help, just say so, and I'll leave. Right now. I'll never speak of your trip to Savannah."

"I don't know, Drew. You're asking a lot."

He stood, and began pacing, turning to face Doña. "I know what I'm asking, but I know that I've given a lot, too, and I know a lot is at stake -- Mary's life, for one.

And many thousands of kids' lives. You've got to help me, Doña. Tell me where to go, what to do, who to talk to."

"Drew --."

"Look," he said, returning to the sofa, "I've made some decisions. One, I'm getting out of the ministry. As soon as this thing is over, one way or the other, good or bad, I'm giving up my ordination."

She stared at him curiously. "You've made that decision? For real?"

"Yes. And, two, I'll use any resource I have, and they are considerable, you know, to help Mary, even if it means going to jail. I am responsible -- in some way, I know -- for Bobby's death. That makes three dead on my account, and if Mary's dead, well --."

"You are serious."

"You're damn right I am."

She nodded. "Sit down, Drew," she said, her eyes narrowing. "Tell me the names."

He sat back. "Senator James Maxwell, democrat from Georgia, for one. 'Charlie', for another. Don't know who he is, though. Some local people, county police, dock workers, others whose names would not be hard to learn, but they're not major players. The senator is. Maybe 'Charlie', I don't know."

Doña poured herself another glass of wine. "Drew," she began slowly, "what you are doing is dangerous." The earlier empathy was gone. Her eyes were cold steel.

He waited.

"But you are on the right track." she said solemnly.

Drew exhaled a huge sigh.

Doña took another sip of her wine and continued. "Let's take this one item at a time. First, they will assume you have the drugs. They have to, until they find otherwise. Two, if Mary is not dead, they'll keep her alive to propose an exchange."

"Mary for the drugs."

"Yes." She looked at him. "Want me to go on?"

"Please."

"Okay. Second, and you're not going to like this, but you need to know now --."

"What --?'

"The senator has a partner." She paused, her turn to stand.

"Who?"

"Rod Gray."

Drew's mouth fell open. His mind swirled in disbelief. "But he --, I don't understand --. Doña, what are you saying, for God's sake? How do you know that --?"

"Later. You asked me to help, to get involved. Now you're in a lot deeper than you ever expected. So keep your head on straight, okay? And listen."

Drew had not taken his eyes off her.

"I'm going to give you another name. In exchange, I want a promise from you."

"What?"

"There is someone I want you to meet."
"Who?"
"A man."
"A man ? What man? Who ?"
"Your promise."
"Hell, what can I say? Yes, of course! Who is the man?"
A pause. Then, "My father."
"But I thought ."
She ignored his surprise. "He can help."
"How?"
She ignored the question. "Go with me to see him."
"And where is that?"
"The Caribbean. More precisely, The Isle of Mujeres, off the coast of Cancun, Mexico." She paused and studied Drew's face. She saw the confusion. "He can help, Drew. I promise you, he can help, and furthermore, I do not know immediately anyone else who can, not like he can. I'll tell you the whole story, later."
"Okay." His word of resignation. "But Rod --? How --?"
"It's a long story, and like I said, later. First, you pay a visit on a Miss Betsy Conners. She's a prostitute, and she's Rod's girl friend."
"This is getting crazy," he said.
"It'll get crazier, Drew, before you find Mary, if at all."
"Why talk to the prostitute?"

"To confirm what I've told you, and get whatever information you can." She got up, wrote on a pad and returned to give the note to Rod. "Miss Conners' address. Go see her first thing in the morning."

"And when do we go see your father?"

"Tomorrow afternoon, at the latest. I have to make a few calls, arrange things, here and there. Then, we can enjoy some more of what has been, don't you think, an interesting evening."

Drew nodded. What would be the next surprise?

Doña was on the telephone for ten minutes. She placed the call from the bedroom and Drew could hear little of the conversation. When she returned, she informed him, "All set," she said, when she returned. Our flight leaves at approximately one thirty tomorrow afternoon."

"What airlines? I need to let my secretary know where to reach me."

Doña said quietly, "You'll be out of pocket for at least two days. Tell her that. The flight will be on private jet. Five hours to Cancun."

"Whose jet?" The question did not necessarily need an answer.

"It belongs to friends," she said, as a matter-of-fact.

He fell quiet and then looked at his watch.

"Why don't you stay here tonight? It's a long way to your hotel. There is another bedroom, or you can have the sofa. It sleeps quite well, really."

He was near to saying "yes" when he acknowledged the stirring in his groin. "Thanks for the invitation," he said, rising from the sofa. "But, I don't think I should accept. I think I should say 'thank you' again and I think I should take my leave. It's been a crazy day, and I need to sort some things out in my head." He started for the door.

Doña watched him walk to the door. "I understand," she said, speaking as she stood and walked toward him. "But I wish you'd change your mind." Her demeanor had changed again.

She ignored his extended hand, slipped her arms around his neck and pressed her lips to his. He caught again the subtle scent of her perfume, felt the warmth of her body against his. Instinctively, his arms enveloped her, lightly at first, then firmly, pulling her closer.

He pulled his lips from hers and looked down into her dark eyes. "It's – it's been a long time," he whispered.

"Maybe too long?"

He did not answer, but returned her kiss.

"Will God be so displeased?"

"I don't know ."

"Me either," she whispered softly. She stepped back and looked at Drew. His face was filled with sadness, and she was more aware than he that his fear of infidelity had more to do with Ellen than with God. She took his hand and gently urged him toward the sofa. He stood firmly for a moment, hesitant, but wanting her. She stopped, their arms extended, their fingers touching. He shut his eyes, squeezing them in a gesture intended to erase his doubts. Opening his eyes, he breathed a long sigh and stepped toward her.

Chapter Fifteen

Drew spotted the apartment number easily and claimed the first available parking. The tree lined street was congested with parked vehicles and a few health conscious walkers. He locked the rental car and joined the people on the walk opposite the line of neatly kept row houses.

He was still processing Doña's incredible revelation of Rod's involvement in drug trafficking. None of what she had said made much sense. An agent into drugs. His friend, no less. The clear implication was that Rod was betraying not only the friend who saved his life in Nam, but his country, too, his oath. And the father, David Moore, in Central America, possessing the power to extricate Drew from his nightmare? That made even less sense. But nothing had made sense to him in the last few days, nothing, in fact, sense Ellen's death. In the residence across the street, according to a woman he had met just days ago and with whom he had slept last evening, was another woman, a prostitute no less, who would confirm Doña's strange disclosures. He shook his head and crossed the tree-lined avenue.

In the entrance way he saw two name plates attached to the wall next to the door. The lower plate contained a man's name, the upper plate was engraved:
ELIZABETH R. CONNORS.

Each plate was accompanied by a small button. Drew depressed the button next to the upper plate and waited. Presently, a woman's voice answered. "Yes?"

"I have a message from Rod."

A buzz. Drew pushed open the door and entered. The narrow hallway led directly to a stairway to the second floor. He climbed it deliberately, going over in his mind what he would say to the woman when she opened the door, or if she did not.

He stepped to the first door on the upper landing and knocked. The door opened quickly.

"Well," she asked impatiently, "what is it?"

Drew hoped the look on his face did not expose his thoughts. The woman standing in the doorway was truly beautiful, in an innocent way, so different from the only prostitutes he had known, those in the back alleys of Saigon. Even in heels, she was small of stature, yet seemed to pull herself up beyond her height. Her light brown, shoulder length hair was highlighted with streaks of blond and tucked neatly behind each ear. The blue silk dress clung to her fine figure. Her makeup, though obviously overstated, was inoffensive. The eyes were deep brown, lined ponderously, and the woman's mouth, not smiling, was painted a glistening pink.

Drew cleared his throat. "I was instructed to give it to you privately."

The woman hesitated, then stepped aside, allowing Drew to enter the small apartment. A mix of used furnishings, neatly arranged, revealed the woman's moderate means. The center of attention was the king-sized bed dominated by a large headboard, the top of which was covered with a dark green velour cloth. Below the cloth were shelves accessed by sliding panels. An overstuffed chair at a window was covered with a brightly colored bedspread. On the window sill next to the chair was a pile of supermarket tabloids. A shimmering picture of Jesus hung between the two windows fronting the street below.

"Well, did he send you to calm me down, or what ?"

Drew turned to face her as she spoke. Her smile was controlled, sarcastic. It was her eyes, he decided, that gave her away. Sad eyes expecting more sadness.

"Rod didn't send me here. I lied. I need some information and I hoped you could give it to me."

She stepped back, toward the door, her eyes wide with a new fear. "I don't know who you are, mister, or what you want, but I suggest you get the hell out of here." She opened the door and held the doorknob, intent on him leaving immediately.

Drew stood his ground. "Ms. Conners, you need to listen to me, even if you don't tell me a thing. I'm not the law, but I know the authorities would be very interested in your connection to Mr. Gray."

The woman opened the door more widely, but it was clear she was not as ready as before for him to leave. "Mister," she said, eyeing him more closely. "You've got one minute!"

He had to make the most of the few seconds.

"Rod Gray is trafficking in drugs. He and his friends may have ordered at least one death, maybe more. If they are discovered, you will be in as much trouble as they. Maybe ten years in jail, if you're lucky, less if you cooperate." He spoke the words slowly, and let it hang there.

"I don't believe you," the woman said, still holding the door open.

Drew, his trained ear listening intently, watched her body language, evaluating the woman's response. Instinctively, he sensed Miss Conners had no knowledge of Rod's activities, if indeed he was what Doña had charged. Again, Drew decided to stand his ground. Now, he had to gain the woman's confidence, and do it quickly. "My best friend has been murdered and I believe Rod had something to do with it. Maybe you did, too."

"You're crazy, mister!" She was nearly screaming. "Now get out!" She pointed through the doorway to the hall.

He ignored her command and chanced a reference. "Do you know a man named 'Charlie'?"

She studied Drew carefully. "What if I do?"

"He telephoned me a few nights ago; he's blackmailing me. He may also have murdered my friend, and possibly my friend's wife." Drew stepped closer. "That's why I'm here, Miss Conners, to try and save the woman, if she's still alive. You can help me do that."

"Rod doesn't do drugs. He gets real mean when I do. He hates drugs. And all he drinks is beer."

"But he's moving the stuff, lady, believe me. Or, at least it looks that way," Drew replied. Then, he took a chance. "Miss Connors, I am a wealthy man. I'll pay you well."

"For what?" she asked. "To rat on Rod? Is that what you mean?"

"Just answer some questions. You can use the money to leave this place. Go somewhere you won't be found. Get out before you make real trouble for yourself. You don't want prison, do you?" He hurriedly considered numbers. It had to be a figure that would get her attention. Whatever he offered would be worth saving Ellen's memory, and getting Bobby's killer. Too, money was no obstacle. He stopped on a number that he hoped would do the trick. "I'll pay you ten thousand dollars -- cash. And I'll help you get set up anywhere you want to go. You name the place. You'll have everything you need to get started. Think about it, Miss Conners. Rod will never marry you, but one day he'll dump you and you'll be back on the streets."

"I was never on the street, mister," she responded indignantly.

"You want your life the way it was before Rod Gray? Huh? That's what you'll get when he's through with you. A different man each time, never really knowing what the man wants. Then, one day, they won't want you anymore. You'll be old and fat. And who'll take care of you then, Miss Conners? Who'll give a shit about you?"

Betsy stared at him for long seconds, then closed the door quietly. "Sit down."

Drew took the only chair he saw other than the large overstuffed chair at the window. The woman sat on the edge of the bed, facing him.

"You're rich, huh?" She crossed her legs and made no effort to restrict her skirt that crept upwards, showing a generous amount of firm thigh. "The money. I want the money first, and I want twenty-five thousand."

Mary's life was worth much more. "I'll go get it for you. I can have it within the hour, and --."

Betsy stood. "Rod will kill me if he knew I was talking to you like this."

Drew rose, walked to the door. "I'll be back in an hour. I'll have the money."

Elizabeth Connors' eyes narrowed. "Twenty-five thousand," she said. "One hour."

"Agreed," Drew said, without hesitation. "I'll be here. And if you value your life, you won't call Rod."

Drew drove to the nearest bank and asked to speak to the manager and told him of his request. Twenty-five thousand dollars, two thousand in small denominations, the remainder in hundred dollar bills. From the manager's office he called the Savannah's Citizens and Southern Bank main office in Savannah, talked to the president of the bank and instructed the money be wired immediately.

Forty minutes after leaving Elizabeth Conners apartment, Drew left the bank with twenty-five thousand U.S. dollars.

Ten minutes later he knocked on Elizabeth Connors' door again.

She accepted the money nervously, fingering the thick envelope. Then she ripped it open and began counting the bills. Suddenly she stopped. "What do you want to know?"

"What you know about Rod and any of his associates."

She sat in the overstuffed chair and spoke slowly. "I have loved him, kind of, a long time. He's been good to me. He's been good to me, really, though there are times when I don't think I know him at all. If you're telling me the truth, I don't know anything about it. I'm just there when he needs me, wants me there. Sure, I can come and go as I like, because I have a key. But I know I can't do that too often. I fix things for him in his place when he's away, you know, get the place ready for when he comes back from one of his trips. And, I give him what he needs when he needs it, if you know what I mean."

Drew understood. His heart was pounding; he was gaining her confidence. Now, he thought, be careful. "Tell me about 'Charlie'. He leaned forward from his chair.

"Charlie ?" she asked, surprised. "That s.o.b.? He's an old Nam buddy. They go back years."

Vietnam! Drew couldn't recall a 'Charlie' from their Nam days, but then he had left Southeast Asia before Rod, many months before. But something was jelling. Obviously their tours, all three of them, had coincided. Maybe..., he thought. "Does Rod meet with Charlie often?"

"Yeah, I think so, but not at Rod's house." She continued to finger the money. "Most of the time he just calls. I've seen him at the house only one other time, maybe two, three years ago. But, like I said, they talk a lot."

She had given him a confirmation of Doña's accusations. The one he needed. He told himself not to rush the conversation.

"What do they talk about?"

"Oh," she said, " about their deals. I don't pay much attention. Meetings. Details of something they're working on, I suppose."

"Do they talk about places, names, anything ?"

"Yeah, places, like you say, and names, too, but I don't pay much attention. Know what I mean?"

"Yes. The names, do you remember any of the names?"

"No , I mean, not really. Of course, the senator, I remember his name coming up a lot. Senator Maxwell. You know, the guy from where is it? Georgia? Yeah, that's right. Georgia. Senator James something."

Bingo! Drew tried to conceal his excitement. "Maxwell? James Maxwell?"

"Yeah, that's him. Seen pictures of him. Tall, grey hair. You know, like senators are supposed to look."

Two confirmations.

"Hey, you're cute, you know that?" Betsy said, pulling her long legs to her side on the bed. A practiced move.

Drew's mind was reeling in a labyrinth of feelings. He stood, and walked toward the door.

"Miss Connors?"

"Betsy."

"Betsy. Thank you." He reached the door and put his hand on the doorknob. He was aware he had put the woman's life in danger. He must try to insure the woman's safety. That was the least he could do. "I warn you again; you are in danger. I don't know how you are going to handle what I've told you, but, you must say nothing to Rod of our conversation, or even that you ever met me. If you're smart, you'll get out of town. Start some other place."

"Where would I go?"

Drew had put her in terrible jeopardy. She could not mean that much to Rod, not if she knew too much. "Betsy, get out of here, right away. I don't care where you go, but make it somewhere quiet. Start a new life. Get married, and have some kids. Just stay away from Rod Gray and his friends."

Then he handed her his business card. "If you ever need help, call this number. Ask for me. Dr. Campbell."

He descended the steps to the street and stood on the sidewalk. He began walking, and reached an intersection where he stood silently. There were voices around him, but they seemed far away. Senator Maxwell! He remembered Bobby's admonitions about the powerful people the reporter had suspected. But the senator? My God! And if the senator, who else?

Drew spent the rest of the day at the desk in his hotel room, committing all he knew or suspected on hotel stationary. He saw more of the picture now. Rod had more than one friend in Nam. Drew had been one. Charlie had been another, obviously. Maybe the senator. If Charlie had been in that room the night Drew killed two people, he could have told Rod. But why? What had been their connection in Nam? And what part did the senator play in all this, if any?

Betsy was packing feverishly when the telephone rang.

"Hello."

"Hey, baby," Rod said. "I've got to be out of pocket for a day or so, but I'll call you soon, okay?"

She hesitated, then drew a breath, trying to act as normal as possible. "Sure, baby, you call me and I'll have things ready." Then she added, for effect: "I've got something real nice planned for you. I'm going to make up for lost time, sweetheart."

Rod smiled into the receiver. Betsy was so predictable. That's what he liked about her. One of the things. "Sure, baby. See you in a couple of days. You have fun while I'm gone. Buy yourself something special." He started to replace the receiver, but stopped. "Betsy, you need some money?"

She responded quickly. "No, sweetheart. I'm fine. I've got money."

"Good. See you, then."

Chapter Sixteen

In a small efficiency apartment in Washington, Markus Williamson, respected national columnist for the Washington Post, tried to contain his fury as he faced Morgan Ann Huntington Maxwell.

"I told you, Morgan Ann, repeatedly, that you should never call my office. We agreed: once a month! That's all we can risk. Once a month, we meet here. If one of us can't make it, we wait until next month, same day plus one, same hour. We agreed! No other contacts. And, leaving your name at the Post was riskier than the call, don't you understand? By now, everyone in the newsroom knows I received a call from you, and every one of them is wondering why. You just can't do ."

"I had no choice, Markus. I needed to talk to you."

"What's so important that it couldn't wait until next week when we were to meet as usual? I can't believe you did this! Someone's going to ask questions, probably of my wife. Worse, if anyone ever found about us, my credibility would be ruined." His double chin ricocheted off his neck when tried to emphasize his point.

"Get me a drink, Markus," she said, "then sit down."

His hands shook visibly when he handed the Absolute on the rocks. "Now, what's so urgent couldn't wait?"

"James. The senator, the fool is involved in a drug ring." She let the words hang there.

The columnist stared her with disbelief. "Drugs? The senator? What are you talking about, Morgan Ann?"

She told him what she knew, what her husband had confided in her. Her information was sketchy at best, and probably incomplete, she said, but true. Then she told him of the pastor's visit, and Drew's threat to go to the police. "It'll ruin everything for us. James will go to jail, I will be disgraced -- and lose everything!"

Williamson had lived in the nation's capital long enough to know one was not supposed to be surprised at anything, but this was too close to home. Suddenly, he wished he had never gotten involved with Morgan Ann Huntington Maxwell. Their trysts had been going on undetected for three years and their secret appeared forever safe. "What are you going to do?" Williamson asked.

"That's why I risked calling; I need your help."

"How can I possibly help?" he asked, but was trying to think of the implications, and how he could somehow extradite himself.

"That's your part of this problem."

"I have no part of this 'problem', as you call it. I have been your lover, but I'm not responsible for that fool you're married to!"

"You're not much of a lover, Markus, and it's your problem now, as well as mine."

"How so ?"

"If I go down, so do you, you pompous ass. Now, you're going to help us get out this mess."

"No!" he said, standing and walking to the shuttered window, peering out, then coming back to his chair. "I have enjoyed our times together, Morgan Ann, and I don't remember you complaining. But I don't want anything to do with this. I'm out."

"You said you loved me."

"In the heat of sex, yes. We both enjoyed the sex, and the talking. But love? Bullshit. It has to end, now, Morgan Ann. I can't get involved. I promise not to divulge what you've told me, ever, but, no, I'm out."

"You don't have a choice lover," she responded with all her feigned southern charm. "You will help, or the Post's most reputable columnist will be exposed by me. Understand, Markus?"

"You wouldn't. I mean, you can't."

"Try me, my dear."

He knew he should not test her. "Morgan Ann, what can I do?"

"You'll think of something. It's time you leave the safety of your word processor, darling. You columnists are all the same. Out from behind the safety of the newspaper and your computer, you're all wimps. Try to be a man for a change and quit telling others how to live their lives for just a few hours, okay?" She stood, put on her jacket and started for the door.

He followed her to the door, knowing that at this moment he could kill her and not think twice about it, such was his rage. But he would think twice, many times over. If he couldn't find a way out of this, she would go down and take him down with her, that much he knew.

At the door, he faced her again. "I'll think of something."

"I'm sure you will."

Markus Williamson thought of everything in the next hour, except a solution. He could see the headline: NATIONAL COLUMNIST LINKED WITH WIFE OF DRUGPEDDLING SENATOR. Markus Williamson sank back into the sofa, even deeper into an unfamiliar fit of depression.

"I'm telling you, he knows!" demanded Charlie. He sat across from Rod at a table in the far corner of the small cafe. He bit off the end of a toothpick, spit it out and began picking at his front teeth again. Why couldn't Rod see it? It is time to take care of the preacher, Charlie thought, and squirmed, waiting.

Rod fingered his coffee cup, staring down into the black liquid. He knew Charlie was right to call him out so early, but to act precipitously, or stupidly, would be a mistake. They still might secure the package, make the delivery. Drew could wait.

"All right," Rod said. He looked up from the cup. "This is what we know. Your men found nothing in his house to implicate us. He was in Washington; for what, we're not entirely sure. You lost him, then picked him up near Betsy's apartment. And, for that matter, where is Betsy? Maybe she's turning a trick somewhere. She does that sometime when I'm gone or when she gets angry with me. But what was the preacher doing at Betsy's place?" Rod paused, then, "You lost him for several hours, picked him up again at the hotel. And we know he had dinner with Doña last evening, and stayed the night. That might not mean anything, except the preacher got some sex. Doña hasn't the slightest clue about us. Drew boarded a flight for Savannah this afternoon. If Taylor told him anything, Drew would have reacted by now. But all he's done is visit Doña.

So, what have we got?" Rod looked past Charlie, thinking further.

Charlie shifted in his chair, trying to keep up with Rod. He trusted Rod. The man was real smart.

"We don't know what the reporter knew, except the senator's name came up unexpectedly in some loose talk among some dock hands. We do know the reporter was asking questions about the shipping lines from South America. We know he and Drew were real tight friends." Charlie continued his silence. Rod rubbed his chin. Listening to himself evaluate the situation was heightening his anxiety. Maybe something did need doing with Drew. He chose the less offensive and potentially more productive option.

"Here's what you do," he instructed Charlie. "Find Betsy. I don't care what you have to do, just find her. And bring her to her apartment. I'll meet you there. If she knows anything, we'll get it out of her. Then, we might pay the reverend a visit. Okay?"

Charlie nodded. "I'll find her."

Betsy waited until the last minute to summon a taxi. The prospects of leaving made her nervous enough, but this thing about Rod was scaring her to death. She would not have believed the stranger except twenty-five thousand dollars was no lie.

She picked up the two large bags and struggled her way down the stairs and onto the street. She hailed the first cab. "National Airport."

She wore the dark blue suit Rod had bought for her the one time he took her somewhere other than to his bed. She felt good in it, like a woman feels when she knows she looks good. Her hair was pulled back in a manner she had seen in a magazine. The dark shades gave her a sense of security. Her aunt in Chicago would be impressed; she could stay with her aunt until she found a place of her own.

She gave her two bags to the airlines attendant and instructed him to wait for her at the check-in counter. She fumbled in her bag for the cab fare, paid the driver and started toward the ticket counter. Everything was going so well. It was an effort to hold herself in check, and not run.

Betsy glanced around the checkout counter. There were a dozen persons in front of her in the line. She saw nothing unusual. She relaxed and felt in her carryon for the five hundred dollars she had put aside for the trip to Chicago. Deeper in the carryon was the remainder of the twenty-five thousand, wrapped in tin foil.

A hand touched her shoulder and she jumped as if a live wire had touched her butt. She recognized the voice immediately.

"Your boyfriend wants to see you, Betsy." Charlie instructed. She froze. "Now don't do anything foolish, or I'll leave your insides a mess."

Half an hour later she was in her apartment again and facing Rod.

"Where'd you get the money, Betsy?"

"A man gave it to me, I don't know his name." she said softly. She did, though, and she had a number to call. She would tell the truth. Maybe Rod would let her keep the money.

Rod poured two drinks and handed one to Betsy. She took it quietly, but held it in her lap. He pulled a chair up next to hers, his face not four inches from hers. "Now, tell me everything," he said, softly.

She did. Every word. Even her plans to go to Chicago. "I was scared, Rod, really, I was scared half to death. If you're really into drugs, if that's what you do, I don't want to be a part of it."

Rod put his hand on hers. "It's okay, baby. It's really okay. You did good, telling me everything. You know I'm going to take care of you. And you can go to Chicago in the morning. Next flight, if you wish. I'll have Charlie put you on the plane. Okay, Charlie?" Rod glanced at the little man with the week's growth of beard.

"Sure, Rod, anything you say."

Betsy had to ask. "Can I keep the money? I mean, I'll need it to get started. And I'll never say anything to anybody about what you do, Rod. I promise." She touched his face lightly. "I really mean it, I'll forget everything. You'll never have to worry about me, I promise."

"Sure. You can keep the money. You're all right, kid. You're all right." Rod patted her on the cheek and stood to straighten his tie. "I have to go now, but I'll leave Charlie here to look after you. The guy might come back, you know. We couldn't have that, now could we?"

"No, Rod."

When Rod left, she went into the bath.

Charlie was waiting for her when she returned. A wide grin was spread across his face as he approached her, deliberately.

"What do you want?" she stuttered.

"You, baby." He continued his slow steps toward her. "Charlie," she said, trying to keep her voice calm. "I know what you want, and I'll give it to you. Just don't hurt me, okay? Say you won't hurt me and I'll make it good for you, I really will."

She threw off her suit coat and began unbuttoning her blouse as he approached. He stepped closer and ripped off the last button. Without hesitating, she pulled the blouse off her shoulders and dropped it to the floor. Charlie watched the performance, leering at his prey. Quickly, she unsnapped her bra and removed it, dropping it on top of the blouse. She was breathing heavily, trying to smile as she did what she was so accustomed to doing in more favorable circumstances. She kept her fingers busy. Her skirt was halfway off her hips when she looked down to step out of it.

She did not see the blow coming. It slammed against her jaw with a force that knocked her off her feet. She tasted the blood immediately, and struggled to regain her senses. Her head was swirling. She could not focus.

The little man pulled at her skirt and yanked it over her ankles. She lashed out with her hands, feeling for his face, clawing. Her nails dug into his cheeks. "Bitch!" he howled, and swung at her head again. This time his fist caught her above the eye. Betsy fell on her back, her arms flailing, grasping for something, anything. She was dimly aware of her clothes being torn from her legs, and then the weight of the man's body forcing itself on her. Another terrible blow. A crunch of bone. A stab of pain below.

Betsy quit fighting.

As he took his pleasure with her, she began to whisper, "Mary, Mother of God ..."

The death blow came as a blessing. She felt herself spinning above herself, rising into the air, through the ceiling. She did not know where she was going. It didn't matter. She was leaving the little man. She was leaving the pain. She was dying, and she was grateful.

Then, the Blessed Mary came, and peace. Blessed peace.

Chapter Seventeen

Doña fidgeted with the small religious figurine her Papa had given her on the occasion of her sixth birthday. It was, he had said, she remembered his words exactly "to remind her of her mother."

She tried to remember what her mother looked like. She forced herself not to look at the picture of the beautiful Mexican woman whose face smiled from the fading photograph on the table beside her. She could remember the black hair. But the only other feature of her mother she could remember without having to have her memory refreshed was the smile. The happy smile. Maybe it was because Papa said repeatedly, "You have Maria's smile." A five year old, she acknowledged, might forget a face, but not a smile. Then, again, it was her mother's smile she looked at every morning for years after Maria's death.

What she remembered most was the warmth of her mother's arms as they rocked each evening. The hot days invariably ended on the open air porch, the smell of salt water in the air, the cool breeze rolling in from the crystal blue Caribbean. Her mother rocked and hummed, singing softly a Mexican lullaby. She remembered, too, that her mother would speak of her father, Papa Maria called him Papa, and taught Doña to speak of him thus as if he were there with them, just gone for a short walk. She learned to love Papa long before she met him. Maria saw to that; one day it would be necessary to love him in her absence. She trusted Papa more than she trusted anyone in the whole world, and she wondered if any daughter had ever loved a father as she loved Papa.

The telephone rang.

She grabbed at it with a rush. "Hello?"

"Eagle One." His voice was as calm as ever, a deep, rolling, caring voice. Every time she heard it, it was like coming home again. She pictured her Papa in the smaller study, the walls crowded with photos of old friends and former bureau colleagues. His ever present pipe was smoldering nearby, a cup of coffee at his fingertips. Black, Columbian coffee. Centered on his impossibly cluttered desk, she knew, were two pictures. Wife and daughter, one an echo of the other. Both smiling at Papa.

"A minor change. The priest has gone home. Maybe we made a mistake sending him to the woman."

"What happened?"

"I'm not certain. I'm going there tonight."

"He must come to Eagle Nest."

"I'll do my best. Have the Eagle stand by."

"Affirmative." Then, "Does your friend like Mexican cooking?"

"He liked mine."

The two men walked to the right of the Washington Monument, avoiding a boisterous crowd of high school students eating box lunches, and started down the tree lined path toward the Viet Nam Memorial. Soon they were engulfed in the sober faced hundreds who quietly strolled the length of the black marble structure. Neither spoke as they weaved their way through the gathering of a cross-section of the American populace, many of whom wept openly, and unashamedly. They stopped once to avoid interfering with a woman photographing a lanky teenage boy who stood at the center of the wall, pointing at a name he could reach only on tiptoe. When the boy turned to face his mother, his face wet with tears, she came to him immediately and swept him into her arms.

They continued to the far end of the wall and stood apart from the crowd. The taller, more distinguished of the two broke the protracted silence. "How long have you been seeing my wife?" the senator asked, refusing to look at his companion as he posed the question.

"Nearly three years," the columnist answered. There was no need to add any details, nor would he. It was over with him and Morgan Ann Huntington Maxwell, except this unwelcomed meeting he had requested of the senator. Normally, he might have felt sorry for the senator. This afternoon, he loathed the man. "But that is entirely irrelevant at the moment, senator. It's over, and unimportant. What we do about your stupidity, that's the issue. Rather, what you do about it."

James Maxwell looked at Markus Williamson. What Morgan Ann had seen in the man he could not fathom. It did not occur to him Maxwell was wondering the same about him, though he knew the woman always did what she did for a reason to get what she wanted. Again, she was getting her way.

The senator raised his head, stared into the blue Washington sky, and then dropped it forward, his eyes on the thick green carpet of grass. He breathed deeply. He had no answer, no solution, except to hope The Man was taking care of things. He had not revealed The Man's existence to his wife, and he had no intention of sharing it with his wife's lover. What he might do is call The Man and ask him to deal with the columnist as well. But he would wait a day or two, to see if things took care of themselves. If Rod was eliminated, then all would be well. The final delivery of coke completed, the money split, the operation closed. Then, he would deal with Morgan Ann and her fatso boyfriend. The scenario comforted him.

"I'll take care of it," he said to Williamson.

"How?"

"I said I'd take care of it, didn't I?" he repeated.

"Like you've taken care of everything else?"

"I can handle it," the senator said, knowing he could not, but The Man could. And would. He always did. The familiar shudder ran through his body.

"Make sure of it."

"You go to hell, you bastard!"

The obese columnist ignored the curse. He turned and walked into the crowd, his estimation of the senator confirmed. Morgan Ann's wimp of a husband could not be trusted with this crisis. If this impending disaster was to be averted, Williamson was now certain, he would have to be the one to accomplish it.

Drew exited the comfortably cooled Savannah airport and caught the blast of August heat squarely in his face. He increased his pace, eager to reach the Camaro and get to the friendlier breezes off Bluff Drive. The trip to Washington had paid off, but at the moment he was quite unsure how he might use the information he had gained. The mysterious invitation to visit Doña's equally enigmatic father was a source of hope, but like other aspirations, it, too, might prove fruitless. Even a waste of time, considering Mary's fate. But he had information, though it might be deadly news, indeed, in the wrong hands. He knew much more than he did when he left Savannah two days ago. But what could he do with it? And, Mary? How did his information help her?

    He found the Camaro after wandering briefly in the long term parking lot. He was unlocking the door when he felt a presence. Turning, he found himself looking into the face of a Chatham County deputy sheriff.

    "Brother Campbell?"
    "I'm Andrew Campbell, yes."
    "This is for you." The man held out a small white envelope.
    "What's this --?" Drew asked, accepting the envelope.
    The deputy said nothing and walked away.

Drew fired the engine and turned the air-conditioner to maximum. He tore open the envelope and read a brief, neatly typed note.

> *The mouth of the river.*
> *Tonight. Midnight. We talk.*
> *R.*

He drove home slowly. If Rod wanted to talk, then the agent was aware of Drew's growing knowledge of Rod's illegal activities, indeed, his criminal operation. Drew reasoned there could be more than one reason for the meeting. One, to recover the package with an offer for Mary's release. And two, to kill him and dump his body where the Savannah River and the Atlantic Ocean meet and where it was unlikely the body would ever be recovered.

But, he understood, he had little choice. Information, damaging as it might be, was useless if he had no way to successfully use it -- successfully, that is, finding Mary, alive!

By the time he reached Isle of Hope he had decided he would take The North Star from the marina at eleven o'clock. There would be no problem navigating even if the moon was heavily clouded. He knew the inter-coastal waters like the back of his hand. He went upstairs and laid out some clothes. Dark, and lightweight, easily removed in water. He removed the .45 from the drawer of the bedside table, ejected the clip and checked the gun's action. Satisfied, he replaced the clip and put the safety on. A few more chores and he was ready. Nothing to do now, but wait.

Markus Williamson liked beer. He liked women, too. In spite of the difficult the first caused to his waistline and the second to his reputation, he could not swear off either. With Morgan Ann he had begun to think he could limit his sexual escapades. It was getting increasingly difficult to secure the services of women he considered safe, politically or otherwise. Before he followed the senator's wife's not to subtle suggestion that he call her "for a little fun", he had tried to control his weight problem, lay off the beer and watch his food intake. But with growing confidence in his relationship with Morgan Ann Maxwell, the bulging tire about his mid-section became less of a concern. It did make conventional sex difficult, but then, their sexual needs were anything but prosaic. And he knew, from the beginning, that it was not sex that motivated Morgan Ann to try to seduce him. She wanted another channel of information, one more way to control the system. Markus did not need seducing, nor did he hesitate to write glowingly of the labors of the Georgia senator. Too, he prided himself in manipulating the senator from the bed he shared with the man's wife. To make things all the more delightful, he discovered early on in his rendezvouses with Morgan Ann that his kinky sexual appetite did not phase her in the least. Markus even stopped soliciting young boys, so good was the sex with Washington's sultriest senator's wife. There was nothing the woman wouldn't try, at least once. And he fed her need for information and for sources of power, ethics be damned.

Now he had a problem. To hell with Morgan Ann. He could find other women, he had always managed. He could lose weight again if necessary. And there were always plenty of pretty young boys around. But he could not allow his name to surface with the wife of a senator convicted of drug trafficking.

He had considered all the options he could imagine. Only one seemed plausible, one that offered the best chance that his name would never appear alongside that of the Maxwell's. He would break the story himself, and he must do it immediately.

Maxwell pushed aside the pad on which he had been listing his options and turned to the keyboard of his word processor. His fingers began tapping our tomorrow's column.

Many of the words I have written in the space of this column have been painful. These words have been torn from the fabric of my heart, so heavy is my despair.

For some years I have applauded the work of the junior senator from Georgia, James Maxwell. But today I confess to you, Gentle Reader, that I have been royally duped, and have made a grievous error of judgment. Even as I write this, I ask your forgiveness. For you have trusted me and my opinions over the last sixteen years this column has appeared. I have terrible news for you folk in Georgia, and equally terrible news for liberal thinking citizens throughout these wonderful United States. I know that in the disclosures of today's column many innocent people will be hurt personally, professionally. But I must not withhold from the American people the truth as I know it. My conscience will not permit it. Even though it may take some weeks, maybe longer, for the information I share with you to be verified, nevertheless, it will be supported in time by the facts.

I have evidence of criminal activity by, not only the junior senator from the great state of Georgia, but likewise by at least one representative of one the nation's law enforcement agencies.

Why have I not taken the information to that agency? Why should I? We have come to expect nothing but the worse of the federal agencies such as the CIA and the FBI. They cater to the far right in every instance and I have no confidence that the damaging information that has come into my possession would be followed and investigated with integrity. Thus, I share it with you, the American people.

Markus Williamson stayed at the keyboard for another two hours, cleverly wrapping his disclosures in thin humility and righteous indignation. As he wrote, he had no idea he was placing in immense and immediate danger the lives of a pastor, a government agent and the widow of a fellow journalist, not to mention the reputations of untold numbers of others. But he would have saved his own kingdom, at least for the moment.

Finally, he completed the column, edited it twice and saved it a final time to the hard disk. With a click of the mouse, he initiated the modem, then hit "SEND". He opened another beer and took it and the cordless telephone to the patio, quite pleased with himself. He estimated it would take his editor at least an hour to call.

Doña arrived, as she promised, a few minutes after eleven. The late hour left them little time to talk. She sat at the kitchen table. Drew leaned against a counter, then walked to the back door to stare into the darkness. He returned to sit at the table. Doña watched his restlessness without speaking. Both understood the gravity of the hour. He would take The North Star from its slip in less than half an hour.

"Drew, listen to me." She reached across the table, squeezed his hand, and held it. "You are in over your head. I know what I'm talking about. Let him sit out there in the water all night if he wants to, but don't go. Come with me tomorrow to talk to my father. He knows how to handle this kind of thing. Think about it, Drew. Taking The North Star out to meet Rod tonight is a big mistake. Please don't do it."

"Doña, you mean well, I know, but I have to go tonight. I have to meet Rod, because I have to know how all this started, and where it might end. I don't know any other way to do it. I've thought it through again and again. I'm ultimately responsible for getting myself and my friends in this mess. One of them is dead, maybe both of them. Three, maybe four people dead because of me. Hell, I don't know how many lives I've put through hell. I have thought of that nameless woman I killed a decade ago. I can still hear her screams, and I remember the sudden silence after I pulled that trigger. I have run through that alley in Saigon a thousand times in the last week. I have to know some things, and I have to set some things right. You can understand that, can't you?" He held her eyes with his.

She knew there was nothing more to say. "Okay, but I stay here." She continued: "Rod needs the package, or he would have pulled out a long time ago. Or, maybe he's just greedy. Too, by now, he knows I know something. I suspect he'll disappear soon. It'd be no problem for him to leave without a trace and to hide comfortably."

Drew was listening.

"But will you promise me this," she asked, "Will you accompany me to see my father tomorrow? We can be there by supper time, or earlier. Then, back in Savannah by late the next afternoon, if necessary. You won't regret making the trip. Otherwise, I have to leave here and decide what I have to do."

Drew considered and said, "Agreed. Unless, of course, I discover something tonight to change my mind."

"Is there anything I can do to help, right now, I mean?"

"No," Drew said. Then, "Yes, there is. Could you check on somebody for me?"

"I'll try."

"There's a woman in Washington. I met her yesterday. She's Rod's girl, or rather, she's a prostitute Rod enjoys frequently. Her name is Betsy Connors. Elizabeth Connors." He gave Doña the address. "I gave her some money to get out of town. I'd like to know she made it okay. I'd hate to think I caused her trouble, too."

"I'll check on it."

"Thanks."

He stood. The black jogging outfit made him appear smaller than he was. He had not shaved today and by this evening hour his stubble of beard was rough, spotty. His hair was mussed, and the gray shone like silver in the low light. He removed a black ball cap from an equally black canvass bag and slipped it on. He checked the remaining contents of the bag. The .45 automatic and a small box of cartridges. A flashlight. His pipe and tobacco. A clean sweatshirt. Satisfied, he zipped the bag and started to the door.

"When can I look for you?" Doña asked.

"If I'm not back by six o'clock tomorrow morning, I'm not coming back," he said. He pushed open the screen as Doña spoke again.

"Drew -."

He turned, put down the bag and reached for her. She stepped into his embrace.

"I'll be back," he said.

"I'll wait for you till six."

Drew eased into the shadows leading to the marina.

The dark shape of the sleek speedboat roared over the water, leaving a rooster tail spray of salt water thirty feet behind the boat. The two men in the front seats stared into the blackness of a moonless night, their heads bobbing in rhythm with each crash of the foot high breakers. The man in the passenger seat leaned toward the pilot and shouted into his ear. "Slow down, for God's sake!" The little man eased the throttle back an inch and the low-slung craft slowed noticeably. Decelerating, the rise and fall of the boat became more pronounced. "We've got plenty of time," the older man instructed, flashing a small light on his wrist watch.

"What if he doesn't come?" the little man asked.

"He'll come. He has to come."

The boat plowed on through the swell of the waves. Aft, a giant rooster tail rose in the shadowed waters. On the starboard side, the low lights of waterfront homes dotted the shoreline. As another mile was covered on the waterway, the lights became fewer as residents turned in for the night. Private docks jutted out from the shore like skeleton arms reaching for passing craft.

Doña walked quietly about the house. She climbed the stairway to Drew's bedroom and sat down on the edge of the large bed. Her eyes fell on a picture displayed prominently on the side table. She had not studied the photograph closely the first time she had waited here, but now she picked it up, aware she was exercising a liberty that was not hers.

    The woman in the picture was seated at the rear of The North Star, one foot planted on the top of the stern, her hands resting behind her, supporting her weight. Her blond hair was swept away from her face by the wind. An engaging smile was exploding across her face. She was a happy woman. And, thought Doña, she was offering that happiness to the photographer, her husband.

    Doña studied the photograph of Ellen. She was, had been, a stunning beauty, Doña admitted. And she was, had been, alluring and sensual. Doña imagined the woman had just shouted some private words intended only for Drew, and then, had exacted the pose. Doña wished the woman in the photograph would speak to her. She returned the photograph to its place, turned and followed the hallway to the top of the stairs. Pausing, she tried to remember where she had seen a photo album several days ago. Then she remembered.

    She descended the steps and made her way quietly to the small study off the spacious living room. There, she risked turning on a small reading lamp and began surveying the sparsely appointed private study. She saw it, a brown leather binder. She took the album to the large desk and opened it under the low light of the lamp.

She began turning the leaves containing photos of Drew and his deceased wife. She had no way of knowing the many others in the photographs, but suspected some of them were family, others, of course, friends.

A page contained pictures of a much younger Andrew Campbell, dressed in army fatigues. One particularly caught her attention. She looked closely. Yes, it was Rod, and Drew, arms over each other's shoulders, smiling happily. Nam, no doubt. She turned the page, then several more pages. There was a page of photographs of Drew and his wife with an attractive black couple. Then, another page of just Drew and the black couple. Bobby and Mary.

Suddenly, she was stunned by the next page of photographs. Pictures of Drew and his wife, but not the same woman, at least not the same healthy, smiling woman whose picture graced Drew's bedside table. This woman was sick, held closely by Drew as if she might fall except for the strength of his arm. Her hair was thinner, her face pale and unsmiling. Her arms appeared small and brittle. Her eyes sunken and lined with the dark shades of death. Doña's eyes filled with tears. A beautiful woman, so filled with life and promise, reduced, in this photograph, to a shell of a human being.

She looked at Drew's face in the picture. Already, Doña could see the approaching grief, the agony of loving so dearly the one who was slipping from his arms and out of his life. She closed the album with a rush. She extinguished the light and left the room, chastising herself for invading their life. Not even her night with Drew gave her that privilege. Strange, she thought, that it is I who waits in his house for his return.

Chapter Eighteen

Drew steered The North Star toward the mouth of the Savannah River. He slowed the handsome boat to a crawl, searching the horizon for a sign of another craft. Then he saw it, bobbing on the swells where the river meets the imposing Atlantic Ocean, its running lights alternating from red to green and the waves tossed the boat about. He kept his course. Let them come to him, he decided, and steered straight for the channel leading to the ten mile buoy.

A light flashed from the smaller boat. Another flash. Drew stood up from the wheel and quickly, unzipped the canvass bag at his feet and withdrew the .45, and loaded the automatic. He worked the weapon's mechanism to put a cartridge in the firing chamber, then pushed the powerful handgun into the waistband of his jogging pants. He pulled the upper garment over his waist. He lit his pipe, and waited.

The smaller boat approached and the two vessels touched. Rod leaped easily into The North Star and tied the rope from the smaller craft to the stern of the cruiser, allowing the smaller boat to drift the length of the rope. The little man sat at the wheel of the low slung boat, riding the swells more than twenty feet behind The North Star.

Rod turned from fastening the rope and faced Drew. The agent found himself looking into the barrel of the .45.

"Sit, my friend," Drew ordered.

"Drew, put that damn thing away," the agent responded with a shrug of his shoulders, and stepped toward Drew.

"Go to hell!" Drew said sternly, knowing at that moment he meant it, literally. He glanced over Rod's shoulder at the little man.

The agent retreated and sat on the seat that stretched across the stern. Drew settled in the pilot's chair facing the agent. "Now, what was it you wanted to talk about?"

The moon had peaked from behind rain clouds and threw a soft glow over the open cockpit area. Still, Rod was more a shadowed outline than clearly visible. Rod tried again. "You don't need that gun, Drew. I came here to talk with you. You're right, I am a friend."

Drew was quick with his reply. "Well, I could have used one several times in the last few days. So, I'll decide when the gun is no longer necessary. You talk."

Rod shifted his position at the stern. Drew was careful to keep Rod between himself and the little man in the boat drifting behind The North Star.

"Okay, Drew." Rod held his hands apart at shoulder width, a gesture of resignation. He tried to ignore the gun pointed at him. "I'm assuming you know the basics. You have reason to be angry, but it need not have happened like it did. And it can stop, for you, for anyone who need not be involved."

Drew's lips tightened. "Like Bobby?"

"It couldn't be helped."

"Like hell it couldn't, you son-of-a-bitch!"

"A point of view," Rod said. "Your friend stepped into something he shouldn't have, and he was about to make trouble for everybody. He could have had his story, but he wouldn't wait. We would have been out of here and gone and nobody would have gotten hurt."

"What happened to Mary?" Drew asked pointedly. Is she dead, too?"

"No, but she could be, if you don't listen to me tonight."

"Where is she?"

"At the proper time, Drew."

Drew was silent for a moment, hoping against hope Rod was telling the truth. He had counted on Rod using Mary whether she was dead or alive, Drew had no way of knowing to control him again. But for now, he had to get some answers.

"I want to know the whole story, Rod. I mean, what the hell is going on? And how did you get involved, anyway? How did I get involved? Why me?"

"What do you know?" Rod asked.

Drew told him. "I know about your association with Senator James Maxwell and that little bastard Charlie, about your long term plan to set up a drug trafficking scheme in the states when the time was right. I know the time became right, obviously, when you made rank in the bureau and when Senator Maxwell gained prominence. The other guy, the one sitting twenty feet from us, I know little, except he's one little scum bag. Nice associate you have there, Rod."

Rod ignored the commentary. "And what else do you know?"

"There are a lot of things I suspect, but I don't have the evidence, yet. I know a woman who will identify you and your associates."

"Betsy?"

"Yes. Elizabeth Connors. A nice lady, at that. She doesn't deserve you."

"A prostitute, and she's dead."

Drew caught his breath.

This time Rod did not smile. "She told us about your visit."

The reason for this meeting. And another death, his responsibility. He had led them to Betsy, put her in danger, and she was dead. Oh, dear God in heaven! How many were going to pay for his sins. There was no turning back now. "What I don't know," Drew said, regaining his composure, "is, why me?"

"Oh, it was perfect. It was too hot to continue the operation the usual way, but we needed one more shipment. We needed someone to help us bring in and transfer the last shipment, someone no one might suspect, nor watch. You were the man."

"I realize that by now. What I don't know is how you knew about the Nam thing." He looked over Rod's shoulder again. The little man, the man who said he was in the shanty the night Drew killed two people in a drunken stupor he was still sitting quietly twenty feet away.

Rod looked in the direction of the boat behind them. "Ah, yes. That night in Nam. Well, Charlie was my runner in Nam. I agree, he is a scum bag, but he is good at what I have him do, and he follows directions." Rod returned his gaze to Drew. "Yes, he was in the room that night. He returned to the base and told me about it. I did you a favor, Drew, I hushed up the whole thing. I went to the officer investigating the sergeant's death and told him the sergeant man was shot by the woman's pimp because she was turning tricks without his permission and keeping the money for herself. The investigator bought it, and that was that. I just filed the information away, and when, several weeks ago, we were looking for a conduit for our last shipment, the little story came back to me. So, you got a call, had a meeting in Rousakis Plaza and, well , the rest you know."

"Is Doña involved in this?" Drew asked, thinking the question might draw away from her any suspicion Rod might be nurturing.

"Doña? Nice girl, as you must know by now. No, she doesn't know. And I'd hoped you had the good sense not to involve her."

"Too late for that."

Rod nodded. "I suspected as much. If Doña does something stupid, the black girl is dead."

Drew ignored the comment. "So, you just up and used me, huh?" he said. "No consideration for my position and, apparently, no thought of whom you might hurt in the process. Very neat, Rod. And I suppose the visit by your two goons the other night was just to scare me off anything I might be thinking, right?"

"That, and to see if the reporter had left you anything. If he did, if you use it, the black girl, well, you know she's dead."

"You may have ruined my ministry, Rod. You've killed a friend of mine, a good and decent man, and you've killed a woman who served you selflessly for years. You've ruined three homes, at least and God knows how many more. Not to mention, of course, the thousands of lives you've wasted with the cocaine you've imported into the states. And all for the almighty dollar. Seems there is a lot of scum floating around these days. And some of it is dressed mighty nicely."

Drew lowered the .45 and put it on the pilot's seat. "Okay, Rod," he said, "Why are you here now? Why didn't you just kill me, too, and get it over with? Surely it hasn't anything to do with what's right, and certainly, your conscience is not hurting you. Why the meeting here?"

Rod stood and looked across the water. The swells were diminishing. The channel waters would soon be calm. "I want you to forget all this, Drew. You're the only loose end. And, I don't want to kill you. But, mainly, I want the package, which I think you still possess."

"You forget Mary ."

Rod seemed uncertain how to respond. "She'll be okay."

Drew could not resolve this thing by himself. He had little choice but to cooperate; the situation was clear enough. All he could hope for now was a little more time; he needed time to talk with Doña's father. Former agent Moore was his last hope.

"I'll tell you what," Drew said, remembering Doña's offer, "I'm going off for a couple days to think it all over. My career is over and I plan to resign this week. I need a few days to get things in order and when I return, say three days, you call me and I'll give you my answer. You guarantee, right, that I will be allowed to live in peace? And Mary. No hassle. No more contacts. No more deals. Right?"

Rod brightened. "That's the deal."

Drew knew Rod's offer was bogus, and he suspected Rod knew his thinking. But he needed time, and Rod's offer, phony or not, was all he had.

Drew stiffened. "I'm not liking the idea of a deal with you at all, Rod."

Rod stepped to the stern and waved to the little man. Then, turning to Drew, he sneered, "You think about it; you think about it real hard. Some mighty important people might want you real dead if you don't deal."

The little man had started the motor of the sleek speedboat and Rod threw off the rope. As the smaller boat pulled alongside The North Star, Rod dropped into it, and motioned to the little man to pull away. "Three days, Drew. I'll want to hear the right answer," he called as the small craft roared away.

Drew watched it disappear into the darkness and began pulling up anchor. Soon, he was steering The North Star toward the Isle of Hope Marina.

It was nearing one o'clock in the morning when Drew stepped from The North Star and began the long walk up the stairs from the dock to the street. He looked up at the darkened house. It was comforting to know Doña was waiting. He stepped onto the front porch, closed the screen and paused.

"Here, Drew," Doña whispered from the side porch. Drew found her in the darkness and dropped into a chair beside her just as the telephone rang.

"Who ?" he wondered out loud.

The answer did not please him.

"Just so you will know," Rod said, "that we are not playing games, Drew, take a look at your boat."

The line went dead.

A warning.

Drew looked toward the marina for a moment, then bolted from his chair. Doña raced after him as he threw open the front screen door. Together, they bounded down the steps and across the darkened street.

"What is it, Drew?" she shouted as they ran.

"The North Star!" he yelled as they reached the top of the stairway leading to the dock.

The explosion knocked them backwards.

A brilliant display of light and cinders rained down on the marina roof and the boats in the harbor. Hissing sounds died in the water as the burning debris hit the surface.

Drew crawled to his knees. "You all right?" he asked, as he looked toward the slip where he had secured the magnificent boat.

"Yes," she said, weakly.

The North Star was engulfed in flames. The stern, where the explosive had been placed, was underwater. The bow hatch was ripped from its hinges by the blast and smoke billowed from the gaping hole. Fire was spreading across the water.

Drew stood, and Doña slid her arm about his waist as they watched in silence the boat's final gasp for buoyancy. Slowly, the bow sank and disappeared into the dark waters. A corner of the cabin roof protruded above the surface as the waters calmed.

"I'm losing everything," Drew whispered slowly. Then, sirens were heard in the distance. The Isle of Hope volunteer fire department was responding. The county police would follow soon. As the firemen arrived and raced to save the other boats, Doña left the dock to avoid unnecessary detection and returned to the house from where she watched the proceedings.

Drew answered questions from the police. No, he didn't know the cause. He had been out on a night cruise and he supposed he had left some switch on, or something. Maybe there had been a leak. Yes, he had smelled gasoline, but decided to check it in the morning. No, he couldn't add anything more to the officer's report. Neighbors expressed their sympathies, and asked if they could assist him in any way. He thanked them, and declined.

When the crowd had dispersed, he stood on the top step leading to the dock and looked through the shadows at the blackened remains of The North Star. Things I love seem to be dying, he thought, one by one. But he had gotten the message: if he wanted to see Mary alive, he had to cooperate with Rod. He was at Rod's mercy. Oddly enough, his only hope was a retiree living in the Caribbean. The prospects of an old man helping him now seemed more ridiculous than ever. But what other option did he have? None, he decided, and turned toward the house.

Chapter Nineteen

Drew watched the ground fall away as the Lear climbed rapidly over the Atlanta Ocean into the Georgia sky and turned south. He sat fixed at the window seat, listening to the smooth whine of the twin jet engines. It would be terribly easy, he thought, to just leave it all behind.

The copilot, a young man Drew guessed was no more than twenty-eight, stuck his head into the passenger compartment. "We're leveling now at thirty-two thousand feet. You're free to get a drink if you like," he said, nodding to the small kitchenette behind the pilot's seat. "Doña, you know where things are, huh?"

Doña, too, had been daydreaming. "Yeah, sure, Johnny," she responded and looked at Drew. "You want something? They've probably got a sandwich on board."

Drew declined.

"Then, I think it's time you know the whole story about my father and me, I mean," Doña offered.

Drew studied her. "Well, I have to admit," he said slowly, "I've been sitting here wondering why I'm off to Mexico when back there," he turned his head slightly, " my friend is dead, his wife probably dead, a woman caught in the cross fire is dead, a trusted friend has threatened to ruin my ministry, and my life is, well, I'm on my way to see a man in Mexico who is supposed to help me. Yeah, if you have some good news, I'd like to hear it."

Over the next hour, Doña revealed the curious story of Eagle One -- David "Papa" Moore. She told how, seven years ago, her father, the deputy director of the FBI, stumbled onto an allegation he found hard to believe. A disgruntled aide to Senator James Maxwell had requested David Moore to meet with him clandestinely. At that meeting, the aide said he suspected the senator of dealing in drugs. He gave Doña's father names of people and places. Enough information to lead Moore to conduct a quiet investigation. When the information appeared trustworthy, Moore informed the Director of the delicate matter involving the senator, and, to his dismay, was instructed to drop all interest in the senator. One week later the aide was found murdered. His death was reported as one of thousands of random street killing in the nation's capital, known even then as the Murder Capital.

Moore did not drop it, but continued the investigation on his own time. What he discovered disturbed him greatly. An illegal tap on the senator's home telephone revealed the senator often made telephone calls to an apartment Moore found was owned by agent Rod Gray. Furthermore, the senator had sizable holdings, and significant income unreported to the IRS. Too, the Georgian enjoyed a lifestyle far beyond the resources he reportedly could muster, even considering what many senators could rip off from the gullible American public. The senator and agent Gray had met secretly on numerous occasions at a location outside Washington. Another man, a Charlie Russell, was seen with the two men repeatedly at the mysterious meetings. Russell was thought to be dealing in drugs, but had no arrest record. The three men were stationed together in Nam. However, when Russell's name was mentioned in the senator's presence, he showed no sign of recognition.

Moore took his developing suspicions to the Director again. That meeting proved to be the end of Moore's career with the bureau. He was once more advised to drop his interest in the senator, and it was suggested he submit his resignation, seeing he was nearing retirement age. Moore refused and stormed from the Director's office, threatening to take his story to The Washington Post.

Later that same night, Moore received a late night visit from the Director. Off the record, the agency chief expressed interest in the information Moore had gathered. He could not permit Moore to pursue the leads in behalf of the bureau for several reasons, chief of which was the senator's influence in the committee which decided the bureau's funding.

The Director, noted for his strong religious convictions, offered Moore an option. He voiced to Moore his growing lack of confidence in the ability of law enforcement agencies to stem the flourishing drug trade in the U.S. The impotence of current drug policies was apparent. He believed -- the President agreed, privately -

- that the bureau, for one, should be given wider liberties in dealing with the drug dealers. The military's entrance into the drug wars was crucial, but congress was weak-kneed, though media polls revealed support for that idea. The Director was convinced: if the President and congress did not face reality, the next decade would deliver the U. S. helplessly addicted. South American drug lords were gearing up for an all-out assault on the insatiable American market. Armed forces must be sent into Colombia immediately. Failing that, the Director confided in close company, others operating beyond legal channels must be encouraged to take up the fight on their own. The bureau, in such a scenario, must never be seen giving sanction to such operations.

The private musings of the Director fell on the ears of an enormously wealthy Texas businessman and his close associates who shared the religious fervor of the Director. The man met secretly with the Director. If he would put him in touch with the right person, he had confided, he would be willing to finance a private war on drugs. His commitment to a holy war, as he termed it, was demonstrated by his pledge of an enormous flow of cash. Two hundred million would be deposited in a Swiss account and made available to a clandestine organization sworn to fight the tide of illegal drugs swamping the American populous. Millions more would be available. A small, yet competent and furtive circle of agents would be recruited and directed by the man of his choosing, a man with a sense of mission paralleling his own. The secret operation would be known to a very few as EAGLE EYE, a reference to the protective gaze of the national bird.

The man selected to run EAGLE EYE would have direct access to the funds for a period of five years, and would be expected to recruit and direct the operation from a remote site outside U. S. borders. He would have a free hand in running the operation. The financier of the antidrug force would not be connected to EAGLE EYE in any manner, but would meet with the chief of the operation once a year to update him on the success or failure of the operation. No reports, annual or otherwise, would be required nor expected. The funds made available by the benefactor would be reviewed in the fourth quarter of the fifth year. A decision to continue, culminate or increase the funding of the operation would be at the discretion of the business tycoon.

The Director of the F.B.I. offered to place David Moore's name before the five industrialists. That done, the Director's connection to EAGLE EYE would be ended. He wanted never to be informed nor consulted, nor did he want to know if the operation was begun, or abandoned.

Moore accepted, on the provision that he would not be required to meet with the businessmen annually, but only at the end of the first five years of operation. Secret negotiations were held, the businessmen accepted the condition, and Moore settled on the Isle of

Mujeres, a small island off the coast of Cancun as the operation's headquarters. He recruited operatives to form the EAGLE EYE team. One of them was a computer programmer. Six field agents possessed backgrounds in covert operations. Two women were stationed at EAGLE EYE headquarters. Sylvia, Moore's Mexican girl Friday, and Catalina, the trusted housekeeper. Two pilots, a chief mechanic and an assistant, and several gofers, completed the team. Each was sworn to secrecy and paid well.

    The team selected its projects carefully, both to concentrate personnel and to remain within the limitations dictated by its financial resources. It was decided to focus on the cocaine trade, one objective at a time.

    At the turn of this century, cocaine was a legal drug in this nation, sold openly for various methods of consumption and for any number of purposes. Its use flourished without restraint in the first decades of this century. Then, when the drug was declared a narcotic and banned in open trade, its use by the populous declined radically. In the sixties, its use flourished again on the black market.

    An EAGLE EYE operation in upper New York State netted more than ninety million dollars' worth of cocaine. Another, in Miami, prevented the distribution of hundreds of pounds of the lethal drug. Other hurts were put on the illegal cocaine trade, none of the operations significant enough to stem the tide of drugs, but each a personal satisfaction to EAGLE EYE and its benefactors. In each of the operations, EAGLE EYE remained unnoticed, its information anonymously filtered with precision to local and federal authorities who grabbed the headlines, a fact which suited EAGLE EYE perfectly. Authorities, eager to make some headway against the selling of death on our streets, were equally ready to ignore what some suspected, but no one could confirm: there was a quiet, efficient group at work in their behalf. If occasional violence, including assassinations, was associated with the anonymous group's work, and particularly if the violence was more often than not directed at the cocaine traffickers, the authorities attributed it to gang wars. Privately, they hoped the violence would not get out of hand and the public demand explanations.

    Shortly after EAGLE EYE became operational, Doña received her law degree. Her father revealed the clandestine operation to her, and assisted in her application to the F.B.I. It was EAGLE EYE'S intention to have her lead two lives, an agent of the bureau and Papa Moore's secret link to the agency. The plan was working, and Doña's access to F.B.I. operations was growing with her acceptance as a dedicated employee of the national agency.

    A second agent, a longtime employee of the bureau in its computer center and who previously worked closely with Moore in many of his bureau assignments, provided complicated yet efficient tap into the agency's computer files.

If the FBI Director knew, or even suspected the presence of EAGLE EYE, he never mentioned it to Doña, nor did he ask of her father's whereabouts. As far as the bureau knew, David Moore was a former shell of himself, a weak and dying old man who could barely communicate. It was assumed Doña did not talk of him because it was an embarrassment to her, and it was also assumed her dedication to duty and intense interest in the bureau's many operations was primarily due to her need to erase the stigma resulting from her father's sudden departure from the agency. Those assumptions suited EAGLE EYE's purposes just fine.

Drew listened without interrupting Doña's long, detailed and fascinating story of EAGLE EYE. The Lear was nearing Cancun Mexico when she finished her telling of the story.

"You've known all along , I mean, you knew what Rod was up to, that he was using me ...," Drew stated in disbelief.

"No," Doña said, "I did not know, not at first, not until I came to Savannah with Rod, not until you told your story to us in the Wesley. Then, it all began to make sense. We knew Rod was dealing cocaine. That's why I requested to work with him. It was a perfectly understandable request. He had worked under Papa when he first joined the bureau and Papa had helped him out of some early jams. I was supposed to be 'indebted' to Rod, to hold him in highest esteem. It wasn't always easy to do that."

Drew glanced at the Mexican coast as the jet began its descent from thirty thousand feet, the nose of the shiny craft pointed toward the Yucatan. The blue waters of the Caribbean contrasted magnificently with the white beaches and lush green of the mainland. In the cockpit, the pilot was receiving approach instructions from the Cancun airport.

Doña touched Drew's arm, and he turned his head to face her. "Drew, I did not know of Bobby's involvement. Our plan was to let Rod conclude his little game with you, then act. Bobby's death complicated things. Mainly, it kept you involved longer than we anticipated. Too, it complicated our plans for the senator. You showed up in Washington, alerted Rod and, well, Betsy is dead. We decided to stretch things out some more, try to help you if we could."

Drew wondered about two nights ago. "Was our night in your apartment part of the plan?" He had to know the answer.

"No," she responded. The question hurt. "We hoped I would have an opportunity to talk with you, but no, our first night was no conspiracy. I would think you could decide that for yourself."

Drew shook his head. "I had to ask. There have been so many games swirling around me, I hardly know whom to believe. Sorry."

"It's okay." She looked across Drew and saw Cancun coming up to meet the plane. "Let's talk more later. We will meet Papa in less than twenty minutes."

The Lear swung over one of Mexico's newest resorts. Only a little more than a decade ago, Cancun was an isolated and practically deserted tropical island. Once largely ignored since the last days of the Mayan empire in the tenth century, it is today one of the most exciting new resorts in the world.

An extraordinary civilization of the Yucatan peninsula dating more than a thousand years ago produced the ruins of the Chichen Itza, Tulum and Coba. The once great culture was abandoned before the year 1200 and no one knows why. Cancun itself rests off the northeast tip of the peninsula, thirty miles north of Cozumel. It is separated from the mainland at each end of the island by channels less than one hundred yards wide. The Lshaped island is a coralbased sand bar, slightly more than a dozen miles in length and only a quarter of a mile wide. Its awesome beaches are composed of white sand derived from old porous limestone and never gets too hot to walk on. Some of the dunes rise thirtyfive feet above the shore.

The Lear touched and sped down the runway, taxied to the far end of an adjoining smaller runway, and waited. Very soon, a Bell 206 Jet Ranger set down within a hundred feet of the Lear. Doña and Drew transferred to the helicopter. Soon, they were airborne again, sweeping out over the azure waters toward the Isle of Mujeres.

"I was born on these waters," Doña shouted above the roar of the chopper's engine, pointing directly to the swells less than two hundred feet below. "My mother made one too many trips on the ferry."

"You were born on the ferry?" Drew asked, shaking his head.

"Yes! Mother almost died giving birth to me."

The helicopter began a wide sweep over the small finger of land known as the Isle of Mujeres and Drew surveyed the terrain of the island. Immediately, Drew could see the vast difference between the resort known as Cancun and this unspoiled island retreat.

"Beautiful, huh?" Doña remarked.

Drew nodded and squeezed her hand.

"We don't know much about its history prior to the arrival of the Spanish in 1517," she added.

"How did it get its name?" Drew asked.

"Isle of Mujeres? It means Island of Women. It came from all the female figurines from Maya ruins."

Drew watched a tiny fishing village draw up to meet them and could see signs of a blossoming tourist resort. Doña pointed to a lagoon bordered by coral reefs. "Great snorkeling!" she shouted above the roar of the rotors. He could see the island was largely uncrowded and better yet, unspoiled.

"It won't take long to ruin it," he offered, eyeing the largely uninhabited shoreline around the small island. "How big?" he asked.

"Five miles long. You can almost throw a rock across it."

As the helicopter swung over the southern end of the island and started back toward land, its speed decreasing rapidly, Drew saw it for the first time: a huge home, hidden by trees and giant shrubs, and nestled snugly into the hillside. It was distinguished from the air by the uncommon site of a heliport adjacent to the north end of the house. The pilot lowered the chopper expertly onto the landing pad and cut the engine. A small, darkskinned man ran toward the craft, waving as he came closer. Doña returned his greeting and bounded from the helicopter to embrace the smiling man. Drew stepped onto the grounds of David Moore's hideaway and followed Doña across the grounds to the house, looking back once to view the helicopter against a backdrop of clear, blue sparkling water. The quiet which surrounded them, now that the chopper engines were silent, was welcome.

As he neared the house, Drew spotted a man seated in a wheelchair positioned at the top of a ramp leading onto a porch that ran the length of the house. So, he thought, David Moore is an invalid. Maybe the stories of his demise aren't so premature, after all. He kept walking until he was at the bottom of the ramp and

Doña was reaching for his hand, eager to introduce him to her father.

"Papa," she said the name with pride, "this is Drew Campbell from Savannah, Georgia. He's the man I talked to you about." Then, to Drew: "Drew, I want you to meet my father, David Moore." She stood proudly at her father's side as each man tried to size up the other. Moore wore a flowered Mexican top, his legs covered with a thin blanket from under which protruded a pair of soft Wejam loafers. His eyes met Drew's and held them steadily. They were the kind of eyes that bore right through you. An unkempt beard intensified the steellike penetration of the eyes.

Drew shifted his feet and stuck out his hand. "I'm pleased to meet you, sir. Doña has told me a little about you, and the operation here. I'm impressed, although I have little to compare it with. I thank you for the invitation." He looked at Doña.

David Moore had not yet spoken. Slowly, his left hand slid from under the blanket, lifted his right arm and positioned it again, then stretched slightly toward Drew. Drew had seen the effects of stroke often enough to recognize the disability. When he spoke, Papa did so with a tortured twist of his lips, the right side of his mouth turned downward as he spoke. The right side of his body, Drew surmised, had been left paralyzed by the attack.

"I'm David Moore," he said with no little effort. "Doña speaks highly of you. Welcome to Eagle Nest."

Drew accepted Papa's left hand, awkwardly at best, and felt the weakness in the grip. "Thank you, sir."

A typical Mexican dinner was complimented by a magnificent view of the presently calm Caribbean rolling its rhythmic greetings on the narrow white beach fronting the house. Doña seldom took her gaze from her father, and when she did, it was a quick glance at Drew. Her eyes asked for affirmation.

"Well, Dr. Campbell " David Moore began.

"Drew, please."

"Yes, thank you. Drew how do you think America is doing in the drug war?"

"Not well, sir, not well at all from all I've heard and read. But I'm no expect on the matter."

"Who is?" Moore responded, then took a sip of wine. "I'll tell you, however, from my perspective, what I think. The President, who speaks a great deal but says little, does little. Talks a good game, though, I grant that. And the Congress is, as ever, so preoccupied with its survival individually, I mean collectively, they are scarcely doing anything. We haven't begun to see the massive effects of the drug trade on American life. The next ten years will introduce new forms of coke which will lower the production costs and the price on the street, and, mark my words increase sales. Until they take the handcuffs off law enforcement, elect judges with courage and jail for life the pushers, our country's bondage to coke, in particular, will only increase. And, I predict, some older, now less popular drugs LDS, heroin and the like will resurface as recreational drugs. Do you agree?"

Drew was holding his wine glass in both hands, touching the rim of the glass to his lips, listening to Doña' father. He lowered the glass to the table and leaned back in his chair. "But, sir," he said, "we are a country of laws, of order. We can't throw away due process without sacrificing one of our dearest judicial rights. We can't give law enforcement agencies the right to arrest without cause, nor give the bench carte blanche in the sentencing process. Too many innocent people will be hurt, not to speak of the Nazilike atmosphere which would prevail in such a society. You don't advocate such a system, do you?"

"No, of course not. Within the judicial processes now in place, there is room for much tightening of the system. We just have to get tougher; it's as simple as that. That's the only language the drug traffickers understand."

"Or," Drew offered, "We encourage operations like EAGLE EYE, right?"

"Yes, to protect our country until those who run it find the courage to do so."

They barely finished coffee when Papa put down his cup with some effort and pushed back his wheelchair. His expression changed, a seriousness replacing the relaxed, though crooked smile of the last hour. He spoke to Doña. "I suggest we retire to my office." He wheeled his chair toward the far end of the great room and passed through a door leading to another wing of the house. Drew followed Doña into the room. What confronted him there boggled his mind.

    A bank of computer terminals and high frequency radios occupied the far wall. An adjoining wall was covered with maps of the world and detailed maps of the western hemisphere. The opposite wall contained photographs, time schedules, charts and graphs a collage which made absolutely no sense to Drew. In the center of the room was a large desk with a deposit of telephones and card files, piles of papers stacked in no apparent order, and a draftsman's lamp looming over the desk. There were no chairs in the room other than the wheelchair in which Papa was sitting. A control room. Everything at the director's reach, or easily accessible. Effortless contact with important points on the globe. Instant communication with his team wherever they might be operating. Everything converted to accommodate a director confined to a wheelchair.

    What was growing more obvious to Drew by the moment was that the man in charge of this operation may have problems with his body, but his mind was unaffected. Papa rolled his chair to face the bank of computers. He entered several commands, and instantly, the first page of a biographical sketch of Rod Gray appeared on the screen. Dates. Places. Assignments. Positions held. Associations. It was all there. No one spoke; Doña looked at Drew and smiled.

Another command was given the computer. An extensive list of Drew's considerable foreign travel was posted. Another series of keys stroked lightly. Drew stared at the screen. What appeared caught him totally off guard. The screen held one paragraph: a succinct description of Ellen's illness, the date of her death, and an estimate of the wealth inherited by her husband.

There was a moment of silence. Then, Papa removed the information and moved to another terminal, and entered yet another series of commands. There was a longer pause than before. Seconds later, a menu appeared on the screen.

FEDERAL BUREAU OF INVESTIGATION
CLASSIFIED
HIGHEST CLEARANCE REQUIRED

Drew permitted a low whistle to escape his lips. Papa ignored the gesture, and moved to a third terminal, entered commands and waited. A map appeared on the third screen, dotted by small flashing cursors.

Doña spoke. "Papa always knows the location of our agents. EAGLE EYE sees all," she said, and laughed.

Moore nodded, and said quietly. "I especially want to know where my daughter is at all times." He entered a final set of commands. Papa indicated with a head gesture he was ready to leave the room. Doña and Drew walked behind his wheel chair into an adjacent room as a printer began to spit out requested information.

The room was no more than twenty feet square. No maps or terminals, charts or photographs. Instead, the room was appointed sparsely. A painting of an eagle in flight dominated one wall. Comfortable leather chairs were pushed against the other three walls. Doña took a seat and motioned Drew to sit next to her. Papa rolled his chair to a position facing them.

"Drew," he began, "we are what you might call a closely held company. You have been permitted to see what no one outside the EAGLE EYE team has seen." Papa waited for the information to register with Drew. When his guest did not respond, Papa continued. "We have brought you here for two reasons. One, to assist you in your present predicament, and two, to invite you to join the EAGLE EYE team."

Drew looked at Doña, then returned his gaze to Papa. He had not been prepared for this. Moore had cut straight to the issues at hand. He admired that, but the second item dumbfounded him.

"Why?" It seemed the only question to ask.

"Because we are in a position to help you, and, in return, you can help us. You are in the perfect position to do that."

Drew eyed him, searching for more.

Papa continued. "You are a wealthy man. You have no need of money. Papa studied Drew's eyes. "Second, and more important, your position as a clergyman, the pastor of a sizable church, provides you the opportunity and the reasons for travel without incurring suspicion. Your vocation, in spite of the recent abuse of the office by noted television evangelists, has an inherent integrity to it. As a mainline protestant clergyman, you possess a certain acceptance into many circles of society. You have no immediate family, and thus, no one to endanger by your involvement in EAGLE EYE. Too, from what Doña tells me, you have indicated you would enjoy putting a hurt on drug traffickers who market death, and that, Drew, is our business. Our only business."

Papa paused, and looked at the clergyman. "If I might employ a cliché -- these are desperate times, Drew."

Drew took in Papa Moore's offer. Suddenly, he laughed out loud. "This is crazy, absolutely crazy! You don't know me, you don't know anything about me, except some data stored in your computer files. That data, correct as it might be, doesn't tell you who I am, or --."

"Crazy? Hardly, Drew." The older man drew himself up in the wheelchair. "You may think we're a bunch of fanatics, as radical as they come, but you're wrong. Appearances deceive, Drew, and the more you learn about us the more what may seem strange at the moment will become prudent as well as rational. If we bend a few laws, if some innocent people get hurt on occasions, those are small prices to pay."

"The ends justify the means?" Drew said to no one in particular.

"Something like that, yes," Moore said. "This is war, and in war -- even if the people's leaders have no will for it -- there is a price to pay to save the country, and future generations." He leaned forward in his chair. "We are making a difference, Drew, and if law enforcement agencies could identify us and if they could speak plainly, they would tell you just that. And they would applaud what we do. Only, of course, once we were known, we'd be shut down, pronto."

Drew said nothing. Something irrational in him wanted to agree with Moore. The words of the old man were correct enough to stir enthusiasm. But --.

"And," said Moore, "there's the matter of your friend." He turned to Doña. "Mary, Is that right?"

"Yes."

To Drew. "She'll die, you know that. They'll kill her without hesitation, as soon as they have the package, or know its whereabouts."

"I know that, sir."

"Then help us, Drew."

"I won't be a minister after this week, or after this is settled."

Moore looked at his daughter.

"I haven't had a chance to tell you. Drew has decided to resign."

Moore's eyes returned to Drew. "Is that true?"

"Yes. I have no choice, none that is, if things turn out the way it appears they will."

Moore continued his stare at Drew. "Understood," the older man said. "Doña," he asked, "would you please bring me the printout." She left without comment, and returned shortly with several pages of copy, and handed them to her father. He, in turn, handed them to Drew who looked down the pages, disbelieving what he read. It was a four page summary of EAGLE EYE'S history, its operations and successes and failures.

"I'm impressed," he said softly. "But even if I were interested, when I leave the ministry I'll no longer be of value to you."

"Not necessarily. We could consider that at a later date. Presently, you can help. We must bring down the team that has raped your future."

Drew was warming to the possibilities, and Papa could sense his interest. "It has been a while since I performed such operations," Papa said. "I'm pretty rusty, as Doña can testify." "You'll lose, you know that, don't you. You'll lose without our help."

"You're asking me to break the law, right?"

Papa did not hesitate. "Yes."

"Well," Drew continued, "there might be reason, in extraordinary circumstances, to do just that." Drew glanced at Doña, trying to gauge her reaction. He could read the anticipation "I'll think about it."

"Good. Then, let's get some sleep. Tomorrow morning we will address your immediate problem. Doña, will you show Drew to his room?" The older man held out his left hand. Drew accepted the gesture and bid Papa goodnight.

Doña and Drew did not retire to their rooms; instead, they strolled down to the beach. When they returned to the house, the lights were out, the house dark. Catalina, the housekeeper, had assigned Drew to the guest quarters off the spacious den and as they came to the bedroom, Drew opened the door and took Doña's hand. Neither spoke as Drew pulled her to him. Her arms closed behind his neck, their lips met.

"I'm starting to care about you, too much I think," he said.

She put her finger on his lips lightly. "Does that frighten you?" she asked, then stepped back slightly.

"I don't know , well, maybe."

She raised to tiptoe and kissed him gently. "Goodnight," she whispered, and left him standing at the bedroom door. As she passed Papa's room she thought she heard the door to her father's room close quietly.

Chapter Twenty

Katherine McKay permitted Markus Williamson to settle his massive self in one of the two dark leather captain's chairs fronting her desk before she picked up the pages containing his column and dropped them back onto the desk. "What is this crap, Markus? Were you sniffing something last night?"

"It's the truth," he replied confidently.

"Background? Sources? Evidence? Give it to me."

"That's privileged, at the moment."

"It's privileged shit!" she roared as she often did when she didn't receive the response she believed she was entitled to.

"Again, it's the truth."

McKay walked around the desk and leaned her over-sized rear against the front edge. "Markus, I've gone along with you on some pretty wild stuff, and I admit you've never truly disappointed me. But this is patently libelous. You can't expect me to print something this ludicrous story without background." She was still shouting. "A senator trafficking drugs? An FBI agent as deeply involved? Come on, Markus." She sat down across from the columnist. "Look, I know you don't usually fabricate stuff. You slant it, sure, and you get your point across and the reader ignores the embellishments and savors the implications. But this is different. You accusing --"

"It's the truth. But," he continued, "If you don't want it, I'll take it elsewhere. And you'll regret it, Katherine. Mark my words."

"Give me one reason, one reason to trust you."

He spit out the name before he realized it. "Morgan Ann Wellington Maxwell."

Drew awoke to a brilliant Caribbean sun rising over the sparkling bluegreen waters. Under normal circumstances the warm sunshine streaming through his open bedroom window would have given him cause to savor the glorious dawn. Not so this morning. He had tossed restlessly throughout the night and awakened with a knot in his stomach. The last five days of hell had torn his life apart. As if the grief of a friend's murder, leaving the ministry and finding Mary were not enough, he was now confronted with another decision -- David Moore's proposal. And there was the other matter of his growing feelings for Doña.

With no little effort, he rolled out of bed and staggered to the bath. Fifteen minutes later the finely ground sand filtered through his toes as he walked on the beach, alone. The waves breaking on the shore slid up to his feet and washed over them. He watched the waves break one by one, throw themselves toward the shore and, retreating, leave tiny levees on the sand. Small shells, thrown forward by the waves, tumbled frantically back toward the sea, as if not to make it was to die. I know how you feel, he thought, thinking of how many times recently he had been tossed on the shore and pulled back again into the turmoil. Hang on, little guys, he encouraged them, and thus encouraged himself.

The prospects of working with EAGLE EYE interested him, he had to admit that. Moreover, the possibility of doing something to stem the drug traffic was inviting. But, when does a 'need' permit one to knowingly and willingly break the law? When does a person step over the line and see breaking the law as a viable solution? Could a person live with the ugly knowledge that, in attempting to help untold numbers of unsuspecting victims children! , certain monstrous acts might be committed? And would such actions become so commonplace that one's conscience is dulled? He knelt on the beach and doodled a finger in the wet sand.

I can stop Rod! That thought shook him. Maybe I can stop many of them, the old Drew reasoned. Drew stood suddenly and bounded up the steps to the top of the dune.

Papa was waiting for him on the porch.

Drew was the first to speak. "I am inclined to say 'yes', but I need more time."

"Of course. And I ," began Moore.

Drew interrupted. "One condition. We wrap up my 'problem' first before I do anything for your operation. I mean, I don't want to talk about my association with EAGLE EYE at all, not until I finish this thing in Savannah."

"Agreed. And I'm delighted. Let's have some breakfast and get to work on your 'problem'. Okay?"

They gathered in the control room after breakfast. Papa and daughter. Trusted aide. And the newcomer, Drew Campbell.

David Moore, who seemed to Drew to grow older by the hour, was staring at the map of the eastern United States. Several minutes passed and no one spoke. Finally, the old man wheeled his chair to face the others.

"Okay," he began slowly, "we have two objectives." The old man's eyes narrowed. "One. We bring the bastards down. Two. We find Mary -- alive, hopefully."

Drew respond quickly. "I'd reverse the priority."

Moore shrugged. "Let's not debate needlessly. The two go together." With obvious pain, he paused to reposition his useless arm, and continued. "Rod Gray. Charlie Russell. And the honorable James Maxwell. Russell, we can take out whenever we like. How and when we do that is not of too much concern to me at the moment. Gray can be exposed and tossed to the bureau which will scramble to cover their asses and save face. But the senator well, he's a different kind of bird. All we have on him are telephone records and sightings with Gray. The latter we can't use without exposing EAGLE EYE. Tax records might lead to fraud, but not to drug trafficking. He will have been too careful to mix funds. If my hunch is right, his cut on the drug trade is safely deposited outside the country."

Drew asked the obvious question. "So, what do we do?" Then, he wondered, "Shouldn't I destroy the cocaine?"

"No." Moore was emphatic. "If you can't produce the package, Mary's dead, and so are you. For some reason other than the profit, they need the coke." Then, "Speaking of which -- is it safely hidden?"

"I suppose," Drew said, aware that anyone could rummage around in the basement. He suddenly wished he had done better at concealing the package.

Doña, who had listened quietly to the two men's exchange, was becoming impatient. "Papa, it's not just the three of them, and Mary. There's the smaller ring of locals, too. What about them? And God knows how many others in the shadows."

Her father smiled. "You want them all, Doña, and I understand that. But the point is, EAGLE EYE's objective doesn't include the little everyday players." He swept his good arm over the modest gathering. "Let me refresh our memories. Mary's presence in this equation notwithstanding, we seek two things: stop significant shipments of drugs from hitting the streets, and put a hurt on big time players. Stop them dead. And," he said, "you can add a third item: we want the big boys to know there is 'someone' who will not permit them to operate without impunity."

Doña nodded. "So, we hit selected targets, hit them hard, and retreat?"

"Until the next time, yes," Papa Moore agreed.

"Sort of like Zorro?" Drew suggested.

Moore eyed the newcomer. "You think we're just kidding ourselves, that this is a game?"

"I don't doubt your successes. I'm just wondering if it will make any difference.

"It might for your friend, Mary. Understand, Drew, we don't pretend for a moment that EAGLE EYE will stop the trafficking of drugs, but we can slow it down in a serious way. Yes, initially we had hoped we could do greater damage to the trade, but we've had to face reality. Our intent now is that there will exist one organization that can make a difference on several fronts. In many instances, the legal avenues are clearly helpless, and only an organization like ours can act and act effectively."

"Outside the law?"

"Yes. Outside the law, if necessary," Moore responded. "But there is something else. Like I said earlier, we want the satisfaction that some big players get hurt, bad hurt. And, again, we are the only operation that can insure that happens regularly."

"Okay," Drew said, "I won't argue the point again. Do you have a plan, now?"

"Yes, but let's take a break. Ten minutes." He wheeled his chair in the direction of the door. Sylvia sprang to assist him. "Yes, Drew," Moore said over his shoulder, "I do have a plan."

A quarter hour later Moore returned. He began methodically outlining his thinking. "We aren't in the business of wholesale murder, so we won't simply execute Gray and Maxwell." He left no doubt 'they' could do so, if they wished. Drew suspected they had on some other occasions.

"Besides," Moore continued, "Mary is -- as Drew insists -- our priority. Gray's people will kill her the moment they know she is no longer an asset. So, how do we get our three leading characters together under one net and, at the same time, locate and deliver Mary safely?" He lifted his head and looked at Drew and Doña, as if searching for an answer.

"This is how," he said with emphasis. "Drew, it will be your responsibility to position Gray and Maxwell in Savannah. That will likely bring Russell." He paused, then, "Really, I don't give a damn if Russell is there. It's the other two we need in the city, together." He looked to Drew. "Can you do that?"

Drew nodded, though he had no clear idea how to accomplish what Moore was demanding.

"Good." Then, to Doña, "I want you out of the action if at all possible. You can play back up, if absolutely necessary, but only then. Understood?"

Doña glanced at Drew, her eyes searching his. A quiet 'Yes'.

"Drew," Moore said, "you must not only get the agent and the senator together, but you must get them together in the same room. You'll be wired. You will demand to know Mary's location and some evidence she is alive. They'll anticipate such a request, of course. We'll have a team listening, ready to rush to that point and do its best to free Mary." He looked a Drew. "No guarantees, you understand?"

"Please. Don't patronize me. I understand."

Moore ignored the remark, and positioned his disabled arm again, grimacing with each slight movement demanded of the useless limb. He wrapped his lap blanket around the claw-like hand and proceeded. "Now, this is the difficult part. You keep them there long enough to get them talking -- on tape. They will be feeling more confident, knowing you have resigned yourself to surrendering the drugs and they, thus, have succeeded. Do whatever you have to do, but get them talking. And keep them talking until we can alert authorities to arrive and make the arrests. You have Bobby Taylor's notes. Mrs. Maxwell will talk, too. And we will supply Doña with enough additional information to make a case that will stick on the two of them. And --."

Drew interrupted. "How do I keep them there?"

"Do you have a weapon?"

"Yes, a .45."

Moore smiled. "That'll do."

"One more thing," Drew said. "What if they won't stay -- or talk?"

"You kill them."

When Doña caught up with Drew he was climbing the hill leading to the street. "Drew, I have an idea. Let's take the motor bike down to Maria's Kan Kin. It's a quaint little restaurant just a few miles down the road. We can talk there, and the food is wonderful."

Drew looked at his watch. It was nearly lunchtime. "Sure. Why not?"

Moments later, the two of them were motoring unhurriedly away from the house. Doña hugged the preacher from behind. A cool breeze buffeted their faces as they maneuvered the hilltop road. The dazzling waters stretching out from the beaches peeked through thick stands of palms.

"There," Doña yelled into his ear, "at that corner, the road to your left. It's a steep downhill incline, so take it easy." She pointed over his shoulder. Drew slowed the bike, leaned it into the turn and started down a concrete drive. At the bottom of the drive was a stone fence with a single entrance into the compound. He braked hard, slowed the bike again and stopped.

He pushed the heavy carved door open and they walked down a palmlined walkway that opened onto a grassroofed patio where half a dozen old tables and chairs were grouped in a dining area. The open air dining room looked out on another breathtaking view of the blue Caribbean. Nearby, a low Hacienda, snuggled under jungle foliage offered sanctuary to weary guests. Behind them was a bamboo bar stretching the entire length of the room. Before them, however, the ground fell off into a small forest of deep green foliage that stopped at the bluff's edge. Far below, the always present and pleasant waters lapping the white Yucatan beaches. Four giant sea turtles swam playfully in a fencedin area of the shallow water. They ate in silence.

"I think you like my island," Doña offered when they finished their meal.

Drew did not respond, but stood and walked to the edge of the patio and stood looking out over the expanse of water. Eventually he turned to Doña. "I'm ready to go. I have to find Mary."

She understood. "Let's go back and I'll get my things together. You can tell Papa to get our transportation ready. I'll be ready in half an hour."

Back at EAGLE NEST Drew informed Papa, "I'm ready to return to Savannah."

The old man looked up from his work. "Good."

"We are leaving as soon as you can arrange our transfer to the mainland. I suppose the Lear can take us back to Savannah?"

"Of course, I thought you would want to get started right away and I've already ordered it. Our agents are on their way to Savannah." The old man, with his good hand, grasp Drew's sleeve. "Anything you need, just call this number," and handed him a note. "Memorize it before you leave and destroy the paper. Use it as you need, but sparingly, if possible. Remember these code names: Eagle One refers to me, Doña is Eaglet. You will be .

"Jacob," Drew suggested.

Papa looked at him curiously. "Jacob? The man who betrayed his brother?" Papa thought for a few seconds. "Okay. Good luck, Jacob, and I hope to see you again, under different conditions, perhaps in the near future." He extended his weakened left hand. "Thank you, sir," Drew said, gripping the old man's hand as firmly as he dared.

Within the hour, the helicopter lifted from the Isle of Mujeres and started for Cancun. Soon they were seated comfortably in the Lear at thirty thousand feet, flying as straight for Savannah as the FAA would allow. Drew tried to relax, but it was impossible. He was no longer afraid of his decision, though he was sure something was amiss. He could not put his finger on it, but the old Drew had a thought: the plan was all too simple and smooth.

Chapter Twenty-One

From the front steps of his home on Isle of Hope, Drew peered into the darkness enveloping the bluff. He sensed a darkness closing in on him, too, and for some reason, he thought about the church. Thank God it's summer, and things at the church were lumbering through the normally uneventful dog days. The expectations of the people were usually low at this time, though soon preparations for the school year would gear up. At the moment he could not have cared less.

That was one good thing about this unwelcomed dilemma. He had not missed the boredom of endless meetings and petty conflicts in the church. Indeed, had it not been for the seriousness of it all, he would have welcomed a little mystery in his life. Something to stir the blood, call forth some courage. Lord knows, there wasn't much of that in his congregation, or any congregation he knew of. He had long thought the death of the institutional church would be its apathy, though the church of his Lord would one day, in God's good time, fulfill its divine purpose. Not so strange, he reasoned, that a crisis would force him to lean so heavily on his faith and at the same time cause him to rethink his calling, even lead him to think of getting out of the ministry altogether.

He peered into the darkness again and thought of Mary. Where was she? The odds were good, he confessed, she was already dead. And why hadn't Rod contacted him? He could not start the plan until --. He slumped against the frame of the door, then suddenly straightened. He would make the contact, start the plan he had decided was "all too easy."

He telephoned Rod's home. No answer, as expected. Call Doña at the Desota Hilton? No, best to keep her out of it as much as possible. Besides, Rod and Doña were no longer a team, except on the books, which made Drew realize even more that this thing was nearing an end. Rod would be gone soon, and the old Drew wanted him, badly.

So, what to do, how to get it moving quickly, get the players together, locate Mary, or her body? And, yes, then destroy the coke. He admitted at this point he cared little about the package. By the moment, he wanted to find Mary, then Rod and the others. But he was stymied for the moment.

Rod, he knew, was not sitting still, waiting for his call. The agent was on the move, getting what he wanted, getting out as soon as possible. Even skip before the deal was made if necessary. If that happened, Mary was sure to die. I must get his attention now, Drew determined. But, again, how? Call Papa? Again, no. Dammit! How? Why hadn't he discussed this with Moore?

A sickening, sinking feeling swelled in his chest. I've been left out here hanging. Rod didn't intend to talk to him again. He had been used! Mary was already dead; now he was sure of it. The coke might have been found! Tomorrow it would be impossible to trace Rod. His enemy had simply bought some time by negotiating for Mary's life. There never was going to be a meeting, an agreement!

Desperation overwhelmed him, until suddenly, his brain rallied. He raced to a side table, flipped open his laptop and clicked on the appropriate icon and typed in 'area codes'. He located the page of area codes and then moved the mouse to turn the power off. He retrieved his cell phone and rang the area code and punched in the digits for information. He listened, remembered an earlier call he had made in Washington, depressed the connecting button and rang another number.

"Senator Maxwell's residence."

"I want to speak to the senator."

"I'm sorry, sir, he's not available. What is the nature of your call?"

"You find the senator. It's a matter of utmost urgency. Find him, and tell him the preacher called, now! You'll lose your job if you ignore me."

"And who are you, sir?"

"My name doesn't matter. You get to the senator with my message."

"Sir, the senator is out of the city. I don't know if I can reach him immediately."

"Where is he?"

"I'm not supposed to give out that information, sir."

"Savannah ?"

The woman on the line hesitated.

Bingo! thought Drew. He is here. "You tell the senator I'll be in the park adjacent to Grace Presbyterian Church for the next hour. That's Savannah. Got it?"

"I'll do what I can, sir. I still don't know your ."

"Have you got it?" Drew shouted.

"Yes, but ."

"Then, do it, now!" Drew demanded, and hung up the receiver. He breathed deeply and started for the garage.

Fifteen minutes later, he was walking slowly through the park fronting Grace Church. He selected a shadowed spot under a large spreading oak and waited. The hour passed. Ten minutes into the next, a tall figure approached the park, stepped onto the manicured grass and strolled to the middle of the square. The man looked about nervously. Drew made the identification even though he could not see the face. He left the shadows of the tree and neared the senator. He stopped a few feet from his prey.

"Well ?" the senator asked.

"You know who I am?"

"Yes."

"I want to meet with you and Rod."

"That's not possible."

"Senator, I am about to expose you all, everything I know about your neat little operation. But I will make a deal with you for the right information."

"Such as?"

"Where is Mary?"

"Mary who ?"

"Don't play coy with me, senator. I'd just soon kill you right here."

"If I tell you what you want to know, what then?" The senator was thinking he had asked The Man to eliminate the wrong enemy.

"Your comfortable life, for one thing. If, that is, you tell me where to find the woman, and help me get Rod."

The senator was shifting from one foot to the other, weighing his options, trying to size up Drew and his demands. He would have to call The Man again, and soon. Even with Rod out of the way, which he was sure The Man was arranging, 'they' were not safe with the preacher alive.

"I can't help you with Rod. But you'll find the black woman in the abandoned warehouse on Broad Street next to the Visitor's Center parking lot. Go to the first block off ."

"I know the place."

"Then goodbye, pastor."

"Wait."

"I have nothing more to say." Senator Maxwell turned and walked into the shadows. Drew watched him go, knowing that the "plan" was being forfeited as the man walked away.

Drew intended no deal. He doubted if Mary or her body was in the warehouse, but he couldn't take the chance of following the senator. Mary was priority now, or the slim possibility of finding her.

He would call Papa later. The plan was voided, but at least he might save Mary. He drove the Camaro to the street Rod identified and cruised slowly until he saw the empty warehouse. It was difficult in the early evening light to make out the faded lettering on the front of the building. Nevertheless, this had to be it. He kept driving slowly, turned around and passed the place again. He then steered the Camaro down an alley next to the abandoned building. He parked in the darkest shadows, retrieved a flashlight from the glove compartment and tested it on the floorboard of the car. It would be adequate at best; he put it in a coat pocket. The .45 he stuck in his belt.

He walked back up the alley toward Broad Street, picking his way along the side wall until he came to a window that looked vulnerable. The height of the window made it easily accessible. He removed the .45 from his belt and slid it into his back pocket. He shined a beam on the lower part of the window and pushed firmly. It moved slightly. He placed the flashlight on the ground and put both hands on the window frame and pushed harder. It responded, opening a bare two inches. Again he pushed and the window swung open and banged against the inner wall.

Drew froze. No sound from within. He picked up the flashlight and pulled himself over the window sill. His feet touched the floor quietly, but his first step was disastrous. A metallic sound echoed through the building. Still no response.

He had to chance it, he thought, and flicked on the beam. He had entered the office area of a former business. An old roll top desk, far beyond repair, dominated the far wall. Rusting file cabinets completely lined another wall. Piles of old papers littered the floor.

The beam fell on a door leading into a large room that contained four old lathes. It was a woodworking shop, at least the remnants of one. Sawdust covered much of the floor, larger piles of the wood shavings gathered under the rusting, antiquated pieces of machinery. Drew swung the beam around the building. At the far end of the large room was another door. He stepped lightly through the clutter and through the door. A small room much like the first. He traced the wall with the beam of light, moving it up and down, looking for any sign of life.

Then he saw it. In the corner of this third room, the torn remains of a woman's clothing. He recognized one piece. Mary's bright yellow wraparound skirt. Drew stepped closer and picked up a blouse. It was spotted with bloodstains. Quickly, Drew swept the beam about the room. No sign of Mary. Where was she?

He saw more stains in the doorway. In the shadows he could see the stains were smeared, as if a body had been dragged from the building through the rear door. He knelt and touched a small puddle with his finger. Still wet. He left the small room, shining the light in all directions. Nothing. Another door to his right. He walked to it quickly and pulled it open, and found himself looking out onto the wooden loading dock at the rear of the building. Drew paused on the dock, saw nothing of interest, and started into the building again when his light crossed over an object that caught his attention. A woman's shoe. He looked closer. Dear God! There was a leg protruding from the shoe! A leg with black skin!

He stepped over a rotting loading crate and shined his light on a woman's body. It was Mary, in a corner between two cardboard boxes. He stared at the body. It was pushed into a sitting position against the brick wall. Mary's head was turned to one side. Drew moved the beam down the length of her body. The shoe on her left foot was her only article of clothing. Her breasts bore crisscrossed slashes from a sharp instrument. Below her right breast, just below the nipple, blood flowed slowly from an ugly stab wound.

Drew gathered his senses and knelt beside the woman. Mary had been brutalized and left to bleed to death. He lowered his light and buried his face in his hands, and a whisper of a prayer escaped his lips. "Forgive me, Mary." He sensed a fog slowly cover his soul. This is what it must be like, he thought, to slowly, surely slip into hell. If he could, he swore to himself and to God, he would crawl up next to Mary and die.

He squeezed, then opened his eyes and forced himself to reach for her hand that rested peacefully on her bare thigh. To his astonishment, the hand was warm.

The realization jerked Drew's mind awake. He put his hand on her thigh. It, too, was warm. He touched her face. Warm. Barely, but warm. With both hands he turned her face toward his. Yes! An eye lid moved. "Mary ." He forced the name from his throat, and waited. Her lips moved, imperceptibly, but they moved!

Drew got to his knees, peeled off his coat as quickly as he could, and covered her upper torso. He put an arm behind her back and lifted her slightly, shifting his body to support her. Her head fell against his shoulder. With one movement, he pulled her to him, sharing the warmth of his body, and gently slapped her face. "Mary! It's Drew. Mary, speak to me!" Her lids fluttered again and open briefly.

"Drew ?"

"Yes, Mary, it's me. Hold on, we're going to get you some help."

She mumbled something. He couldn't make it out. He was frantic. What to do? Leave her and call for help? What ?

"Drew they they killed my Bobby!"

"I know, Mary, I know. But you are alive! We have to get you to a hospital." Drew struggled to get his feet under him. Coaxing all his strength, he lifted the limp woman and stood. Slowly, because he could not see well in the shadows, he carried her across the loading dock to a set of steps leading to the ground.

"Drew , just let me die. Please, Drew ..."

"Stop it!" he said, firmly. "You are going to make it, Mary. You have to make it." He found the narrow alley and, shifting Mary's weight, started for the Camaro. Several agonizing minutes later he was able to make it to the car and position Mary in the front seat. Climbing in the driver's seat, Drew realized he was covered with her blood. He glanced at her quickly. It did not require a physician to recognize she was near death.

The Camaro roared from the parking spot and sped away to Memorial Hospital, screaming through traffic, horn blowing, tires grabbing at pavement with a vengeance. Shortly, Drew wheeled the car into the emergency entrance of the hospital and screeched to a halt. A uniformed paramedic ran to the car, jerked open the door to the passenger side. Soon two other attendants rushed forward with a stretcher. The paramedics rolled Mary though the automatic doors. Drew followed. A nurse stopped him outside the trauma room.

Drew sat in the surgery waiting room. He had filled out papers and answered questions as best he could. Most of the emergency room personnel knew him by name. He was grateful for their attention to Mary.

He had no consciousness of the time. His body ached; his mind was exhausted. Others in the room looked at him, whispering the rumors they had heard. His silent prayers for Mary were drowned in the rage that held him captive. Rage, and fatigue.

The minutes passed into an hour. Another hour. Finally, his head back against the wall, he drifted unintentionally into sleep. A touch on the shoulder awakened him.

"Reverend Campbell "

He opened his eyes and looked into a familiar face, Ms. Johnson, the nurse supervisor of the intensive care unit. It took him a moment to focus clearly, to remember why he was where he was.

"Yes?"

"Mrs. Taylor is going to make it."

Drew stared at her.

Yes," Ms. Johnson smiled, "she's going to make it. And you can see her now, for a moment. She's demanding to see you. But just for a moment." She offered him her hand and he stood, and followed her down the hall to the intensive care unit.

The scene was a familiar one. Attendants stepped intentionally but calmly from bed to bed. Complex apparatuses beeped their coded messages into the serious air of the large room. Mary already looked better, in spite of the presence of several tubes taking fluids to and from her body. The clean white atmosphere was not something he was afraid of. He knew its purpose. He touched her hand lightly and bent to kiss her on the forehead.

"Thank you, God," he whispered.

Mary opened her eyes, blinked them, and tried to focus on Drew's voice.

"Drew ?" she whispered.

"Yes, Mary, I'm here. Just take it easy. You're going to be okay." Drew leaned closer and Mary's eyes found his. She raised a finger in recognition and her lips formed words Drew could not understand. He leaned over her bed and put his face just inches from hers.

"I'm here, Mary. Please, take it easy." He listened carefully as she spoke each tortured word.

"I heard them ... talking," she whispered softly.

"Shhhh. Easy Mary."

"No !" It was a terrible effort for her to talk. It must be equally important, Drew thought.

"Drew. It is much bigger ... than Bobby thought. That's why they ... killed him."

"We'll find them, Mary. You have to save your strength."

"Please ... listen ... you don't ... understand ."

He would not be allowed to stay much longer, and he was not helping.

"Mary ."

"No!" She spit out the word. He wondered where she found the strength. "Listen to me ... I heard them ... it's bigger ...."

Drew tried to understand. What was she trying to say? Bigger? Bigger than what? Than Savannah?

"Mary, what do you mean? Bigger than what?"

She spoke again in a strained whisper. "Tonight, Drew. The riverfront ." She could not sustain her speech. Her eyes closed.

The nurse stepped to his side. "I think you'd better leave now, pastor."

"One more minute, please," Drew requested. He did not wait for her answer. "Mary, tell me, bigger than what?" Her lids opened, closed, and opened again.

"Bigger than ... your friend."

Drew watched her eyes close again. Reverend Campbell, you will have to leave now." The nurse edged between him and the bed, checking the monitors over the bed, indicating clearly that she wanted Drew out of the room.

Drew thanked her. Then, he added, "I'm the only family she has in Savannah. Her brother is in Africa. She is to lack for nothing, understand? I want her to have the best of care, and do not worry about cost. Everything. Understand?"

"Yes, Reverend," Ms. Johnson replied indignantly. "She's already getting that."

It was nearly nine o'clock when the police concluded their questioning. He was commended by the questioning officer, and told to go home and get a good night's rest. He would be needed for further questioning later, but they would call him.

Drew sat in his car, trying to recall Mary's words in their distorted conversation. What did she mean, 'Bigger than your friend?' What friend? Bobby? She had no way of knowing about Rod. Doña? No, that wasn't it. There were no other friends except Papa Moore.

Then, he remembered his talk with Bobby. He had told him about his agent friend in Washington. Had he mentioned his name? He could not remember. Yes, he did remember. He had told Bobby, 'I have an old friend from Nam. His name is Rod Gray.'

Did Rod identify himself to Mary?

They had come to Mary's house after they had killed Bobby, looking, probably, for any notes, any kind of evidence he might have left there. They took Mary because they could not leave her behind, or because they wanted information. They had tortured her, then talked in her presence, or she had overheard them. It did not matter. She knew something. When they were through with her, they had abused her, stabbed her and left her for dead. But Mary had survived God only knows how she had listened to them talk, and remembered. "Bigger than your friend."

It had to be! What she had heard something that stuck in her mind even as she was being violently abused she had connected what she heard to something Bobby had said. Drew felt his body stiffen. It was becoming clearer. Yes! Bigger than Rod? How could that be? The entire operation was bigger than Rod? Bigger than anything Drew had suspected? Bigger, even, than Papa Moore suspected!

Abruptly, he sat up straight. He had completely ignored Mary's other admonition. "Tonight. The riverfront ." His mind was racing. There was something else going on tonight. The riverfront! But what? Then he understood. They were meeting at the riverfront. For what, he did not know. Drew was to be anywhere but the riverfront; that's why the senator had directed him to Mary, and Mary was supposed to be dead. He started the car, pulled from the emergency parking lot and the Camaro roared toward the heart of the city.

Chapter Twenty-Two

"What do mean, you've lost him?" bellowed Papa Moore.

"Just what I said," replied the EAGLE EYE agent. "He tore out of the parking lot near the church and we lost him in the traffic."

"What about the senator?"

"At the Hilton."

"And Gray?"

"He's in a small inn downtown. If there is a meeting, we'll follow him. Charlie's whereabouts will come to light."

"Okay, just sit tight. We have to wait, otherwise we lose the package. Campbell will show up; he won't walk away from Rod. There was a pause in the international call. Shortly, Moore continued. "Leave Eaglet out of this. It's probably going to get nasty soon and I don't want her involved. You stay clear, too, for now. Just don't lose Gray. We can always find the senator, and Charlie doesn't matter. If a meeting occurs, if the cocaine surfaces ."

"What do we do with Gray?"

"That's up to Campbell. Gray's choices are limited. He must get out soon, it's all falling to pieces, and the preacher knows that by now, too. He wants Gray, badly. Let him try."

"Gray may kill him."

"Yes, I know."

"And Doña? She'll sit still for that?"

"She won't know we allowed it," The Man said with only a hint of emotion."

"If that happens ?"

"Hit Gray. It's time to stop him. The charade is over. We'll expose the senator later. He's history. And it's time we operate on our own terms."

"Understood."

Drew positioned the Camaro among a dozen automobiles in the shadows of one of the several parking areas fronting Bay Street. From his vantage he could watch the entire upper plaza; a direct line of sight to the front door of every office of most of the buildings. No one could go in or out without him seeing his or her movements. But would it happen here? All Mary had said was, "Tonight. The riverfront." It had to be the upper plaza. The riverfront itself was too open. He was sure he had it figured correctly. He checked the time: 9:27. If he had not missed their arrival, he was in perfect position.

He lifted a newspaper on the seat and picked up the .45, checked its readiness and slid it under the afternoon edition again. If just once, he thought, I could initiate ."

Suddenly, he sat up straight. Someone had stopped at a door at the near end of the row of offices. A smallish man. Dark hair. A baseball cap. Seconds later, Charlie opened the door and entered, closing it behind him. Drew's breathing slowed noticeably. It won't be long now, he assured himself, and slid the .45 from under the newspaper and placed it in his lap. For the first time in days, he felt a measure of control.

"Come on, come on ..." he whispered, his eyes sweeping the upper level of Factor's Walk. Maybe, just maybe he was about to get a crack at them on his terms. Then it occurred to him how easy it was to hate. He strained to see under the glare of headlights that momentarily blinded him. He rubbed his eyes and his vision quickly cleared.

Another figure approached. Rod? The strong shoulders. Head erect. Yes! Rod paused at the door, his eyes taking in the area wholesale, and disappeared inside. Two down, one to go.

Drew did not have long to wait. Soon, the tall, distinguished man he had met earlier walked to the front of the office and entered without hesitation.

Time to move. Drew set his pipe in the ashtray, grasped the .45 and opened the car door. Reaching back into the car, he retrieved the newspaper and wrapped it around the automatic. He opened the trunk and took a tire tool from the compartment. He made his way quickly, carefully, down a grassy slope to the rear of the building. The office was like many on Factor's Walk; a metal stairway stretched up the back of the building. It served as a fire escape and a rear entrance. Two windows, painted quickly and poorly, bordered the rear door. He climbed the stairway quietly, stopping when he reached the landing at the top of the fire escape. Below, the street was filling with tourists and sidewalk vendors. Good, he thought. The more noise, the better. But there was no time to waste. He positioned the tire iron under the window frame and slowly applied pressure. If this did not work, he would lose the element of surprise. The front entrance would be much more risky. The window gave quickly and Drew raised it easily. He eased himself over the window sill with no problem. Inside, he found himself in a small, seldom used room. Except for a basin on the wall, it was completely empty. Light peeking from the street below through the crack in the window was sufficient. He crossed the twelve feet to the only door; a thin shaft of light shone under it. He could hear voices beyond the door. Good, again; they were occupied with conversation. He leaned against the wall and inched closer to the floor, putting his ear to the door. The voices were barely intelligible, but enough for him to make out bits of the conversation. An argument.

"I say we kill the bastard now." The senator.

"No. We get the package, then take care of the rest of business." Gray's retort.

An undecipherable curse from Charlie.

"We've messed around long enough. Charlie, what about the black bitch?" Rod again.

"She's taken care of."

Drew decided he could not wait any longer. Slowly, he stood and slipped the large automatic from his belt and took a deep breath. With one continuous movement, he jerked the door open, fell to a crouch and whipped the gun in front of him with both hands. "No one move!" Drew shouted. "Hands out where I can see them."

The three men were seated about a box; they froze in surprise. Senator Maxwell's mouth hung open, his eyes bulged with fear. Charlie made a move for his weapon, then stopped, convinced by the large bore of the .45. Rod stared at Drew with rage.

Drew's eyes scanned the room. A door led to the front office area. It was closed. A side window's blinds were drawn tight. There was no chance of anyone seeing this drama being acted out two stories above the Savannah River. From the opened door behind him, he could hear the excited voices of the evening's trade. He stood, his eyes fixed on the threesome, searched with his foot for the door and finding it, slammed it shut.

"Well," Drew said, motioning for Charlie to move closer to the other two men, "we all meet at last. My dear friend from Nam. The distinguished senator from Georgia. And Charlie, a bag of quality scum."

"Drew, what the hell do you think you're doing? We made a deal!" Rod's voice shook with anger.

Drew's eyes narrowed. "Some deal. Right now, Rod, I'm trying to decide which of you I'm going to kill first, and I think I've decided it will be the senator." He leveled the gun at Senator Maxwell. His finger tightened on the trigger as his hand squeezed the grip. The truth be known, he had no idea what he would do next.

"No! Stop!" It was the senator, looking wild-eyed and pointing at the other two. "They are responsible! They had your friend killed. The girl, too. I didn't --."

Drew decided what they didn't know wouldn't hurt them. "I found 'the girl', as you call her. Her name is Mary, and she's dead."

Rod spoke. His voice was as sober as his eyes, ignoring the sniffling senator. "How did you know we were here?" He looked at his two companions. "They wouldn't tell," he said. "The only other person who knew was ."

"Yes. Mary," Drew said. "Before she died."

Rod stopped. His eyes grew cold with a sudden realization of betrayal. "No," he said, "not the woman." He rubbed his upper lip. His eyes narrowed. "No, I don't believe it, but it has to be." He looked hard at Drew. "Who told you, Drew? I mean, you've found us, you've got the stuff, so tell me! Who was it? I want to know who it was that told you where to find us! Was it David?" Rod shouted his demand.

Drew thought he heard his heart stop. For an instant, his hands wavered, and the gun shook. His stomach was suddenly filled with a hard emptiness. He could not focus his mind. The name, David. David Moore. Papa Moore! It would not compute. How did Rod know about Moore? How much did he know? He released one hand from the automatic to wipe the sting out of his eyes. The motion was a mistake.

Charlie's rush was too quick for him. The small, compact man crashed into him before he could react. The body blow knocked him to the floor as the gun exploded, then fell from his grip and bounded across the floor as Rod and the senator ran out the front door. Charlie fell on him, swinging wildly at Drew's face. A fist landed on the side of his temple, and Drew fought for consciousness. He grabbed at the man's throat, located his windpipe and squeezed it shut. Charlie raised his fist to swing again, and that was all Drew needed. He uncoiled his body with all his strength. Charlie tumbled to the side and quickly rolled to his feet to face Drew who was now crouched and ready to strike. The little man lunged awkwardly, and Drew permitted the force of Charlie's thrust to carry him into Drew's kick to the chest. Charlie staggered and Drew smashed his elbow against the side of Charlie's head. The little man fell in a heap at Drew's feet.

Quickly, Drew retrieved the .45 from the floor and turned back to Charlie. "Get up!" Drew commanded, motioning with the gun.

Charlie stood slowly, his eyes wild with fury. Drew walked toward him, the .45 pointed at the man's midsection. "Ever see what a .45 does to a man's belly?" Drew asked, moving closer. He put the nose of the gun in Charlie abdomen, his anger barely under control. "You can live, Charlie, if you tell me where Rod is headed."

Charlie grinned. "You're a dead man, preacher." He spit in Drew's face, and grinned even wider.

A rage exploded within Drew. He backed the man to the wall and rammed the muzzle of the .45 deeper into Charlie's stomach.

"Pull the trigger, preacher! If you've got any guts, you'll do it!" His grin grew wider.

Even the old Drew had never experienced such a hatred. He wanted nothing so much as to pull the trigger. He stared into the man's eyes and saw nothing but contempt. The loathing frightened him. He paused, then eased back from the man several inches. His hand holding the .45 withdrew slowly from the Russell's midsection and Russell's grin increased. The smile was short lived. Drew swung the heavy weapon upward and the muzzle of the automatic whipped across Russell's face.

The small man screamed and threw his hands over his face. Instantly, blood streamed through his fat fingers. "You broke my nose! You bastard! You broke my nose!"

Drew took a look. The bridge of the man's nose was shattered; an ugly gash exposed the bone. He swung again. The weapon slammed against Charlie's cheekbone and he crumbled to the floor. Drew stared down at the man. Russell's eyes were closed. His left leg jerked once, twice. If he wasn't dead, he might be soon. That will be just fine with me, Drew thought, his rage still shaking him.

Drew stepped back slowly. He stared at Russell's lifeless face. He started from the office, no longer afraid someone would see him, or that he might be stopped for questioning. It was too late to worry about that now.

In his study, Drew sat in the darkness, looking out over the park below his office window. He closed the draperies and switched the reading lamp on his desk to low intensity. He listed the questions in no priority.

> Why did Rod ask about Moore?
> Get in touch with Doña?
> Rod's location?
> The senator, what to do, where was he?
> A missing link? What was it?
> If he were Rod, what would he do next?

He drew a line through the last question. Rod was an enigma. There was no way to predict his next move. The senator was the most vulnerable, and the easiest to find. While he tried to decide what to do, he dialed Memorial Hospital and asked for the nurses' station just down from Mary's room.

"How is Mrs. Taylor," he asked.

Who's calling, please?"

"This is Reverend Campbell, her pastor ... and her friend."

"She's fine, pastor. She'll be okay in a few weeks." "Thank God."

"Dr. Campbell?"

"Yes."

"I thought you would want to know. There is a police guard at Mrs. Taylor's door."

"Good. And thank you."

Drew replaced the receiver and breathed a prayer of thanks. He sat back and pondered a thought. The senator was probably registered at one of the city's finest hotels. If that was so, the man would return to his hotel room, check out early and high tail it back to Atlanta, or Washington. If I can find him, he will crack under pressure. Drew reached for the telephone book, found the number he was looking for and dialed.

"Desoto Hilton," the woman answered politely.

"Yes, this is Mr. Hail, Senator Maxwell's aide. I must speak to the senator immediately. Please connect me with his room."

"One moment please."

Drew heard the distant ring of the in-house system and replaced the receiver quickly. He turned off the desk light and ran out of his study, down the hallway and through the darkened sanctuary. He did not bother to lock the front door.

The Hilton was three blocks from Grace Church. Drew covered the distance in less than three minutes. Dashing up the steps of the front entrance, he passed through the flowered arcade and slowed his steps as he walked through the electronically controlled sliding doors. He held his hand at his side, hiding the bulge of the automatic stuck in his belt.

Which room? Damn! I don't know which room the man is in! He stopped in the center of the lobby and looked about. On the registration desk, he spotted a large Federal Express envelope. A conventioneer passed him and Drew read his name on a label. Alex Garner. He stepped to the registration desk. A young woman offered assistance. "Would you see if Alex Garner has any messages, please?"

The smartly dressed woman examined a small box behind her. Drew lifted the Federal Express envelope and held it at his side below the countertop. She turned back to Drew. "Sorry, sir, no messages."

Drew thanked her and started for the elevator. On the second floor, he stepped from the elevator and walked down the hall. No one appeared. He returned to the elevator and repeated his plan. Again, no one. The fourth floor. He scored. A maid entered the elevator as he left it. He stopped, held the door a moment and asked. "Miss, I have an urgent delivery for Senator Maxwell, but I seem to have forgotten his room number. Can you help me?"

"Room 449, sir. At the far end of the hall."

"Thank you." He allowed the door to slide shut. Number 449. He walked quickly toward the end of the long hall, pausing to slide the Federal Express envelope under a door marked SUPPLIES. At the door to 449, he removed the .45, gathered himself and knocked.

"Who is it?"

Drew recognized the senator's voice.

"The assistant manager," Drew called out.

The door opened, and Drew threw his weight against it, knocking the senator back several feet. He threw up the muzzle of the automatic.

"You !

"Easy, senator," Drew ordered and closed the door quickly. "Step back, please."

The senator's eyes bulged. He obeyed Drew's instruction instantly, retreating to the center of the room as Drew approached. Senator Maxwell's hands trembled noticeably. Drew thought: how interesting that a man whose arrogance preceded him on every political front could be so quickly reduced to jelly.

"Sit down, senator," Drew instructed, waving the gun in the direction of one of the large king-sized beds. "Now," he continued, taking a seat opposite the pale faced politician. "I am going to tell you what I want only one more time."

The senator nodded. Drew began with what he hoped was a lie. "Charlie's dead. You're going to get the same, without any hesitation from me, if you don't tell me what I want to know, and if you don't tell me quickly. Understood?"

The senator nodded, his lips trembled noticeably at the sight of blood on Drew's sleeves.

"Good," Drew said. "We understand each other. Now, I want to know where I can find Rod. You've got ten seconds." Drew raised the automatic to the senator's eye level and pushed him on his back across the bed. His trigger finger tightened.

The man was near hysteria, and Drew feared he might begin screaming at any moment. Or, crying. "Seventeen Ninety."

"The restaurant?"

"No, one of the rooms above it."

Drew was silent. Seventeen Ninety was a historic restaurant only blocks from the Hilton. He could be there in minutes. First, he had to get some other information.

The senator wanted to negotiate. "I don't care about my life, but so many people will be embarrassed. My wife will be humiliated if she finds out what I've done. And my daughters! They aren't responsible for what I've done. Please! Let me go. I'll give you money, lots of it. And I'll clean up my act, really I will. I'll do lots of charitable work, get lots of things for people who need some help ." The spirit of the man was totally broken.

"Is Rod at Seventeen Ninety now?" Drew demanded.

"I don't know."

Drew allowed the man to sit up.

"Keep talking."

"Gray's a dead man. 'The Man' will take care of it. Then we'll all be free."

"The Man? What man?"

"Moore, of course."

Drew's mind was disjointed again. Moore again! What did he have to do with this? Damn! There were too many questions, too many pieces to an ever growing puzzle.

"Don't move!" Drew instructed the senator.

He stood and walked to the French window leading to the balcony overlooking downtown Savannah. From the fourth floor, he could see lights blinking over the entire city. Something was terribly wrong! He needed to get to Seventeen Ninety as soon as possible, but he had to have an answer to the question he didn't even know how to ask. He returned to the bedside opposite the senator. "Now," he said, "one more question. Don't lie to me."

"I'll tell you, just ask."

But Drew did not know how to ask the question. He stared at the man opposite him. Moore. The senator. Rod. What was the connection? Finally, words formed in his mind and he let them out slowly. He knew the wrong answer would destroy his senses. "Have you ever heard the words, EAGLE EYE?"

It was the senator's turn to stare. "You don't know, do you?" the senator asked. "You don't know anything! You're guessing, all the way!" The senator began to laugh a deep, sinister laugh. Wicked. Almost hysterical.

Drew held his eyes on the man's face, a silent rage filling his throat. He stood slowly and bent toward the man. He grabbed the senator's neck with one hand, tossed the .45 on the bed beside them and with the other hand forced the man on his back. Both his hands encircled the man's neck, tightening, closing the circle. The laughter stopped abruptly. "Tell me what I don't know," Drew growled.

"Let me up," the senator pleaded in a desperate whisper. Drew released his grip and leaned away from the man. It was his second mistake of the evening. The senator rolled off the bed in the direction of the open window. He scrambled to his feet as Drew watched in amazement; he had not considered the senator might have a gun in the room. He dived for the automatic with one hand, managed to finger it precisely and rolled to the floor between the two king-sized beds. In one continuous motion, he raised to fire in the direction of the senator.

But the senator was not after a gun. He had rushed to the window and onto the landing of the balcony. One leg protruded over the waist high ledge. The man was going to jump!

Drew lowered the gun. The senator was framed in the opening of the draperies, lights dancing behind him from a thousand homes and a million stars. "Don't ," Drew said, the rescuer coming out in him.

"I have no choice, pastor. You won't let it go. I know your kind, you won't forget. EAGLE EYE won't forget."

Drew watched incredulously as the senator rolled over the edge of the balcony and disappeared into the night. A guttural scream was quickly swallowed up in the sounds of the evening.

Drew continued in his kneeling position for what seemed an eternity, gazing at the empty balcony where moments before a man had stood. Then, a woman's scream filled the air. The cry jerked Drew from his paralysis. He ran from the room, down the hall to the elevator. Thinking better of it, he bolted to the stairway, racing down the steps, taking three, four steps at a time. At the bottom, he opened the door slowly and watched the flurry of people running back and forth in the lobby. He stepped into the flow of hotel attendants and guests.

    He began walking slowly from the hotel. In the distance he heard the howl of an ambulance. Each passing second brought the screaming sirens nearer the Hilton. The old Drew kept walking. Seventeen Ninety was only blocks away.

Chapter Twenty-Three

Drew dismissed the chaos at the Hilton. No time to rethink that scene; he had to think more clearly now than ever. If he had not been lied to again, Rod was close again, and with Rod there absolutely no room for error. He turned a corner and started down a narrow side street which emptied into the west boundary of Lafayette Square.

Drew was sweating profusely in the steamy Savannah night after only a few blocks. The gas lights glowed through the humidity, punctuating the evening eeriness. Heavy shadows lurked about the square. Ahead, Seventeen Ninety was barely visible at the next corner. He slowed a hundred feet from the charming old restaurant. A large oak offered a vantage from which to survey the entrance both to the dining area and to the several hotel rooms on the second floor.

He considered his options. If he entered the hotel, he had to get into Rod's room. If he waited here, he would have to confront Rod in the street. He had to assume Rod had transportation; he simply could not allow the agent to escape again. If he did, Rod would disappear. That might not be so bad, in itself, except Drew's objective would be lost. He intended on stopping the man, period. He had a debt to settle.

What other option did he have? If somehow Rod knew about EAGLE EYE, well, surely he would not contest the resources Moore had assembled. Then a question: was Moore connected in some way he did not understand? Another thought came to Drew: he had the drugs safely hidden away. Rod would not chance trying to recover them. The man probably had enough money for two lifetimes. No, the only reason to stop him now was very personal, and Drew knew he could not go through whatever life he had left knowing Rod had walked free. If Drew was the only one who could stop him, it had to be.

He looked about him. One couple was entering the restaurant, otherwise, the streets on either side of Seventeen Ninety were clear. Drew made his decision. He pushed himself away from the tree and started toward the entrance to the hotel rooms. He was only a few steps toward the restaurant when he stopped abruptly. Rod was exiting the hotel in a rush. Walking away! No! His brain cried. He was within seventy feet away; so close, yet so far. At that moment a woman and a small child came around the far corner of the restaurant. They were too near Rod for Drew to risk calling Rod's attention. I have to follow, Drew thought, and broke into a run in Rod's direction. When his feet hit the pavement, the agent turned and saw Drew coming at him.

Drew slowed to a walk. He would confront him here. He started slowly toward Rod; the agent froze, his eyes fixed on the shadows beyond Drew. Abruptly the scene changed. Drew heard a rush and whirled in time to see the shadow of a man upon him. The shadow attacked. Drew took the force of the blow on his left arm, but it was enough to knock him off balance. He hit the old brick pavement hard. His attacker quickly followed up his assault, bolting at Drew. Drew sprang to his feet and spun away from the man, coiling his strength as he rotated his body. His right foot whipped out like a hammer and his shoe hit its target with precision. His assailant's forward charge was stopped instantly. The man staggered under the effect of the devastating kick. Drew moved instantly, stiffening his empty right hand and drawing it back beside his body. He stepped forward and thrust it into the man's midsection. It struck with the force of a jackhammer. Drew could hear the man's breath expel with a rush. The attacker was gasping for breath as he fell in a heap in the middle of the street. Drew slammed his foot into the man's face. The assailant lay still.

    Drew whirled around to relocate Rod. The agent was gone. Then, Drew saw him. Running from the restaurant area, more than a block away. Drew bolted after Rod; he must keep the agent in sight. Within seconds, Drew was gaining, cutting the distance between himself and Rod with every step. He was within half a block when Rod stopped suddenly, turned and raised his revolver. Drew dived to the street as Rod fired a first shot, and prepared to fire again.

    Drew completed several rolls, finally stopping against the front wheel of a parked pickup truck. The second shot ricocheted off the brick pavement inches from Drew's head. Now Drew had the .45 in front of him and knew he had only a moment to aim and fire. Rod would not miss the third time. The awesome automatic exploded and the shot tore into Rod's left shoulder, spinning him around and knocking him off his feet. Incredibly, he rebounded, firing indiscriminately in Drew's direction. A shot hit the brick again, this time in front of Drew. Small missiles of brick bit into Drew's skin.

He wiped his eyes with the back of a hand, frantically trying to clear his sight, certain Rod was positioning himself to fire again. He could feel the warm presence of blood on his face. His vision cleared and he raised the automatic, but Rod had dragged himself from the scene and disappeared into the night.

Drew forced himself to his feet and staggered to the spot from where Rod had delivered the shots. A puddle of blood marked the site. Quickly, he ran in the direction Rod had to have gone. Nothing, the street was empty. Screams came from the direction of the restaurant three blocks away. He had to get out of the area, he realized, and began walking slowly away; don't attract any more attention, he cautioned himself. At the corner he looked back and saw a crowd gathered in the street outside Seventeen Ninety.

Darting into the shadows, he made his way back to Grace Church. The front door was standing open as he had left it earlier. By the time he had reached his still darkened study, he was aware of a hundred aches. And he was aware, too, that he was fortunate to be alive.

In his private bath he switched on a light. His face was peppered with red dots, each with its tiny flow of blood. He splashed cold water on his face liberally and with a clean hand towel, began wiping away the blood. There were not as many bites in his face as it had first appeared, but his skin was stinging fiercely. He stripped off his shirt and found the nasty scrapes on his elbows. He cleaned the abrasions as best he could. He slipped on the clean shirt he kept at the office for emergencies, turned off the light and went to his desk.

He sat in the darkness. Until he got some answers regarding Moore's connection to Rod and the senator, he dared not make contact with Mexico. He hoped Doña could furnish the answers he needed. Something the senator had said shortly before he leaped to his death was bothering him. He had not had time to think about it earlier. "You don't know, do you?" the senator had said, and had begun to laugh hysterically.

What was it he did not know? It had to do with Moore, surely. There was a sound outside his study window. Drew parted the draperies and peered out. A Chatham County Police car was parked directly below his window and a heavy set patrolman was walking away, toward the front doors of the sanctuary.

Lord! Why didn't I think of that before, he said to himself, remembering Bobby's warning? The county police, some of them were in this thing! Rod would have called the officer and told him where to look for Drew. He could be charged with the senator's death!

He remembered he had not locked the front door of the sanctuary when he had entered. The patrolman, if he was here to arrest Drew, detain him, whatever, he would find the open door. Drew slipped quietly from his study, making his way to the sacristy which had a seldom used door leading to the sanctuary. The passageway was darkened, but the shadows were no hindrance; he knew the area. Drawing near the worship area, he opened the door slightly and looked out into the shadows, and listened. Quiet filled the large room. He moved silently into the sanctuary, keeping the large inside columns between himself and the front door.

A shaft of light pierced the room briefly and disappeared. Someone had entered the sanctuary. Drew knelt beside a row of pews and waited. Presently, he saw the shadow of the large man moving slowly down the center aisle. Drew crawled between the pews until he was only a few feet from the aisle. Now he could see, it was the officer and the man was coming toward him. Drew slid his feet beneath him, braced himself and waited.

When the officer was directly in front of him, Drew sprang like a cat at the man's knees. With all the force he could generate, he crashed into the side of the officer's knee. He heard the crack of ligaments. The man let out a scream, dropped his revolver and clutched his wounded knee with both hands.

Drew jumped to his feet. The man's eyes were closed as he tried to force away the pain of freshly torn ligaments. Drew crouched over the man and forced him to his back. The officer opened his mouth to protest, but the words were garbled. Drew had the barrel of the .45 in the man's mouth. "One wrong move and the back of your head is gone!"

The man tried to speak. Drew withdrew the automatic from the man's mouth and positioned it against his left eye. "What do you want?" the officer asked, trying to still the pain in his knee.

"No, the question is, 'What do you want?'" Drew corrected him.

"I was told to come here!"

"Why? By whom?" Drew demanded, pushing his weapon into the socket of the man's eye.

"Because I told him to." A voice from the rear of the sanctuary. Rod! Drew whirled in the direction of Rod's voice, crouching below the pews as he turned. He crawled away from the moaning officer, retreating to the safety of the pews. He had not yet located Rod, and he knew the agent would not be foolish enough to expose himself.

"Drew," Rod said with an evenness that surprised Drew, "let's talk."

Drew did not answer.

Rod again: "I'm coming down the aisle, Drew, like a repentant sinner."

295

Drew peered over the pews. Rod was standing at the far end of the center aisle. The agent began a slow walk down the passageway. His left arm was in a makeshift sling.

"Here's my gun, Drew." Rod tossed the weapon down the aisle. It bounced toward the communion table, coming to rest only a few feet from where Drew was crouching. Drew stood slowly, the automatic trained on Rod with both hands.

"Don't," Rod said calmly, and walked toward Drew.

Then they were only feet apart. Rod continued past Drew and sat down on the steps leading up to the chancel. He held his hands out in front of him for Drew to see clearly, even in the dim light. "You can leave now," Rod said to the officer, who struggled to his feet and hobbled from the sanctuary, dragging his busted leg.

Drew sat down on the front pew, his gun pointed at Rod's heart. "Okay, talk," he said.

Rod adjusted the sling holding his useless left arm. It was obvious he had lost a considerable amount of blood. A .45 caliber bullet leaves nothing to the imagination. How he was sitting so easily was a wonder to Drew. "Where do you want me to start?" Rod asked.

"Start with 'why'!" Drew said, the automatic still at the ready.

"Cocaine is power, Drew," Rod replied. "You know that. America is captive to the stuff. I'm not saying everybody is on the powder, but more and more are addicted daily. We, Maxwell, Charlie and I we could see the effect on our troops in Nam. It didn't take a genius to know its use would soon be rampant in the states. We decided to get in on the ground floor. It's as simple as that."

"So you planned, waited and then ," Drew said, "when the time was right and your positions solidified, you opened shop. Is that it?"

"Precisely."

"And the senator's appointment to the upper chamber's Committee on Drug Abuse gave both of you the cover you needed. Right?"

"Yes."

"It also provided you a vehicle to manipulate people and obtain information. Am I right again?"

"Go on. You're doing very well, pastor."

Drew stared at the man whom he had once counted as a dear friend. Somebody began to close down your supply routes."

"Well," Rod corrected him, "we decided long ago that Savannah would be our entry point. It did begin to get a very hot in the area, but they'll never close it down, Drew. The stuff is coming in like the tide. Savannah will rise again a drug entry point, I mean."

Then, "Why me?"

"Because we had promised one more shipment to our northeast buyers. We had to try to deliver one more shipment, but the freighters were really being watched. Then I remembered your problems in Nam. Charlie had told me about what he had seen that night in Saigon. It

297

was for your sake I had shut down that investigation. I figured you owed me a favor, but I never figured you to get hurt. I thought we would get in and get out, close down shop and nobody would be worse for wear."

"You must have taken me for quite a fool."

"Well, no, but you did cause us some concern, but even then, it all would have worked out if others had not intervened."

"Like whom?"

Rod was silent.

"Like whom, dammit!" Drew shouted.

Rod looked at him closely. "If I tell you that, your life won't be worth spit."

"Let me be the judge of the value of my life!"

Rod stood, and Drew leveled the .45 at his chest. Drew snarled his words. "Don't do something stupid, Rod. You tried to have me killed, remember. I won't hesitate to kill you."

Rod ignored the warning, shifted the sling to change the direction of the pain and sat down again.

"Okay, Drew. Here's why I'm here. This is the deal. I tell you everything you want to know and, in return, I get the package. I'll disappear and you'll never hear from me nor see me again."

"Brazil, maybe?"

"Something like that."

Rod was weakening by the moment. There was no way he could carry the package even if it were given to him, Drew thought. There must be others nearby. At least one. The officer? He'd be in no shape to carry a hundred pounds. Then there were others, at least one.

"Keep talking," Drew said.

"Then, it's a deal?"

"You're getting weaker. Much longer and you'll not make it. I destroy the coke and expose the senator."

Rod eyed him closely. "But you'll never know how you have been betrayed, will you?"

Drew saw Rod's shoulders drop steadily. If he was to learn anything, it had to be now, and decided one betrayal deserved another. "Okay, deal."

"Good," Rod said, and leaned forward. "Shortly after we started our operation, the senator received a visit from David Moore. The old man is brilliant, you know. He had an interesting proposal. Seems someone had made an offer to him to set him up in business to counter the drug trade. They were willing to put up considerable seed money to fund the operation. Moore, obviously, decided he wanted more than a gold watch for his retirement. He proposed an organization he called EAGLE EYE, an organization funded by a right wing religious capitalist, supposedly established to counter drug trafficking. A clandestine operation, connected to no one, directed solely by David Moore. He would supply us all the information at his disposal to insure the success of our operation. In turn, he would hit competitive groups, giving evidence that EAGLE EYE was doing its job. In return, he got a one fourth cut of all proceeds. I run the operation. He supplies information we needed. Maxwell keeps the feds off our butts. Moore hits other operations, not ours."

Drew had not spoken as Rod detailed the hidden fabric of EAGLE EYE. He could believe, finally, what he was hearing. For the first time everything was falling into place. Except one detail.

"And, Doña?"

"She knows nothing. Straight as an arrow. And she adores her father."

"Yes, I could see that."

"You see? Then, you knew?"

"No, I bought the front. I met Moore on Isle of Mujeres the other day. Doña and I went there to get help in stopping you and the senator."

Now, it was Rod's turn to be silent. When he spoke it was with a voice of a weakened man. "It doesn't matter now. I'm going to deliver that package and get the hell out."

Rod started an attempt to stand, but the effort was feeble at best. He sat back down on the steps.

It was beginning to make sense to Drew. The way he figured it, Moore had helped set him up, and then was planning to use him to take out Charlie, the senator and Rod, and then, Moore would take over the whole operation. The only thing that bothered him was what did Moore plan to do about his daughter? At the moment, however, Drew had to deal with Rod, and whomever he had brought along with him to carry the package and get rid of Drew.

"I want the cocaine, Drew."

"All you get, 'friend', is a chance in a court of law." Drew was thinking fast. Whoever was outside, or, was he inside, would make his move soon, and Drew had to be ready.

"Get up, Rod."

Drew stood, pulled a weakened Rod to his feet and shoved him toward the door. He was not ready. A shadow stepped from behind a column on the far side of the sanctuary. The shadow had a voice. "Mr. Gray, this is from EAGLE EYE." The shadow squeezed a trigger. The shot echoed through the vaulted sanctuary as if someone had fired a howitzer. Rod spun in a grotesque, twisting motion. Another shot drove him back against the communion table. A final shot ripped through his abdomen. The agent was dying on the table of sacrifice.

Drew dropped to his knees at the first series of shots. He squinted in the darkness at the rear of the sanctuary. In the brief flashes of fire, he had seen a figure outlined against the back wall. He prepared to fire, but the door opened and closed quickly. The assailant was gone; he had done his job.

Drew searched the semidarkness of the great room for other shadows. There were none. Watching the rear of the sanctuary carefully, he moved to Rod's side. The agent was barely alive. His sunken eyes tried to focus on Drew. His lips moved slightly.

Drew leaned forward, his ear at Rod's lips.

"It was ... hollow ..."

"What was, Rod? What was hollow?"

Rod's throat gurgled.

"The blackmail ... hollow ..."

"What do you mean, Rod? Try! Tell me!"

The words were nearly imperceptible. "The sergeant ... woman ... they ... they were ... part of it ..."

"Dammit Rod! Part of what? Tell me!"

"... part of ... the ring in ... Nam ..."

Drew recoiled from the dying agent. "No! No, No! All of this ... you mean, I killed two drug dealers?"

A belabored "Yes."

A madness enveloped Drew. He grabbed at Rod's bloody shirt with both hands and began shaking him, a rage enveloping him. He continued shaking the man violently until finally he released him, and let Rod's limp body fall against the table. Drew slumped back on his heels. Exhaustion claimed him.

"For nothing," he whispered into the still air of the great hall. "For nothing."

Rod stared at him with lifeless eyes. Drew moved to the side of his former friend. Sadness swelled within him, and he could not control the tears that filled his eyes. He knew he should be running. Someone must have heard the shots and he could not be implicated directly. There were questions remaining, questions he had to find answers for ... but he did not move. Instead, he thought of the day, years ago, when the Viet Cong had infiltrated their post, catching them off guard. He and

Rod had been ready that day to give their lives for each other. It seemed ages ago when they had been friends.

Drew waited for the doors of the sanctuary to open and police to enter. Strangely enough, the police did not come. Perhaps the great room had absorbed the deafening sounds of the shots, he thought, his thinking returning to the present. He walked to a panel of switches near a side door and turned on a light which illumined the chancel. It was barely enough light to reveal the desecration. Rod's body was propped against the communion table, his legs stretched before him in twisted fashion. His head had fallen back against the table, and his mouth frozen open in death as if a scream might yet escape his lips. Drew stood in front of the table and stared down at the body of the agent. Somehow, it seemed only right that the violence of moments before should have ended at this table of sacrifice. The table of the innocent One smeared with the blood of the guilty. Our violence, our guilt, he thought, laid at the altar of love. He pulled the paramount from the communion table and covered Rod's lifeless body. He turned and walked from the shadowed great room.

Drew made his way through the darkened halls and stairways to the basement. There he removed the cocaine from its hiding place and dragged it to the center of the room where a drain was fitted into the sloping floor. He hooked up a water hose, laid the nozzle at the edge of the drain and turned the water on, producing a steady flow of water into the drain. He slashed the package open, took out the first smaller unit of cocaine and began dumping the white powder into the flow of water. It required nearly thirty minutes before the last of the drug was washed down the drain. Then, he split the wrapping open and laid it flat on the floor, and washed the final specks of powder from the material. Finally, he rolled the empty package into a tight wad and pushed it into the nearest trash can.

Returning to his study, he dialed the police and reported a homicide in the sanctuary of Grace Church. As quickly as he could replace the receiver, he rushed to the sanctuary to throw open the front doors and wait for the arrival of several patrol cars. The response was immediate.

The next hour was a media circus. Television flood lights illumined the front of Grace Church as reporters stumbled over each other in frenzied competition for every gruesome detail. The police established the accustomed barricades at the entrance to the church, accented by the orange ribbons strung ominously around the boundaries of the investigation.

In the sanctuary, transformed from a place of worship into a secular pageant, Drew stood quietly aside and watched as Rod's body was lifted from its distorted position against the communion table and placed on a stretcher. The body was covered and strapped. Finally, it began its slow journey from the holy place to the morgue.

Drew thought the scene resembled a funeral of sorts, except no one offered words of comfort. As the body passed up the aisle, a police officer whispered, "This is spooky." No one said, "I am the resurrection and the life ..."

Finally, Detective Mosely motioned for Drew to join him at the far side of the sanctuary. Drew had confirmed in his mind the details of the story he had sketched earlier.

"I was working late when I heard the shots. They were muffled so I couldn't make out for sure from where they were coming. When I ran down the hall to the side door, I heard another series of shots. They sounded as if they were coming from the sanctuary. When I opened that door," he pointed to an entrance just beyond where he and the detective were standing, "I saw the front door close. I started to follow when I saw the body against the table."

"You didn't see the killer?" Mosely asked.

"No."

"Go on."

"That's it. I was horrified, to say the least. I called the police. That's it."

"The coroner says the body had been dead about thirty minutes when we arrived."

"Maybe so. I guess I looked at the body for several minutes. Then turned on the lights to see if there were others. And I straightened the candles and the Bible. I don't suppose I should have done that, huh?"

Mosely just looked at the preacher.

"Then, I called the police."

The detective asked several more questions. Finally, he told Drew he could go. "I'll want to talk to you again in the morning. "Say, nine o'clock in your office?"

"Someone has to clean up the mess," Drew responded.

"Not until tomorrow, not before we can look at everything in the daylight," the detective said sternly. Drew nodded, and left for his study. A few minutes later, he left for Isle of Hope. He was shaking noticeably as he turned the Camaro into the garage.

Doña watched Drew enter the house and it seemed to her that he had aged overnight. If he had not slept in an alley, it appeared that way. He was unshaven, and generally unkempt, his clothes noticeably wrinkled. Dark circles lined his eyes.

"What are you doing here?" he asked.

"I got a call from Papa. He was worried when he didn't hear from you."

He embraced her in the center of the kitchen, holding her silently, and so intently she could feel him shaking in her arms.

"Drew," she said softly, "what is going on? You look like hell."

"That's where I've been," he responded, his tone underscoring the words, "in hell."

"Tell me for God's sake."

Drew took her hand and led her to the kitchen table and sat, indicating for her to join him. "Doña, I'll tell you what has happened since I arrived in Savannah, but there is something else, something I dread talking about."

She looked at him, saw the fear in his eyes.

"First," he said, returning her gaze, "Rod is dead. So is Senator Maxwell and probably Charlie."

The news stunned her, but her trained mind told her there was more, something worse.

Speaking slowly, he told her everything that had transpired since he had returned to his city, ending the report with Rod's death and the final conversation with Detective Mosely.

She listened without speaking a word. "Then, everything's worked out, not exactly as we wanted, but it's worked out, hasn't it?" She knew instinctively that was not the case.

He looked away.

"Drew, what is it? I want to know."

His face was etched with disbelief. "The man and woman, the ones I killed in Nam?"

"Yes."

"There were in it with Drew. The drugs, I mean. I killed two drug dealers that night. I'm sure Drew meant to kill them himself before he left Vietnam. It doesn't lessen my quilt, but it does explain why they never reported me. The blackmail was an empty threat!"

"Oh, Drew. What an ass Rod was. He used everyone."

He looked at her. "Yes, everyone, Doña," he said very slowly. "Everyone used everyone. Even your father."

"What? I don't know what you mean."

So he told her. About Papa's visit to the senator. About her father's role in Rod's tight little group. And about his suspicion: that Papa Moore had used him to rid Moore of his three partners in the cocaine trafficking operation. "Your father is a first class con man, Doña. Worse, he has deceived not only those who put him in business; he has deceived his own daughter! In the process, he used me to do his dirty work."

"I don't believe it! It's a lie!"

"Then, who was the man who killed Rod ?" Drew asked. "He identified himself as a messenger from EAGLE EYE? Why would Rod go to such lengths to implicate your father? How did he know about EAGLE EYE, information known only to a limited few?"

She was silent.

"Doña, you have to face the truth. And now, with your help, I trust, I have to stop your father! I have to destroy EAGLE EYE."

She stood, and walked away. Then, turning, she said, "There is a simple way to find the truth. We go to Isle of Mujeres and talk to Papa. If you're right, we will know."

"Good," he said, standing, and walking to face her. "But we do not call for the Lear. Instead, and this is how we have to do it, Doña, we go commercial. We go to the island unannounced. We don't give your father a chance to prepare for our visit. And we don't call before we go."

She considered his demand. "Okay. Let's go."

"Tomorrow, at the earliest. I have to meet the police in the morning. And," he paused, "I'm going to announce my resignation. You make the flight arrangements."

"Okay." Then she asked, hopefully, "Where do I sleep?"

"Take my bed," Drew offered. "I'll sleep in the guest room. Besides, I'm not very sleepy. I need some time alone, if you don't mind."

She nodded, and stood. "Goodnight." She started from the room, stopped and turned to face him. "Drew," she said quietly, "I'm scared to ask Papa if he , I mean, what if he ." She put her hands to her face. "And what if you're wrong?" She turned and left the room.

Drew sat on the darkened side porch until long after midnight. He recalled his earlier life in Savannah, event by event, trying to focus on better things. It did not help. He began thinking of tomorrow. Tomorrow, he would begin sorting out an uncertain future. He walked to the front screen door and looked out over the waterway. He could not see it, but he knew The North Star rested quietly in its grave. The sky was darkened with threatening clouds. He heard a rumble of thunder. Good, he thought. Let it rain. Come on, Lord, bring me a terrible thunderstorm.

Chapter Twenty-Four

"Oh, Dr. Campbell! Thank God you're here!" Jackie exclaimed, rushing to greet him. "Sir, it's awful! There is blood everywhere! On the communion table, the carpet, everywhere!" She began to sob.

"I know, Jackie, take it easy. Everything will be all right. I was here until late last night. I'm supposed to meet the police again this morning. They want to ask some more questions."

"Perhaps we could do that, Dr. Campbell," said a man standing at the door to Drew's office.

Drew turned. The smartly dressed man was joined by a uniformed officer from the Savannah Police Department, and Detective Mosely. The man stepped forward and offered his hand. "I'm Daniel Miller, F.B.I. You know Detective Mosely, of course. This is Officer Norman."

Drew shook hands with the agent. "How can I help you?"

"Dr. Campbell, could we talk in your office?"

"Of course. Jackie, hold my calls, please," he instructed, and walked past the three men.

Mr. Miller nodded to the uniformed man. "Please wait outside, Officer Norman," he said, and closed the door. Inside, the three men sat about the center coffee table and Miller began the conversation.

"Dr. Campbell," the agent began soberly, "The record of this investigation will report an F.B.I. agent was killed in your sanctuary last night while in the line of duty. The report will also reveal a drug cartel whose operation he had traced to this city is responsible for his death. There will be a continuing news story about this terrible thing that happened in your church. Public outrage will be predictably fierce. Local officials and the bureau will promise to continue the investigation until the attackers are found. Then, ever so slowly, the story will die. You, sir, will not be implicated."

Drew glanced at Mosely. The detective's expression said it all: he did not like what Drew was being told, but he had been briefed earlier, and told he had no choice in the matter. It was, as he had been previously instructed, a highly classified matter.

Drew sat silently. Miller continued. "A connection will be made between agent Gray's death and the murder of the reporter."

"Bobby Taylor," Drew corrected. At least, his name could be spoken.

"Yes, Mr. Taylor," Miller repeated. "A connection has been leaked to the press to give credence to the story. Taylor and the agent were working together, undercover. That's our story, and the newspapers are jumping on it. There is no reason not to believe it, of course. Your name came up immediately, and, naturally, they want to speak with you. You should honor that request as soon as possible and tell them of your anguish over this terrible series of events."

Drew stared at the man. "Why am I being given this option? That's what it is, isn't it, an option?"

"Only if you consider it so, Dr. Campbell. We prefer it this way, and I think you, of all persons, will understand that, and why."

"I don't think that's all of it," Drew retorted.

"No," Miller said, "but the rest of it will remain classified. All I can tell you is that the Director has taken a personal interest in this case. Though I suspect you are, somehow, implicated in this matter, my instructions are clear: hands off where you are concerned. Clear your name at all costs. Now, I don't understand that ."

"Neither do I," echoed Mosely.

"As I said, I don't understand," the agent continued, "how you were involved, nor do I need to know. I follow orders, Dr. Campbell; so from this moment on, you are free of any involvement in this matter. You may, I should tell you, be called for further questioning, but the implications are that this operation is much bigger than any murder, or several murders. I hope you understand what I have said to you." The agent sat back in his chair.

"I do understand," Drew said. "Oh, yes, I understand." Yes, he thought to himself, I understand. Doña had called the Director, or was it Papa? The Director was told enough to convince him it was in the best interests of the bureau and all concerned for Drew not to be implicated. The Director himself, of course, understood that better than anyone. The media would delight in bringing down, not only the Director himself, but the bureau, too, should his involvement and Rod's, and the senator's, become public knowledge. Too, the presidential elections were in full swing. The sitting administration would be literally destroyed, and its candidate devastated. Understanding the offer Miller had just presented was no problem whatsoever.

"Then, we will be going, Dr. Campbell. We thank you for your time." His hand was on the doorknob when he turned, withdrew a folded newspaper from his briefcase and dropped it in the chair next to the door. "Ever read Markus Williamson, the columnist? You'll find his column on the editorial page. It may be of interest to you. As you will see, the whole thing would have unraveled within days, anyway. Goodbye, Dr. Campbell."

Moments later, Drew was alone in his study. He picked up the newspaper Miller had left and opened the Washington Post to the front page. Today's date. Quickly, he turned to the editorial page, found the column and began reading. Williamson had most of the facts right, though they would woefully incomplete. Drew dropped the paper on his desk and began mulling over the startling developments. It's time, he decided, and summoned his secretary. "Jackie, I want you to call the officers of the church and tell them I want to meet with them within the hour. Then, I want you to call a press conference to follow my meeting with the officers. Set it up in the fellowship hall."

Jackie looked at him. "What's this about, sir?"

"I'm sorry, Jackie. I wanted to tell you earlier. I am resigning my position with Grace Church."

Tears swelled up in her eyes. "But why, Dr. Campbell? We'll get over this terrible thing. You don't have to resign. It wasn't your fault. And --."

"Jackie, please, do as I say. We'll talk later."

"Of course, sir," she said, regaining her composure.

The officers of the church sat in stunned silence following Drew's statement to them, which of course, was brief and not altogether the truth. He begged the strain of the ministry, Ellen's death, from which, he told the elders of the church, he had never recovered. Simply put, he needed extended time to get his head and heart right. Too, his friend's death had added a burden he simply could not handle and perform his duties, too. It was not an impetuous decision. He had been considering it for months. They wished Drew well and assured him they would be praying for him.

At the news conference, Drew answered the questions of the reporters, careful to follow the Bureau's line. How did he feel about a murder occurring in his church? Simply terrible, but he was certain God was offended more than he. Did he know the agent? Yes, they had been in Nam together, and had talked occasionally over the years. No, it was only coincidence that the agent was murdered in his friend's church.

Would he describe his feelings? He repeated what he had said earlier. Would this have an effect on the church? Of course, but the church would survive the terrible ordeal. Why was he resigning? He repeated the items he had shared with the officers. It was simply time for him to seek emotional rehabilitation. When was he leaving? Today. Would he care to share his feelings about the death of Bobby Taylor? Yes, he cared, and no, he would not talk about Mr. Taylor, not now.

Then, he announced he would be placing in a trust a hundred thousand dollars for the purpose of establishing the Bobby Taylor Journalism Award to be given annually to the reporter who most exemplified the professional qualities and commitment demonstrated by Bobby Taylor's professional life. In addition, a similar trust would be established in honor of Mary Taylor and the annual yield of the trust given to the shelter for abused women.

Finally, Drew announced that the bulk of his assets would be placed in the Ellen North Campbell Foundation which would be established shortly. The annual income of the Foundation would be distributed in various grants to charitable causes, primarily in Chatham County. He would serve as president of a Board of Directors which would determine which causes would receive the grants. He turned to his secretary. "And I intend to offer Miss Starling the position of Assistant Administrator."

"My wealth," Drew further informed the reporters, "came from my wife's estate, and I have wondered since her death how I might best invest her memory and her money in this city that she loved. The foundation is my answer."

Drew stood outside Mary's hospital room, listening quietly to her brother, Dr. Benjamin Denton, detail her condition. Dr. Denton, a general surgeon, had returned to Boston from Zaire, where he was serving in a bush hospital as a volunteer in mission with his wife. The news of Bobby's death and Mary's disappearance brought them to Savannah on the next available flight.

"The loss of blood was considerable," Dr. Denton was saying, "but the internal injuries are not life-threatening. It's the emotional trauma I'm most concerned about. She'll need a lot of care just to find the courage to go on. We'll take her home with us until she can decide what she wants to do. I have a feeling, though, knowing her as I do, that she'll return to Savannah. At least for a while."

Drew offered any help he might provide. "If there's anything, anything at all ."

"I would call you," her brother said.

"I'd like to come to Boston to see her, if you don't mind -- in a week or so."

"That would be better timing."

Drew agreed, and wondered if Mary's brother had also been briefed by the bureau.

An hour later, Drew and Doña were sitting silently on a flight to Dallas. Two hours later they caught a Mexicana flight from Dallas to Cancun, arriving late in the Caribbean afternoon. The taxi ride from the airport to Puerto Juarez took twenty-five minutes. From there, they paid their thousand pesos each, about fifty cents in U.S. money, and boarded the lumbering old ferry and began the final leg of their trip to the island. The five miles of the Caribbean Sea separating the mainland and Isle of Mujeres was a forty-five minutes ride.

Drew and Doña found seats in the rear of the ferry, avoiding a boisterous group of Mexican teenagers occupying the front of the wide berthed, sturdy vessel. They had spoken little during the last seven hours. At the rear of the ferry the noise from the engine was less dramatic, and from their seats they enjoyed a wider view of the blue green waters. The ferry plowed methodically toward the Isle of Mujeres.

"Doña, I wish there were some other conclusion I could make, but I have gone over it again and again. Unless Rod was lying and why would he? There just isn't any other answer. I know it must hurt like hell!"

She could not deny the obvious any longer, but that recognition deepened the hurt beyond belief. Her Papa, who had loved and nurtured her for twenty-five years! How could he do such a thing? And, for God's sake, why? The obvious simply did not make sense!

She turned to Drew, unable to hide the hurt. "I don't know how I will feel when I see Papa. I should be furious, and I am. Yet, I don't know where to focus the anger. I keep hoping there is some other explanation."

Tears filled her eyes and she turned away. The ferry's captain cut the engines and the ponderous craft settled easily into a slow crawl in the shallow harbor waters. Ten minutes later the ferry docked and the pier was inundated with the hundreds of Mexicans who made their way to the street fronting the sea.

Doña and Drew stepped into the moving crowd, neither of them eager to hurry the last few miles to EAGLE NEST. Moments later they walked into a small motor bike shop, rented two mopeds and rolled them into the street. Doña touched Drew's arm as he was about to depress the kickstarter. "Drew, I want to speak to Papa first. That's my right, you know."

"Sure. But I want to be present."

"Okay," she said. She started her bike and guided it into the crowded street. Drew followed. They motored along a mile long lagoon, past Maria's Kan Kin, toward the southern end of the island. Just short of El Garrafon, less than a mile from the lighthouse, they took a left turn up into a densely wooded area. Within moments they drew up to EAGLE NEST. The place was quiet, as usual, and as they cut the motors of the mopeds, the stillness increased.

The helicopter sat motionless on its pad. A welcomed breeze touched their faces as they walked toward the seldom used front door.

The silence was broken suddenly. The front door opened quickly and Sylvia emerged. Papa's assistant leaped off the small porch and ran to embrace Doña.

"Oh, señorita! I'm so glad you've come! I've tried to reach you all day."

Doña broke the embrace and grabbed Sylvia by the shoulders.

"What is it, Sylvia?"

"It's Papa Moore! He's suffered another attack. The doctor says it's his heart, and maybe another stroke." She was nearing hysteria. "He's dying, Doña, and he keeps asking for you."

Doña pushed Sylvia aside and bounded up the steps and into the house. Drew followed quickly, leaving the weeping Sylvia to follow.

Doña entered Papa's bedroom with Drew at her heels. The man appeared much older than Drew remembered him. He was propped up in the bed to enhance his breathing. An oxygen tube ran from a large tank beside the bed to his nose. His eyes were closed, his arms resting motionlessly at his side. She pulled a chair to the bedside and took Papa's hand in hers. She spoke softly.

"Papa? Papa, it's Doña. I'm here. I love you."

At first there was little response. Then, the old man's eyes fluttered, opened. "Doña? Is it you, baby?"

"Yes, Papa. You are going to be all right."

Moore's eyes closed slowly, then quickly opened.

"No, baby. I'm dying. I know that. I made the doctor tell me the truth. I have been holding on just to see you, my darling." A tear rolled down his cheek.

"Oh, Papa," she said faintly, "you can't give up. You can't leave me!"

Drew stepped closer to Doña, peering over her shoulder into Papa's eyes. His hand rested gently on Doña's shoulder Papa recognized him. "Drew ."

"I'm going to be here with Doña, Papa, and I'll stay with her. Don't worry."

The old man struggled for some hidden strength. His head raised slightly, then dropped weakly on the pillow. "I have to tell you something, both of you."

"Not now, Papa," Doña protested.

"Yes, now baby," he demanded feebly, and gripped her hand with a strength that surprised her.

She relented. "Okay, Papa. But then you must rest."

Drew leaned closer. "Papa," he said, hesitantly, "we know about your association with Rod, and with the senator. What we don't know is, why ?"

The director of EAGLE EYE struggled for breath. "The man who financed me ," he said, obviously getting weaker by the moment, "he didn't come through with all the money he promised. I had far too little to do the job. I knew about Rod and Maxwell from my investigations. He drew a deep breath, "I made a deal with them. I offered to provide them with all the intelligence they needed to stay ahead of the feds, or anyone else."

Doña was crying softly. "Why, Papa?"

"I had to have capital, a lot of it. This was the only way I knew to get it. I was willing to let a limited amount of cocaine enter the country to get the financing I needed. I thought I could make up for it later." Papa winched as a stab of pain grabbed his chest. But the old man was determined to finish. "EAGLE NEST's cut of the take has amounted to more than seventy-five million dollars. Sylvia has the books. It's all there. Every penny accounted for."

"Oh, Papa, it's not right. You should have told me."

"But you would have stopped me, baby, and I needed the money to make EAGLE EYE work! Don't you see? I never intended to let it go on. When I saw it was getting too big, and even EAGLE EYE might not be able to stop it, I devised a plan to stop them."

Drew, still trying to take in Papa's revelation, asked, "That's when I entered the picture?"

"Yes. I told Rod my intelligence network showed a major crackdown coming soon in the Savannah area. I even told them their identities were close to being exposed. I wanted to convince them to stop. But they insisted on one more shipment. The package. A hundred pounds of pure cocaine, worth millions."

He rested a moment and continued. "That's when Rod made the suggestion that we use you to bring in the last package. The plan suggested another scheme to me. I did a background check on you. What I found was a man I thought could be useful to EAGLE EYE. My bet was you could be angered enough to take out Rod and his associates, keep the cocaine from hitting the streets and end EAGLE EYE's connection with drug trafficking. At the least, you would be my tool. I had enough money to make EAGLE EYE work. I needed Rod and the senator eliminated. And I needed it done without any connection to EAGLE EYE."

"What went wrong?" Drew asked.

"Too many things."

"How could you have possibly thought I could pull off your plans?" Drew asked.

"It was a great risk. But EAGLE EYE was more important than your life, don't you see that?"

Drew was silent. The old man's eyes widened. "In the end, it worked, didn't it? Not like I planned, but it worked. You did a great job, my boy. And I suppose you have the cocaine, right?"

"No. I destroyed it last night."

"Ah, Good," Papa said, "That's a relief."

Doña put her head on Papa's arm. She was crying softly. Then, she looked at her father and whispered, "Papa, you were wrong to do what you did, but it's over now. I love you more than ever. You must rest now."

"No, there's one more thing." He looked beyond his daughter to Drew. His eyes watered, but held steady as he spoke. "I am dying. I know that."

"No, Papa!" Doña squeezed her father's hand. "Don't say that."

"Doña, I know the score. We all know it. I can't pretend I'm going to make it when I know better. EAGLE EYE is far too important, far more important than either of us for me not to face the truth. The doctor says I am dying. I accept that. But I can't accept something I believe in dying with me." He turned his eyes to Drew again. "EAGLE EYE must endure. It must go on. Right now, it is poised to make its influence felt. No matter how you feel about how I secured EAGLE EYE'S future, it must go on. And you, Drew, you are the man who must see that it does what it was intended to do hit the drug trade hard, again and again."

Drew was taken aback. "Me? Lead EAGLE EYE? No way, Papa Moore! You're asking the wrong man."

Drew looked at Doña who was as stunned as he. Moore did not relent. "Listen to me, Drew. Just listen to me, please. There is no one else. I know you are new to all these crazy games we play, but you learn quickly. Sylvia can teach you everything I know, everything I do here. And you can bring someone else in to actually run EAGLE EYE, so you can be in the field more, like I wanted to do before I was struck down by my first stroke. I have ten good men out there."

"The answer is 'no,' and that's final." Drew turned to leave the room. There was little to say, except, "I will return to Savannah and try to put my life back together. My life! My life you almost ruined, probably did. No thanks, Papa Moore," he said, "I made a mistake getting involved with EAGLE EYE the first time. It did me no good, actually. I won't make the same mistake again." He left the room.

Drew had been sitting on the back steps nearly an hour, watching the lights of the mainland dance on the horizon. He did not hear Doña open the door, nor hear her approach until she stepped to his side and sat beside him.

She eased herself beside Drew. "Papa is very weak. I don't think he will make more than a few days. I'm going to stay with him. He's my father, and I love him dearly. I'll inform the Director."

"I'm truly sorry."

"I know. I believe you, so I'll ask you this special favor. Will you just let him die, not expose him?"

"Yes, but EAGLE EYE must be dissolved, stopped, you understand that, don't you?"

Yes. I'll see to it. The Director will know what to do."

He looked at her, but did not reply. It was her problem now. "Will I see you again?"

"Should we?" he asked.

"Why shouldn't we? My God, Drew, I thought we meant something to each other! Nobody's talking long term commitment. I know we live in vastly different worlds. I'm not stupid, but we don't have to throw it all away just because --."

"It's not that."

"Do you feel anything for me? I want to know, do you care?"

"Of course I care! That's just it, I may care too much. And what future is there in it?"

"You're not being truthful, Drew. I deserve better than that."

He looked at her.

"You are feeling unfaithful to Ellen, aren't you?"

"No, I."

She ignored his protest. "I can't complete with your wife's memory, Drew. And I won't try. I wasn't asking for marriage, just a simple acknowledgement that we experienced something special, and the willingness to let it go where it might."

"It's not that simple for me."

"No, it's not. I can see that."

"Doña ."

"Let's leave it at that, shall we?" she said and stood. "The helicopter will take you to Cancun when you're ready."

"I'm ready."

Chapter Twenty-Five

The Allison 250C20 turbo shaft power plant of the Bell 206 Jet Ranger began its familiar whine, initiating a slow revolution of the two blade main rotor. The action signaled the man and woman walking quietly on the beach that the pilot had concluded the preflight checklist for yet another quick trip to the mainland. The pair turned toward the steps leading to the house perched at the top of the dunes.

The rotors whirled steadily as they neared the circle of safety just beyond the reach of the blades. The woman stopped, their hands parted and the man continued with bowed head to the chopper. Goodbyes had been said on the beach.

Drew fastened his shoulder harness, nodded to the pilot and waved goodbye to Doña standing a safe distance from the helicopter. The pilot, a Vietnam veteran of the Air Force's search and rescue missions, rolled up the throttle to bring the rotor rams to maximum, pulled pitch on the collective and simultaneously added left pedal. The Jet Ranger lifted smoothly from the pad. EAGLE EYE fell away from the rising chopper at three hundred feet per minute. As the pilot rotated the aircraft and pointed the cyclic toward Cancun International Airport, Doña disappeared from view.

The pilot leveled the Allison 250 turbo shaft powered chopper at five hundred feet for the ten minute flight to Cancun. The 700 horsepower chopper thundered toward Cancun from the Isle of Mujeres. Drew swept his eyes across the horizon. The blue green waters of the ever rolling Caribbean Sea dominated every view. Cancun was already drawing near. At 152 mph maximum cruising speed, he reasoned, he would step from the chopper within minutes and cut his last tie with the covert operation. If he had his way, he would be in Savannah soon, then on the next plane to Dallas and to the Rockies and a few days of quiet.

The pilot touched him on the thigh and pointed to the second set of head phones. Drew acknowledged the instruction and fitted the headset over his ears. He adjusted the microphone before his lips and glanced at the older man at the controls of the sleek helicopter. He appreciated the diversion.

"Thought you might like to listen in, "the pilot said.

"Thanks," Drew replied.

The pilot pointed toward Cancun. "Need to check in with Cancun," he said and began the proper flight dialogue with an anonymous controller less than five miles away. The pilot spoke calmly to the nameless controller. "Cancun International. This is Copter 697. Five miles out. Request left base for heliport Alpha."

The tower responded immediately. "Roger, Copter 697. Report airport in sight."

The helicopter continued its straight path for Cancun.

"There it is!" The pilot pointed to the rapidly approaching heliport less than a mile away.

Suddenly, a frantic voice screamed in Drew's ears. "Copter 697! This is EAGLE NEST. Return to base. I repeat: return to base!"

The pilot jerked his head toward Drew who had quickly covered his ear phones with his hands in a fruitless effort to recognize the voice. Drew returned the pilot's gesture with a questioning stare. Drew frowned, and started to speak. "What?"

"That's Sylvia!" the pilot shouted. "There's trouble at EAGLE NEST."

"What kind of trouble?"

"I don't know." Then, "NEST base. This is Copter 697. What's going on?"

Sylvia's voice cracked over the radio again. "We have a security break! Return to base immediately! EAGLE NEST is threatened!" Then Sylvia lost her composure. "Papa's hurt! Eaglet in danger! Please, return to base!"

Drew stared at the pilot for a second and made a decision. "Do as she says."

The pilot hesitated. "I'm in the traffic pattern. I can't break now."

It was Drew's turn to waver. Something was terribly wrong if Sylvia had panicked. What? He grabbed the pilot's arm. "Turn this thing and get us back!"

"But!"

"Now! I mean now!"

The pilot heaved a deep breath and initiated a sixty degree bank and, at the same time, pulled maximum torque. The Bell 206 Jet Ranger shuddered as it entered a tight high-G turn. The pilot ignored the Cancun control tower's inquiries about the aborted approach.

    The Isle of Mujeres immediately appeared directly ahead. "Get me there as quickly as you can," Drew ordered. The pilot eased the Jet Ranger to within twenty feet of the water and pushed the chopper to its maximum speed of a hundred and fifteen knots. The bright morning sunshine was dancing on the peaks of the waves.

    "Can't you go any faster?" Drew implored.

    The pilot shook his head. "I'm at VNE now!"

    The Jet Ranger covered the five miles to Isle of Mujeres in scant minutes. Drew strained to see any movement at EAGLE NEST. Nothing.

    "Forget the pad," Drew shouted. "Put it on the beach," he instructed. "There!" Drew pointed to the white sand below the house where Papa Moore had died. The pilot shot a tactical approach to the beach. He executed a side flare to quick stop the Jet Ranger and the chopper settled over the white sand. Before its skids touched the beach, Drew released his shoulder harness and threw the door open. "Do you have a weap ?" he screamed at the pilot, jerking off his headset. The roar of the turbine drowned the rest of the question. But the pilot understood the request. Wrestling with the controls, he nodded to the box behind Drew's seat. Drew lifted the lid and retrieved a nine millimeter Beretta automatic.

"Thanks!" he shouted to the pilot. "Stay near, okay?" he shouted again and dropped to the beach. The Jet Ranger roared away like a frightened bird.

Drew ran toward the steps leading up the dune to the house. The automatic swung in his hand. He hoped to God it was not needed. He received an answer to his first wish at that moment. A shot rang out from the house, and another. A rifle; he recognized the report. Sand flew about him as the rifle shots tore into the beach in front of him. Drew kept running until he reached the thirty foot high dune and dived into the bank of sand. He had no idea what was happening, but it did not require much argument with himself to sense the trouble above him was serious. If they had tried to kill him, it was quite possible Doña was dead. Sylvia, too, and the others occupying EAGLE NEST. He had to get to the house. But how? Then he remembered that the only approach that offered any kind of cover was at the north end of the property. There, a dense accumulation of foliage blocked one's view of the water from ground level. He made the decision quickly. Rolling to his left, he pulled his legs beneath him, paused to collect himself and then bolted across the sand.

Another shot rang out. Not even close, he thought, as the sand erupted twenty feet to his left. Twenty more yards and I'll be out of the gunman's sight. He ran as fast as he could, but the sand refused to release his pounding feet. He stumbled and fell face down in the warm sand. No rifle crack. Drew looked over his shoulder and saw he had passed the point where he could be seen from the house.

Quickly, he gathered himself and raced for the thicket of brush and palm trees. He squatted in the covering of shrubbery and trees and surveyed his situation. He could see the eaves of the house one hundred feet beyond his position. He had another forty feet of cover before the open space to the house. He moved quietly toward the house, working his way to within five feet of the naked lawn.

Then he saw him. A man stood up from a vantage point overlooking the beach where the chopper had deposited Drew. When the man turned toward the house, Drew's heart jumped. There was no mistaking the face. Charlie Russell! And Drew knew instantly what was happening. Russell had survived; he had come to EAGLE NEST to exact payment.

Then another thought, the worst kind, came to Drew. Russell had come for revenge! His neat operation had been destroyed. Now he would destroy his destroyer! That was it. I should have killed him when I had the chance, thought Drew.

If Russell is outside, Drew reasoned, then that means those inside are unable to help themselves or they are dead. If they are not dead, then I have to help. I have to get in there and take Russell out.

Drew checked the clip in the automatic. He took off the safety and fingered the weapon. The handgun resembled the .45 he preferred, and for a moment he wished he had his more familiar .45, but this would have to do. Actually, in the right hands it was a much more accurate weapon. He decided to rush the house. He glanced at the sky and spotted the Jet Ranger circling in the east at three hundred feet, a quarter of a mile from shore. He trusted the pilot to stay near.

He was prepared to spring toward the house when an explosion ripped the north end of EAGLE NEST, tearing a hole in the wall of Papa Moore's bedroom. Fire erupted through the opening.

"Damn!" Drew sputtered. The crazed man inside the house wasn't satisfied with killing people. He was going to literally destroy the house, too. Drew sprang toward the house, running with all his might to the end of the porch that fronted the beach. Without hesitating he leaped through the smoke onto the porch and pushed himself against the wall. The operations room was at the far end of the building. That's where Doña might be; possibly the others. But, where was Russell?

Drew could feel the heat building from the fire at his end of the house. Nobody in this end, they couldn't survive the heat, he reasoned, and snaked his way down the wall toward the rear door, bobbing beneath each window to escape attention. At the door, he paused, lifted the automatic to chest level and drew a deep breath. He lunged through the open door and dropped to a crouch, his weapon held with both hands at the ready. The den was clear. Then he heard voices. From the

333

computer room, he guessed. He crept slowly in that direction. The den was filling with smoke quickly.

Reaching the door leading to the room he sought, the voices were more distinct. Drew raised the automatic again and crossed the open space of the door, whipping the weapon to the ready. Charlie Russell saw the movement and started to whirl in Drew's direction.

"Don't!" Drew shouted at the squat little man who had started his journey across the Jabbok two weeks earlier. Russell stopped his turn instantly and trained the rifle on Doña. Drew held his gun on Russell and permitted himself a quick glance at Doña. She appeared unhurt. Sylvia stood rigid at her side.

"Drew! He hurt Papa!"

"Put the rifle down, Charlie," Drew said slowly.

"Go to hell, preacher!" the diminutive man yelled angrily. "I'll kill her in a second. Now, you just back off or the girl is dead!"

"He means it, Drew," Doña said.

Drew was thinking. The automatic was trained on Russell's right ear. Could the man get off a shot if I fire? Drew wondered. The familiar rage was filling his senses. A strange quiet filled the room as the four desperate people held their positions. Russell stared at Doña, his eyes flickered right, trying to catch a glimpse of Drew. Doña looked first to Drew, then to Russell, then repeated the act again. Drew stared at the right side of Russell's head.

He made a decision. He aimed carefully and squeezed the trigger. The explosion filled the room. But he missed his primary target. Russell moved when he heard the sound of the firing mechanism. The shot tore into the side of his neck, spinning him toward Drew. He raised the rifle as he spun, firing in rapid succession, not seeing, not caring where the shots landed. He was a dead man still firing.

Drew dropped to his knees and fired three shots in rapid sequence. Each found its mark like a hammer in Russell's chest. The third shot straightened him up and Russell fought to keep his balance. He was facing Drew now, the rifle held at his side. Blood erupted from his lips and his death stare focused on Drew. Drew held his weapon at the ready, waiting.

Sylvia bolted past the dying man to the far wall where a red metal box was mounted. She opened the cover and a piercing siren sounded throughout EAGLE NEST. She ignored the alert signal and pushed the red button at the top of the exposed panel. Below a lower black button the arm of a small clock began a slow counter-clockwise circle.

In a split second, Drew watched the woman's strange, swift action, then instantly returned his attention to Russell who tottered with the last energy in his body. The man won't die, thought Drew. The rifle began to rise slowly in Drew's direction. When it moved a foot from Russell's side, Drew squeezed off another shot. It slammed into Charlie's upper chest. The rifle fell to the floor a split second before Russell crumpled in a pile in front of Drew.

Doña was the first to react. She stepped over Russell and stood before Drew. He was still kneeling, his hands gripping the gun, his eyes glued on the dead man.

"Hurry! We've got to get Papa! We've only got a few minutes! The place is about to go!" she shouted. Sylvia disappeared through the smoke into the den.

"What?"

"The emergency destruction! Sylvia has set it off! Papa had a system installed to destroy everything the computers, the records, charts everything. It won't leave anything at EAGLE NEST for the authorities! Drew, hurry, please! Help me get Papa out!"

"Where?" Drew shouted.

"That way!" Doña was pointing as she reached inside the red box and retrieved a three by four inch plastic box. She tossed it to Drew. "Guard this with your life!" she said.

"What is it?" Drew asked, turning the small container over in his hand.

"EAGLE EYE. On computer disks." Then, "Come on, We have less than two minutes now," she said, and turned to leave the room. The fire was stretching toward the south end of the house. The smoke had filled the den behind them and was quickly engulfing into the computer room.

Drew followed quickly. The den was black with smoke. They felt their way across the room toward the dim light of open door to Papa's bedroom. Then the light vanished. They felt their way in its direction, found the door and tried to open it.

"It's locked!" Doña screamed.

Drew pushed against the door. The heavy oak door was bolted solidly.

"Sylvia!" Doña cried. "Open the door!"

Inside, the sad voice of Papa's trusted aide replied. "No, señorita. We die together."

"Sylllviaaa! Open the door, please."

There was another piercing sound of the siren.

"What's that?" Drew shouted.

"One minute, we've only got sixty seconds! God in heaven, Sylvia, please, my God, open the door." Doña pounded her fist on the door. She was near hysteria. Both of them were breathing the thick smoke as they gasped for air.

Drew threw his arms about her from behind and started pulling her toward the only light he could see.

"No! I can't leave him!"

Drew dragged her screaming to the light, found the door to the outside and forced her onto the lawn. He grabbed her again as she bounded to her feet, coughing, struggling for breath. But Doña was no longer fighting.

"Doña, come on!" He pulled her by the arm toward the landing pad. Overhead, the Jet Ranger had changed positions and was hovering over the water a few hundred yards directly opposite them. The pilot spotted them and the aircraft began moving quickly toward the house, the rotors' distinctive sounds drawing nearer. Drew could hear in the distance the sirens of the village fire truck.

Drew held Doña's hand as the Jet Ranger circled, then descended quickly to the pad. They fought the crush of wind from the rotors and crawled into the chopper.

"Get out of here, quick!" he shouted to the pilot who needed no encouragement to follow the instruction. The pilot had kept the rpms up. In a split second, he pulled up the collective and kicked right pedal. The chopper lifted off and swept away from EAGLE NEST in one grand motion. As they crossed the shoreline a deafening blast sounded and Drew jerked his head in the direction of EAGLE NEST. An enormous fireball formed over the remains of the house. Debris floated down in slow motion from all angles. The eruption shook the Jet Ranger momentarily. The pilot quickly corrected his course and made for the mainland.

Drew held Doña tightly as she sobbed against his chest. He took a last look at the site of Papa Moore's headquarters. The devastation was complete. EAGLE NEST was gone.

Chapter Twenty-Six

In a motel fronting the cloverleaf near the Pentagon, the columnist and the senator's wife sat nervously with the Director of the F.B.I. Markus Williamson had initiated the contact, trusting his candor would exonerate him from any connection with the senator's death. He had convinced Morgan Ann to attend the clandestine meeting on the promise he would testify to the Director in her behalf. Together, they hoped to convince the Director that any exposure of their trysts would add nothing to the inquiry except an embarrassment to the Senate. The Director had listened attentively, relieved that the two confessors had only limited knowledge of the extent of the EAGLE EYE operation, much less his involvement. But there were unanswered questions.

"The government will attempt to recover your husband's account in Switzerland, Mrs. Maxwell. But as far as you're concerned, it doesn't exist. Is that understood?"

"Yes," Morgan Ann acknowledged.

"And both of you will go to your grave with the information you possess. Is that, too, agreed?"

Williamson and his former lover nodded their heads.

"The senator's death will be reported as a suicide, tragic, to be sure. The report will suggest an incurable illness. The man was depressed. You'll indicate that, Mrs. Maxwell, relating how his behavior in the last months was consistent with the story. You're grieved beyond words, for yourself, your daughters, and for the country. A great loss for all."

"Yes."

"Then this matter is resolved." The Director stood and left the room. In the corridor he paused, painfully aware the matter would never be so easily laid to rest.

Markus Williamson and Morgan Ann Huntington Maxwell remained seated when the Director left. Now, they were silent still, each aware of the burden they would carry the rest of their lives.

Suddenly, the columnist covered his face with his hands and muffled an agonizing scream into his palms. Then, dropping his hands into his lap, he wept.

Morgan Ann watched her erstwhile former lover in arrogant silence until she had endured enough of the crying. There was little sympathy for his distress in her eyes, but rather a contempt for his weakness. Finally, she gathered her purse and started for the door where she stood for a moment with her hand on the knob. Then, she turned slowly and spoke to Williamson.

"I've known some weak men in my time, but none more so than you and James. I've lost everything. My position in this town, my reputation, my husband and my lover, in that order. Not to mention millions in Switzerland. If you were a real man, you would have handled it."

He looked up at Morgan Ann, his hatred for the woman clearly evident.

"You!" he shouted, "all you've ever cared about is yourself. At least I was honest with you from the beginning. My integrity is marred, to be sure, but at least I have some."

"Well," she said in her best, liquid southern drawl, "enjoy it, my darling, but don't try to spend it. It's not worth much."

In the main office building of the Bank of America Bank in Savannah, Drew and Doña studied the large sterile chamber in which they stood. Rows of safe deposit boxes lined the walls, hundreds of small vaults, each solidly in place and undisturbed. Drew considered their contents, certain he was surrounded by a great sum of cash, bonds and certificates of deposits, and, of course, jewels and other items of immense value. Important papers, too. And some very private documents, no doubt.

His hands rested lightly on the sides of the long, slim metal box opened before him. Glancing at Doña, he drew a measured breath, reached inside his cost and slid his hand into an inner pocket. One quick look toward the door satisfied him; they were not being observed. He withdrew a slim, plastic container with a snap on lid and held it before him momentarily, stared at it, then carefully placed it in the safe deposit box. An innocent looking container with a red star drawn in the upper left hand corner of the label. Two words typed in capital letters on the upturned side: EAGLE EYE.

He studied the container a moment and withdrew it. He carefully peeled the paper label from the container, then returned the plastic container to the metal box, closed the lid and called for the bank attendant. The threesome walked silently to the slot from which the box had been taken. The attended inserted it, and he and Drew turned the proper keys.

Satisfied, Drew and Doña walked out of bank into a cool Georgia breeze. For the first time in weeks Drew relaxed. They had placed in safe keeping the computer disks containing the digits needed to retrieve more than seventy-five million dollars from a numbered Swiss bank account. Were they really safe? But that wasn't the whole of it. The diskettes had other files in addition to the secret numbers. There were names, important names which, if revealed, would effect a national scandal. And strategic information, too. Lives would be destroyed should the data fall into the wrong hands. The diskettes held the history of EAGLE EYE. And they, the Reverend Dr. Andrew Campbell and agent Doña Moore, were the only persons who knew its resting place. The decision had been made: the diskette would remain hidden, and EAGLE EYE defunct, at least for the foreseeable future.

They walked into the light breeze as Drew inhaled deeply. He was feeling surer of himself than he had in weeks, though he was quite unsure the feelings were appropriate. They stepped into Johnson Square and started slowly through the park.

"What will you do now?" Doña asked.

"I've been thinking about that. I need to try to answer some lingering questions, I suppose."

"Are you still planning to leave the ministry?"

"Yes. There are some loose ends to tie up, like meeting with the presbytery reps, that sort of thing. I want to do it honorably, what little honor there is left to save. In my heart, even now, I am no longer a pastor."

"Well, what then?"

"I don't know," Drew answered quietly. They continued walking. "I have the establishment of the Foundation to pursue, and that'll take some time. I want to do it right. And," he remembered, "I have to meet with the bank's Trust Department to set up the funds to provide the awards in memory of Bobby and Mary. Then, well, I just don't know. I need some time to think things over."

They walked another block in silence before Doña asked the obvious. "What about the money? I mean the seventy-five million? We can't just let it sit there, can we? Somebody will begin asking about it, try to get their hands on it, that's for certain. Not today, but someday."

"You're right, but we don't have to make that decision today, or tomorrow. Its time will come, soon enough."

He was still thinking about the myriad of events the last week, even as he answered Doña's concern about the money. What had this ugly odyssey of betrayal and violence done to his soul? Did he need professional help to unravel the intricate web of grief, guilt and complicity?

Doña slipped her arm inside his. "And Viet Nam?"

"I think that's gone, for now, anyway." He stopped, looked at her. "No, it's not gone. It's still there, just pushed back again." Would it come back to haunt him? Probably. They began walking again. That's when she hugged his arm a bit tighter, then pulled him to another stop.

"And what about us?" she asked. "Is there something in you for me?"

The question jumped out at him, not as if it surprised him, but more like he expected it, was waiting for it, yet was not prepared for it. It was a totally honest question, and he knew Doña well enough to know it required a truthful answer. Where did the extraordinary woman at his side fit into his life? Could they have any meaningful future together? More to the point, the primary question -- could he answer that now? Had his grief, Ellen's death, her haunting presence, finally released him?

Drew was suddenly aware of the beauty in which he was standing. He permitted the warm sun to bathe his face, and listened to the sounds of life about him. He studied the people hurrying through the park, saw the child pulling at her mother's skirt. Across the green the massive, reassuring columns fronting First Baptist

Church dominated the plaza. The city was alive, people were going about the business of living, and he knew he desperately wanted to be part of both, the city and the people. And, he could be! That was the message he was getting. All the questions did not have to be answered immediately for him to go on living, and doing so with purpose. Then, quickly, he knew! He had crossed his raging Jabbok River and survived his Esau, as had Jacob. The delight was so satisfying, he almost laughed. He looked at Doña who stood quietly to one side, observing the man she loved. He nodded to her with a smile and reached for her hand.

He stopped and turned to her, their eyes met. "Doña," he said softly, "I love you. That I know. Whatever there is for us, we have to try to find it. But not at this moment. In time, at the right time. For now, let's just enjoy the freedom to love."

A block later Doña broke the silence. "I love your city," she said, and tightened her grip on his hand.

"Our city," he said without breaking stride, feeling almost whole again.

- End -

About the Author

Dr. Lawrence (Larry) Wood is an ordained Presbyterian minister who served churches in Mississippi, Arkansas and Georgia for 45 years. A large part of his ministry was in Savannah, GA, scene of much of the story in *The Jabbok Condition*. Larry served as a counselor in an alcohol and drug treatment center and led a mental health association. He was president of various local human need agencies boards of directors, and was chosen for the Leadership Georgia and the Leadership Savannah programs. He retired from active parish ministry in 2008. He and his wife, Helen, sold their properties in north Atlanta, GA and are travelling the United States in their 32' Fifth Wheel RV, spending much of their time in the West. On invitation he preaches and teaches in local churches. He is a graduate of Presbyterian College in Clinton, South Carolina, where he served as a member of the Board of Trustees and of Columbia Theological Seminary in Decatur, Georgia, where he served as President of the Alumni/ae Association.